Previously published Worldwide Suspense titles by
JUSTIN M. KISKA

NOW & THEN

VICE & VIRTUE

JUSTIN M. KISKA

W🌐RLDWIDE

TORONTO • NEW YORK • LONDON
AMSTERDAM • PARIS • SYDNEY • HAMBURG
STOCKHOLM • ATHENS • TOKYO • MILAN
MADRID • WARSAW • BUDAPEST • AUCKLAND

W**O**RLDWIDE™

Recycling programs
for this product may
not exist in your area.

ISBN-13: 978-1-335-01221-0

Vice & Virtue

First published in 2022 by Level Best Books.
This edition published in 2024.

For questions and comments about the quality of this book,
please contact us at CustomerService@Harlequin.com.

TM is a trademark of Harlequin Enterprises ULC.

Harlequin Enterprises ULC
22 Adelaide St. West, 41st Floor
Toronto, Ontario M5H 4E3, Canada
www.ReaderService.com

Printed in U.S.A.

VICE & VIRTUE

To Mum & Dad—
How proud are you that your son knows so many
interesting ways to dispose of a body?

PROLOGUE

Summer 1984...

LANCE HAGGERTY SLAMMED on the brakes, bringing the beat-up old Ford pickup to a screeching halt at the corner of Thomas Jefferson Drive and Third Street. Cursing, he watched the bright yellow VW Bug that ran the stop sign continue down the street. It was four-thirty in the morning. No one else should have been on the road right now, he thought as he put his foot back down on the accelerator. The pickup lurched forward through the intersection and continued on its early morning journey.

Getting into an accident before the sun was even up was not the way he needed his day to begin. He already knew it was going to be a long day at work, which he wasn't looking forward to, and the fight he'd had with his wife the night before was still playing on his mind. Haggerty figured it was too early for a real drink. But a shot of the whiskey he kept in the glove box might help to calm him down a bit. Maybe he'd pour just a drop or two in his thermos when he got to the construction site.

The rusty pickup rattled down the empty street as Haggerty made his way through downtown Parker City. A thick fog had rolled in overnight making the visibility extremely difficult in some spots. With the weather being as back and forth as it had been the last few days—eighties and nineties during the day, then down into the forties at night—this was the recent norm for this time of the morning. Haggerty hated it.

Yeah, his morning cup of coffee was going to need that whiskey, he thought to himself. He was not in a good mood today.

The early hour had nothing to do with the fact that the streets in this part of town were completely empty. It had everything to do with the fact that this was a part of the city that was quite literally, falling apart. The closer the pickup got to the construction site, the more and more decrepit the buildings became.

Even before the flood that devastated the city's downtown several years earlier, this section of town had been in decay. Industrial buildings and warehouses built in the 30s and 40s had sat empty since the economic downturn in the 70s. These buildings were now a breeding ground for vagrants and illegal activities. Even the police rarely ventured into this area, opting to focus their resources where they thought they would actually do some amount of good.

Four square blocks of boarded-up, derelict buildings greeted Haggerty every morning as he drove to work. The site was depressing as hell. But one to which he'd become accustomed. The general feeling of defeat that hung in the air didn't do anything to help the construction worker's mood that morning. And with the fog hovering in the streets between one dilapidated building after the next, it looked like the set of a zombie movie. He expected a swarm of the living dead to come around the corner at any moment.

Pulling his truck into the temporary parking lot

across from the construction site, Haggerty parked on his usual patch of dirt. As was the custom, he was the second person to arrive. The first being the foreman, a guy who seemed to work all hours. He was always the first one there in the morning and the last one to leave at the end of the day. Haggerty wondered if he even had a home to go to. He couldn't stand the guy. But then again, he'd always had a problem with any type of authority figure.

Grabbing his lunch pail, thermos, and silver flask from the glove box, he locked his truck and started across the street to the metal trailer that served as the construction office. Next to it, a large billboard read "Coming Soon, Parker Plaza!" in giant red letters. It was one of several locations in the downtown area targeted for redevelopment in the mayor's plan to revitalize the city. This specific project was the construction of a brand new commercial shopping center that would have stores and restaurants and be a beacon to help attract other businesses to locate in what was once a thriving industrial corridor, albeit half a century earlier.

Before the new complex could go up though, the old structure on the property needed to come down. Haggerty had no idea what used to be stored there, but like every other building he saw through the dim light of the streetlamps, it was an old brick warehouse.

He remembered the first time he saw the place. He couldn't understand how it was still standing. The doors and windows on the ground level were boarded up with sheets of plywood that were decorated with brightly colored graffiti. Entire chunks of masonry were crumbling from the lack of upkeep, as sections of the exterior walls bowed and leaned dangerously out of place. Once inside, he'd seen that every window that hadn't been covered with plywood had been broken, leaving shards of dirt-covered glass everywhere. The flooring itself was nothing but wood, so with the giant holes in the ceiling, nature and its elements had ravaged the surface. In some areas, the wooden planks were completely disintegrated revealing the dirt below.

While Haggerty would have liked to have used a wrecking ball on the whole damn building, they'd needed to go through the place first to make sure there was nothing of any historic value and then come up with the safest way to bring the structure down. Again, he'd suggested a wrecking ball. Or, to make it more entertaining to see the whole building come crashing to the ground, sticks of dynamite placed around its foundation.

Finally, after weeks of "study and prep"—as the foreman was calling it—they were ready to really get to work and tear the place down.

Haggerty was just closing his locker when the foreman came into the construction trailer. He was a grumpy little man with a massive beer belly. It was clear he was in one of his "we-have-so-much-work-to-get-done-why-are-you-only-getting-here-at-quarter-to-five-in-the-morning?" kind of moods.

"Mornin', Joe," Haggerty said, trying to start things off on the right foot for a change.

"I need you to take one last walk through Area B-2 before any of the guys start work there this morning," was the response he received. "Make sure nothing got left. If we can get that section signed off on today, we'll only be a week and a half behind schedule."

"I'll do it now and get it over with."

The construction supervisor grunted a reply before heading toward the back of the trailer and his make-shift desk. Once seated, he could barely be seen over the stacks of papers and design plans piled in front of him.

Haggerty grabbed his hardhat off a hook next to the door, along with a flashlight and walkie-talkie from the shelf, and headed for what was designated as "Area B-2" of the warehouse's ground floor. The sun would start to peek over the mountain range off in the distance soon, but for now, he needed the flashlight to help guide the way. There were a few work lights set up outside around the warehouse and construction trailer, but he didn't want to deal with starting up the generator that would power the work lamps inside the building. It would take him longer to get that old thing to turnover than to just walk B-2 using the flashlight. He wasn't sure what Joe thought he was going to find, having just made a final sweep of that part of the building the day before. All of their tools and equipment had been moved out already and there wasn't anything of any significance found there to begin with. But the less time he needed to be confined in the construction trailer with Foreman Joe, the better.

Making his way across the decaying floor, the wooden boards squeaked in some places and cracked in others. In one spot, Haggerty's weight caused an entire board to crumble under him, causing his boots to sink into the dirt beneath.

"Sonofabitch," he cursed, as he kicked the rotting debris to the side.

On the demo plan, Area B-2 was an odd little ten-by-ten room sticking off the back of the main structure. Haggerty could only assume it used to be an office or some sort of workroom because it wasn't big enough for much else. It did have an exterior door, so it could have been an entrance area for the workers, but it didn't show up on any of the building's original plans filed with the city, so there was no way to tell. Not that anyone really cared.

Standing in the doorway, the flashlight's beam crisscrossed the room. It was empty. Just like it had been the day before. At least this little bit of the building was ready to be torn down, Haggerty thought stepping into the room and looking around one last time. He didn't know what Joe expected him to come back and say that was any different from when he said the area was all clear yesterday.

Frustrated, he turned to leave. As he did, the tip of his boot caught a gap in the floor and Haggerty found himself stumbling and crashing to the ground. Hitting the floor hard, he heard a crack, followed by another, then the boards under him completely gave away. He didn't fall very far, just about two feet into a gap under the warehouse floor.

Lying flat on his stomach, pieces of the broken floorboards under him, his flashlight somewhere at his side, Haggerty tried looking around. There was no way the floor would have been put down over a hole like this with no support. Judging by the stream of mud in which he found himself lying, this empty pocket under the floor must have been caused by erosion over the years.

Screw the coffee, Haggerty thought. He was just going to have the whiskey by itself when he got back to the trailer. Starting to pull himself up, he caught a glimpse of something stuck in the dirt about a foot away. The light from his flashlight was just catching a glint of something that had been partially uncovered when the floor collapsed. Reaching out, he pushed away more of the soggy earth until he had a better view of what had caught his eye. All six feet two inches of the hard-drinking, tough construction worker recoiled as he looked into the empty black eye sockets of a human skull.

ONE

BILLY ROSCOE WAS a household name in Parker City. Some knew him as a philanthropist, others as a businessman. The one thing everyone agreed on was he was a self-promoter. He liked seeing his name in the paper, so he made certain everything he did became newsworthy. It was a brilliant masterstroke on his part because he was able to use the limelight to overshadow his more illicit projects—the sort of activities not looked too highly upon. In his mind, he figured as long as he kept everyone's attention on things that were positive and shiny, he wouldn't have to worry about anyone questioning his shadier dealings that were far outside of the public eye.

An attractive forty-something, Roscoe was the embodiment of charm poured into a Fortrel suit. His ruggedly handsome face with wavy blonde hair and piercing emerald green eyes made every lady who crossed his path swoon. For the men, he always had an iron-gripped handshake and a hearty slap on the back. The man's self-confidence level was off the chart. He loved himself and expected everyone around him to do the same. Most people that entered his orbit usually did. There was just something about the guy. If he chose you as the focus of his attention, even for just a few moments, it was like the sun's rays shining down on you and only you.

Though he was one of the most popular and recognizable public figures in town, he held no official title. But that didn't stop many residents from thinking of him as the city's honorary mayor. If City Hall wasn't able to fix your problem, all you needed to do was ask Billy Roscoe. No one really understood how, but he could make things happen. That's why it wasn't uncommon to see him walking down the street flanked by a group of admirers and those seeking a favor. In the small Western Maryland city, he was the celebrity equivalent of Frank Sinatra.

Not everyone in Parker City had fallen under Billy Roscoe's spell, however. There were those who were extremely leery of the young, energetic "snake-oil salesman"—as a few referred to him—who seemed to appear from nowhere and build a very successful business empire without much effort.

Parker City, after all, was very much a community built upon tradition and steeped in history. The words "change" and "new" were not part of the city's vocabulary. Originally settled as a trading outpost along the Tasker River in the late 1700s by five prominent families, the city had grown up along with the rest of the country. On several occasions, playing a part in its storied history. But even after almost two hundred years, it was still those founding families that influenced much of the goings-on in the city. And these leading members of society didn't care much for the rabble-rousing, status quo-challenging, nouveau riche Billy Roscoe.

While families like the Tildons, Worthingtons, Bak-

ers, Mosses, and, of course, Parkers ran established and
esteemed institutions that included banks, land companies, and newspapers, Roscoe owned flashy restaurants,
a hotel, and a shipping company. He and his businesses
were hardly the type with which the elite of Parker City
society associated.

Roscoe never let that stop him.

He'd grown up playing on the streets of Trenton,
New Jersey during a particularly difficult time in a not-
so-good neighborhood. His father was abusive and his
mother an alcoholic. Not that there was all that much
of a difference between the two of them. As soon as he
was able to get out of the house, he did. Working odd
jobs here and there to pay his way through school, he
was a proud graduate of Rider University…with hon-
ors. Roscoe intended on making something of himself
and wasn't afraid of hard work. Or doing *whatever* it
took to get ahead.

Why and how he'd made his way to Parker, a city an
hour outside of both Washington, DC and Baltimore,
at the foot of the Blue Ridge Mountains near the site
of two major Civil War battles—South Mountain and
Antietam—no one really knew. While the gregarious
entrepreneur was all too happy to talk about his early
life as a child or attending the business college, or his
current endeavors, he rarely spoke of the time in between. And those closest to him knew not to ask. Some
things were strictly off-limits.

Most evenings, Roscoe could be found holding court
at his private table in the back corner of the Derby
Room. His newest eatery, it was located on the ground
floor of his ParkMar Hotel just a few blocks from Park-

er's Center Square. On the day of its grand opening, the line of restaurant-goers stretched around the block. Roscoe was thrilled because it made for a great photo that ran on the front page of both of the city's newspapers. Business hadn't slowed since. It was the most popular restaurant in town.

Inside, the wood-paneled walls, sparkling brass fixtures, and orange leather seats, along with the mouth-watering smell of grilled steak wafting from the kitchen, welcomed all those starving for a hearty, feel-good meal. Bustling waiters kept the kitchen's swinging doors in constant motion as they hustled plates with giant slabs of meat and seafood from stove to table.

Whenever possible, Roscoe liked to work the room and greet as many of the diners as possible. He especially relished when he could do something special for one of the tables. If a nervous young man finally worked up the nerve to ask his girl to marry him, Billy would happily send over a bottle of champagne and pick up the check. If a family had saved up to enjoy a special night out, he'd have the waiter deliver an extra scoop or two of ice cream for the kids for dessert. His saintly behavior downstairs in no way matched the activities going on three floors above.

That particular week, a heatwave had settled over the area, pushing temperatures well over what most people expected in mid-May. While central air conditioning was still not very common throughout Parker City, Billy Roscoe, once again, was benefiting from his forward-thinking. As the thermometer outside registered 100 degrees, steam visibly rising from the pavement, it was a crisp sixty-nine inside the Derby Room. As other restaurants were seeing a drop in the number of diners walking through their doors, Roscoe was raking in the dough hand-over-fist because his establishment was a refreshingly cool refuge from the stifling heat.

Scanning the dining room from his seat, Roscoe couldn't be more pleased. The tables were full, the waiting area was stacked with those ready to be seated at the next available chance, and when he'd arrived, there was a line outside the front door running halfway down the block of those hoping someone didn't show for their reservation. Finishing off the last of his scotch, he'd not even placed the empty tumbler on the table before another appeared before him.

A slim, young waitress with big blue eyes, who could very easily have gotten a job as a pin-up girl, gave her boss a mischievous smile as she took the empty glass from his hand.

"Thanks, Rose," Roscoe said, returning the smile.

Inside, Rose's heart melted. Outside, she blushed. The fact that Billy Roscoe knew her name was almost too much for the girl who was barely old enough to drink, let alone serve alcohol. She skipped back to the bar knowing full well that Roscoe and the other guys at his table were watching her go. Happy to give them a show, she threw in an extra little swing of her hips for their entertainment.

"Where'd that one come from, boss?" one of Roscoe's table companions asked without taking his eyes off Rose's firm butt as she disappeared behind the giant mahogany bar at the other end of the room. Freddy Quinn was Roscoe's personal driver and unofficial bodyguard, though "lackey" might have been a more apt job title.

"I have no idea. She's just one of the girls," Roscoe answered, scanning the room to see who he recognized in the crowd of diners.

"Yeah, but you knew her name. She's obviously made some kind of impression on you, Billy," said the man sitting to Roscoe's right. Much more distinguished than Quinn in his appearance, Marty Schulman also had far better manners. Next to Freddy, Marty was the only other guy Bill Roscoe really trusted—even if he was a lawyer. But he was Billy's lawyer and a bit of a father figure at times. He was also a calming influence when Roscoe's temper started to flare. In Billy's orbit, Marty Schulman was the brains to Freddy Quinn's brawn.

Giving a slight shrug, Roscoe said, "It was a lucky guess. All those little girls look the same to me."

"Until you get 'em undressed," Freddy offered, letting out a laugh that drew the attention of those sitting around them.

"Down, boy," Roscoe said through clenched teeth. Practically inaudible, Freddy heard and got the message loud and clear.

Looking around the dining room, Billy was happy to see the mayor and chief of police at their usual tables. Having such fine upstanding men like that around helped to add a good deal of legitimacy to his establishment. Not that the city's *establishment* would ever see it that way.

"Fuck 'em," Roscoe said to no one in particular. "Freddy, go have some more drinks sent over to the mayor. Let's make sure he leaves feeling real good to-night."

With a quick nod, the six-foot-four hulk of a man pushed himself to his feet and lumbered off in the direction their waitress had just a few minutes earlier.

Swallowing the last bite of his Porterhouse, Roscoe wiped his mouth with the crisp linen napkin and tossed it on the table next to a black leather notebook. Reaching over he began flipping through the pages with the most recent dates at the top.

"Are these numbers good?" he asked Marty without taking his eyes off the figures.

"I think you'll be happy. We're up over last week and the week before," the lawyer answered before taking his last bite of salmon.

Tapping his fingers on the table as he read over the handwritten numbers in the ledger, Roscoe was in fact pleased with what he saw. Everything's coming up roses he thought, coincidentally, just as Rose reappeared with another round of drinks for the table. The waitress made it a point to brush against him as she was clearing away some of the empty glasses. Under the table, Roscoe ran his hand along her stockinged leg as she reached across him to pick up an empty wine glass. Had he not been distracted by a sweat-covered Freddy shuffling up to the table, who knows where his hand might have landed.

"What's wrong?" Roscoe asked, casually pushing the waitress away.

Leaning down and whispering in his ear, Freddy said, "We've got a problem out back. It's that cop again."

Roscoe's demeanor changed instantly. In a split second, his twinkling emerald eyes turned to pools of darkness as the smile on his lips twisted into a frustrated sneer. With just a few words, the jovial restaurateur that had been at the table all evening was gone. Freddy hated having to be the one to deliver the news and interrupt his boss's dinner, but he knew it needed to be done.

Trying to attract as little attention as possible, Roscoe stood, straightened his tie, and gave a subtle nod to one of the maître d's at the front door. He watched as the little man disappeared through a side door before he himself made an exit from the dining room.

The kitchen was a beehive of activity, everyone moving at a breakneck pace. Cooks shouted back and forth to one another as dishes of food seemed to fly through the air. Billy paid no attention to any of it as he deftly weaved his way around the busy kitchen staff. Freddy and Marty did their best to keep pace. In one of the cramped back hallways, Freddy couldn't help running into a busboy carting a bin of dirty dishes. The force of the unexpected collision caused the young man and everything he was carrying to fly into the air then land on the ground in a giant heap.

Before the final dish hit the yellow linoleum floor, Roscoe shouted over his shoulder, "Clean it up!"

Pushing through the back door that lead out into the alley behind the restaurant, Roscoe and his associates found Freddy's younger brother standing with his arms crossed and a scowl on his face. As tall as Freddy, but almost twice as wide, Jimmy Quinn was a giant compared to the little man leaning against the patrol car.

"Officer Ramsburg, I'm so surprised to see you here," Roscoe said, his words dripping with sarcasm and a hint of disdain.

Bert Ramsburg was a twenty-five-year veteran of the Parker City Police Department and a pain in Billy's ass. He reminded Roscoe a lot of the bumbling characters Jerry Lewis always played in the movies, with one exception. Unlike Lewis's comedic buffoons, Ramsburg was actually pretty damn smart, which is why he was causing such a damn problem.

"You don't look all that happy to see me, Mr. Roscoe. Am I interrupting something? Maybe about to interfere with some illegal activities, am I?"

"You caught me, officer. I was just inside counting all the illegal T-bone steaks I smuggled into town. What is it you want, Ramsburg? Don't you have more important things to do?"

"Yeah. Like help some old lady get her cat out of a tree," Freddy said with a sneer.

Ramsburg was a gangly twig of a man. But when he went toe-to-toe with someone, his confidence made up for his physical shortcomings. Even though Roscoe was a good six inches taller, Ramsburg didn't flinch or back down. He walked straight up to the man who had become his nemesis over the last several years and never blinked. Out of the corner of his eye, he saw Freddy reach into his jacket and rest his hand on the .45 he always had in a holster tucked under his arm.

Without taking his eyes off Roscoe, as cool as ice, Ramsburg said, "You're gonna wanna take your hand out of there so I can see both of them or we're gonna have a real problem here, Mr. Quinn."

Roscoe nodded, letting Freddy know it was alright to relax. No need to escalate the situation any further. Then he said directly to Ramsburg, "I don't know what you think is going on here. Or what you hope to find. But I have half a mind to walk back into the restaurant and ask the chief to come out here right now. Yeah, that's right. Your boss is inside right now eating a nice big spaghetti dinner with his boss, the mayor. Either one would be happy to throw your ass off the force if I asked them to."

Marty could see the telltale signs that Billy was beginning to get a little too hot under the collar. So, to make sure his boss didn't say anything else that he'd regret, he stepped in.

"Officer Ramsburg, this is bordering on harassment. This is private property so unless you have a warrant, you're going to need to leave. Otherwise, I will be filing a complaint with the PCPD about your unwarranted *persecution* of my client."

It wasn't the first time Ramsburg had been threatened by the lawyer, who himself was crooked by most accounts. Schulman had been to the station several times raising hell about Ramsburg. But as long as he was doing his job, Ramsburg wasn't much worried about the attorney's warnings and threats.

"You don't scare me, Billy. You or your counselor here. I'm about to get everything I need to put you away for good. And once Mayor Albert and Chief Stanley see what you've been up to, they're not gonna have any interest in doin' you any favors."

Roscoe took a deep breath and thought very carefully before saying anything else. He could feel the anger rising inside of him but knew he needed to play it cool. There was no way he could let this little insect of a man get to him. That's exactly what Ramsburg wanted. If he lost his temper and slipped up, saying something he shouldn't, or worse, taking a swing at the guy, he'd have landed square in the officer's trap. Instead, Billy Roscoe flashed his thousand-watt smile, turned on his heels, and walked back inside without saying another word.

TWO

No sooner had the door closed behind them, Roscoe's calm, cool demeanor vanished—replaced by fiery rage. With no warning, he slammed his fist square into the wall. Neither Freddy Quinn nor Marty Schulman knew if the crack echoing through the corridor was caused by the bones in Billy's hand breaking or the backing of the wall snapping from the force of the blow.

Without showing any sign of pain, or even discomfort, Billy turned on Freddy. Tearing into him, he shouted, "What the hell does he mean he's going to have enough to put me away? What could that little prick possibly know?"

"He's gotta be bluffin,' Billy," the thug stammered, watching his boss flex his bruised fingers. Freddy was shocked that his hand wasn't broken and bloody.

Even though he was a good five inches taller than Billy and carried about fifty more pounds on him, in that moment, he thought he might be the next thing Billy took a swing at. Freddy had seen the charming, easygoing façade crack from time to time, but nothing like this. There was a blazing inferno behind Roscoe's eyes that actually scared him. And it took a lot to scare him.

"Look, Billy," Marty began, trying to defuse the situation. But he was quickly cut off.

"And you! You're my lawyer! Why the hell can't you get that little shit off my case? What am I paying you for? You're supposed to be so smart. Why can't you get that prick to back off?"

Before Schulman was able to answer that Ramsburg technically hadn't crossed any lines so therefore there wasn't much he could do without making it *look* like they were trying to hide something, Billy turned and stormed off down the hall. Whether he wasn't paying attention, or just didn't care, he ran into the same bus-boy from earlier, sending a bin of glasses crashing to the floor this time. Again, without breaking his stride, over his shoulder he shouted, "You're fired! Get the fuck out of my restaurant!"

To be completely honest, even Billy wasn't entirely sure why this particular encounter with the annoying police officer was causing him to lose his cool so uncontrollably. Ramsburg had been hounding him for almost a year, making it more and more difficult for Roscoe and his organization to actually do the things Ramsburg suspected they were involved in. He just seemed so much more confident with his threat this time. Like he might have a solid lead. Heaven help anyone who might have talked, Billy thought as he pushed through the door into the hotel's lobby.

An Art Deco theme ran throughout the entire hotel. Years before, Billy spent a weekend in New York City and had fallen in love with the style when he had the good fortune to dine with a female companion at the famed Waldorf Astoria. Even though his hotel was 43 stories shorter and about 1,200 rooms smaller, he still wanted to bring as much of the luxury hotel's elegance to his own.

In addition to the Derby Room Restaurant and all the guest rooms—which were filled every evening, the hotel also boasted a lounge with a stage for entertainment, two different bars, a club room for small private functions, and a ballroom for grander affairs.

Some thought the hotel's "fancy" interior design didn't fit with Parker City's style, and that Roscoe was simply trying to put on airs so people thought better of him. Those were the same people who looked down their noses at Billy no matter what he did. In his mind, he was doing everyone in Parker City a favor and bringing a little class into their lives. Just like when one of the greatest men Parker had ever known, Bernard Parker Moss, built the Harlequin Theatre. No one thought it was needed at the time, but Parker Moss wanted to broaden Parkertons' minds with "big city" entertainment.

They were all going to come around, Billy thought as he quickly crossed the lobby. The sound of his heels clicking rapidly against the polished marble floor rose above all the other commotion. Roscoe was heading for the door next to the Reception Desk marked "Private."

Catching one of the desk clerk's eyes, the man behind the counter hit a button, unlocking the door for his boss. Once through, Roscoe strode down the small corridor towards his office.

Slipping through the door at the end of the hall, he was glad to finally be alone and able to drop the charming façade everyone always expected. Tossing his suit jacket on the back of a guest chair and loosening his tie, he poured himself a large scotch and drank almost the entire tumbler in one gulp.

Billy's office was his sanctuary. It was the one place that was his and only his. Even Marty and Freddy knew how important it was to leave him alone when he was locked away in his office. Here, private meant private.

Having grown up with next to nothing, Billy now surrounded himself with everything he always thought represented success. Vibrant colored paintings hung on the walls between bookcases that held everything from first edition prints to random objet d'art he'd purchased from around the world. Each was its own little treasure in his personal collection.

One of his favorite pieces was a Fabergé egg he'd purchased at an auction several years earlier. Not that he was a Fabergé enthusiast. He'd only bid on it to impress the woman he'd been with. But once he held it in his hands for the first time and was able to examine its fine details, there was something about it that made Billy…happy. A feeling he was finding more and more difficult to experience on a daily basis. The jeweled egg's deep purple, almost black hue, was mesmerizing in itself, only to be enriched by the shimmering gold filigree with which it was encrusted.

As elegant as the Fabergé masterpiece was, it stood in stark contrast to the Colt Single Action .44 revolver which it sat next to. Reportedly owned at one time by William Henry McCarty, it gave Billy Roscoe great pleasure to think sitting on his shelf was the favorite gun of Billy the Kid—the name by which McCarty was better known.

Letting out a deep sigh as his eyes floated over the

oddly assorted collection of antiques and trinkets, Roscoe was so wrapped up in his thoughts and frustration from the run-in with Ramsburg that he hadn't noticed the figure casually sitting behind his desk. Or the gun lying on the blotter in front of the man.

THREE

1984

ON HIS DAYS OFF, Detective Sergeant Benjamin Winters still liked to get up relatively early so he could take advantage of every minute of the day. He wasn't one who liked having too much extra time on his hands. For as long as he could remember, he always felt he needed to be doing something productive. When he was a child, he was one of those kids that hated summer break because he genuinely loved going to school and learning. To keep him occupied while school was out, his parents signed him up to be a part of everything from the local youth summer soccer league to the YMCA. Ben was always on the go.

But today was different. He'd promised his fiancé that he wouldn't set his alarm so they could both sleep in for a change. Yes, things had changed quite a bit since Natalie Kirkpatrick had come into his life. Before Nat, on his days off, Ben usually wound up at the station to "check on something" that could quite easily have waited a day or two. That was on top of him regularly working fourteen-hour days. All without complaint, of course. It was just his way. And though Natalie never actively forbid him from working long hours, completely understanding how important his job was, she'd managed to help Ben see how taking some time off wasn't a bad thing. It helped to recharge and reenergize him, not to mention clear his head. She showed him how a little time off could actually make him even more productive.

Ben was the first to say that Natalie was the best thing that could have happened to him.

Not that he'd been all work and no play before Nat, he'd just let the balance between work and play tip further to the work side of the scale. Even though his best friend and partner had tried to get him to rebalance the scale on numerous occasions, it took a feminine touch to finally do the trick.

Now, he enjoyed having a leisurely breakfast on a Saturday morning or taking a day trip to the Chesapeake Bay. But at the end of the day, Ben was still a workaholic.

Which is why, even without the assistance of his alarm clock, he still found himself wide awake at a little past seven that morning. Lying in bed, not wanting to get up and take the chance of waking Natalie, he'd become enthralled by the rays of early morning sunlight cutting through the blinds. They'd created shadowy tiger stripes on Nat's shoulder where her sleep shirt had fallen away.

The two had met three years earlier under extremely unfortunate circumstances. She was a teacher at Tasker High School and he was investigating a case in which three women were brutally strangled—two of which were students at the school. It was his first big case and one that still bothered him whenever he thought about it.

At the time, their meeting was strictly business. Romance was the last thing on Ben's mind as he was hunting a killer causing panic throughout the city. Not long after the case was closed, Ben and Natalie began running into each other in the most random of places. It was these brief and unexpected interactions that lit the spark that was missing during their first encounter. Natalie, always willing to say she was the smarter of the two—something Ben never disagreed with—made the first move. One day, while both of them were sitting at the Department of Motor Vehicles, waiting to get their driver's licenses renewed, she invited Ben to speak to her classes about what it was really like being a police detective. Wanting to show them that real life wasn't like what they saw on television. It was after the final bell rang and the last class of the day was packing up their things to head home that Ben asked Natalie out for dinner. It was after that first date that they knew they were destined to be together.

Now, with their wedding day approaching, Ben hated thinking about how they'd first met but was eternally grateful they did.

"Are you just staring at me?" Natalie asked without rolling over to look at him.

Ben didn't realize she was even awake. After an awkward pause, he answered, somewhat sheepishly, "Yes."

"Stop it. It's creepy," she said with a laugh.

"I thought it was romantic."

"It's only romantic in movies. In real life, it's a little weird," she said, finally rolling over bringing them face-to-face.

She couldn't help but smile looking into the eyes of the man she was going to spend the rest of her life with. The fact that he was a police detective hadn't really settled in yet. In reality, his life could be in danger every time he went to work. Natalie knew that in the back of her mind. But she also knew that Parker City wasn't exactly a hotbed of criminal activity. Sure, there was the case back in '81, but murder wasn't common in the small Western Maryland city. In fact, there hadn't been a crime like that in the last three years. Which is why Natalie was able to breathe a little easier about Ben's profession than if he were a detective with the Baltimore Police Department or the Metro Police in DC.

"What would you like to do today?" Ben asked, brushing an errant strand of hair from her cheek.

Natalie's nose wrinkled like it always did when she was trying to make a decision. They could go out and spend the day shopping at the mall or go see the new *Ghostbusters* movie that everyone was talking about. Or, they could spend the whole day at home just lounging around.

Before she could answer, the telephone in the kitchen began ringing.

Glancing at the clock, Ben saw that it was only seven-twenty. No one should have been calling that early.

"You can just let the answering machine do its job," Natalie pointed out as Ben rolled out of bed and started for the door.

"It could be the station."

"It's your day off."

"Exactly. It's my day off, so if the station is calling, it's important."

"Suit yourself," Natalie said, rolling over and pulling the blankets up around her. "But it could also be my mother."

For the briefest of moments, Ben paused in the doorway. Weighing his options, he couldn't *not* answer the phone. Besides, he liked Nat's mother…most of the time.

The couple shared a one-bedroom apartment that gave them just enough room for the both of them. Though, they'd decided after the wedding, it was time to look for an actual house. Crossing through the living room into the kitchen, Ben picked up the receiver just before the answering machine clicked on.

Clearing his throat, Ben answered, "Hello."

"Ben? Sorry to call you so early. I know it's your day off and all," said the unmistakably deep baritone of Nicholas Brent, Chief of the Parker City Police Department. "I was hoping you could check something out for me. A construction crew found a skeleton buried under the building they're tearing down over in the old Warehouse District. Since we don't really know what we're dealing with, I'd rather you just take the lead on this from the get-go."

"Of course, sir. I'll be there as soon as I can. You said a skeleton? Not a body?"

"That's what I've been told. There are a couple of our guys there already. I told them to lock down the area and not touch anything until you get there. I'll get state police to roll out a crime scene team."

Ben scribbled the address down before promising to touch base with the chief later in the day, then hung up. Standing there, he looked at the notepad in his hand, then at the bedroom door, then back at the notepad. He hoped this would turn out to be some sort of prank and he would be able to get back to spend the day with Nat.

As he padded back across the apartment to the bedroom, he admitted to himself that the idea of a skeleton buried under an old warehouse did intrigue him. Maybe it was the schoolboy deep inside of him that was still fascinated by the macabre. The grown-up part however, knew that skeletons didn't just turn up under buildings unless they were put there. Which in turn, meant there were a lot of questions that needed to be answered. That's where he came in. As one of the department's detectives, it was his job to ask the sort of questions that would uncover why there was a skeleton buried under an old building.

For her part, Natalie took Ben having to leave extremely well. It wasn't as if they had any plans. Plus, even though school had ended a couple weeks earlier, this was the first day she had nothing she needed to do and nowhere she needed to be. So, she was more than happy to roll over and go back to sleep while Ben was rushing around getting ready.

After a quick shower and shave, Ben threw on the first suit he grabbed out of the closet and was out the door.

Ben knew a bunch of people at the PCPD who wouldn't be too happy to be called in on their day off, but he was in a different situation than most. He was the head of the department's Detective Squad. Albeit a squad made up of just him and his partner, Tommy Mason.

The two had grown up together, gone to school together, and joined the force at the same time. Then, three years ago, when the mayor ordered the then-chief to form a detective unit for the PCPD that would specifically focus on criminal investigations, he and Tommy were tapped for the new post. It started out horribly. As two of the youngest members of the department, they were given no respect. Many of the more senior officers questioning why they had been the ones selected over everyone else when they were still so green. That was exactly why the mayor wanted younger officers for the job. He knew, like Ben and Tommy, that the department needed to move forward and couldn't keep doing everything the way it always had. The PCPD needed to evolve with the times.

Edgar Stanley, the chief at the time, thought having a Detective Squad was a waste of time. He was perfectly happy with the way things had always been done. But it was the mayor's order, so he did what he was told. Ready and eager to point out how he was against the idea when the new detectives went down in flames.

For the first few months, their cases were pretty basic. A few car thefts and some breaking and entering were as exciting as it got. Then came the fateful day in 1981 when the Spring Strangler killed his first victim. Beverly Baker was one of the most powerful and prominent women in Parker City and she'd been murdered. All eyes turned to the two young, inexperienced investigators to solve the case. Unfortunately, there were two more victims before the case was finally solved. But in the end, Ben and Tommy looked like heroes. Even Chief Stanley was forced to say they'd done well. Begrudgingly, of course.

Since then, thankfully, they hadn't been faced with anything as terrible. Ben knew that most police officers would go their entire careers without having a case like the Spring Strangler. It was the kind of thing you'd only find in the movies—two fledgling detectives faced with hunting down a killer on a rampage. But low and behold, that was his and Tommy's first big case. It was a real trial by fire. Now, he was being called in because a skeleton had been found under a building. Ben wasn't sure what to think about this one. But again, he was intrigued.

FOUR

In the 1950s and '60s, Parker City was thriving. It was a small city at the base of the Blue Ridge Mountains, with picturesque surroundings and a warm, friendly atmosphere. Even though the population hovered between forty and fifty thousand, it was a tight-knit community where everyone knew each other. When the weather was nice, the streets would be filled with people wandering around Downtown, popping in and out of shop after shop, or dining at one of the numerous restaurants along the main thoroughfares. That's what Ben vaguely remembered from his childhood.

What stood out in his memory the most was Christmastime when all the stores were decorated for the season and a festive feeling floated through the air. To his young eyes, everything was so shiny and bright. It was magical.

Then came the '70s. Things changed when the economy took a downturn. The vibrant commercial corridor began to lose its luster. Shops began closing. Restaurants shuttered. And the population dropped. People began moving away as the jobs disappeared. It wasn't a story unique to Parker City. The same thing happened elsewhere but only Parker could say the nail in its coffin was the Great Flood of 1978.

Several days of torrential rain caused the Tasker

River, which ran through the heart of Parker's Downtown, to burst over its banks like an invading army and flow through the streets showing no mercy to anything standing in its way. By the time the floodwaters finally receded, there was nothing but devastation left in its wake.

Six years later, though the outer limits of the city had built up, only now was the Downtown area beginning to show signs of turning around and coming back to life. It had been a major priority of the mayor to revitalize and restore what was once a booming city center.

No matter when he drove along Commerce or High Streets, Ben just couldn't help thinking about what it used to be like. He only hoped he would still be around to see it return to its former glory one day.

Ironically, the Warehouse District hadn't been touched by the floodwaters. These buildings were left dormant due to economics. But under the mayor's revitalization plan, this entire section of the city was to be torn down and rebuilt.

The warehouse at the corner of Fifth and Antietam looked like all the others, Ben thought as he stepped out of the unmarked squad car and looked up and down the street.

Clipping his shield to the lapel of his jacket and adjusting the holster under his arm, Ben crossed the street to the metal trailer set up at the front of the construction site. He counted two PCPD patrol cars and a state police cruiser already on the scene. Ben paused for a moment next to the Maryland State Trooper vehicle to look at the new design of the car. He hadn't seen it in person yet. The tan paint job on the new line of Crown

Vics was so much better than the hideous yellow-green color of the old fleet, Ben thought. Though he was still partial to the gray and blue of the Parker City police cars when all was said and done.

Normally, as he'd enter a crime scene, Ben would be more focused. Much more serious about the task that lay ahead. But as he still wasn't entirely sure what *this* was yet, he didn't know how to be thinking or how to mentally prepare himself.

He immediately snapped to attention when the door of the construction trailer opened and two men in flannel shirts and hardhats walked out followed by a PCPD uniformed officer.

"Why is it always LuCoco that gets here first?" Ben sighed under his breath.

Officer Buck LuCoco was one of the biggest pains in the ass in the department. Literally and figuratively. He'd been on the force since several years before Jesus was born and weighed close to six hundred pounds. Okay, those might have been serious exaggerations, but it was how Ben saw the aging, overweight patrolman in his mind's eye. LuCoco was one of those members of the PCPD that hated anything new and just wanted to live in the past. He would have been absolutely fine beating a confession out of an innocent person if it meant he got to clock out early. He'd also been one of the harshest critics of the Detective Squad when it was first established. After the Strangler case in '81 though, his open hostility toward Ben and Tommy wasn't as vocal. It had turned into a cooler and quieter disdain.

"Good morning, Officer LuCoco," Ben began as pleasantly as possible. "What have you got for me?"

Leaning against the trailer—Ben wondered how his girth didn't knock the entire thing over—the officer flipped through his notepad and said, "This here is Joseph Warner, the site foreman, and this is Lance Haggerty. He found the…um…remains when he was inspecting a portion of the building earlier this morning."

Ben noticed several more construction workers milling about on the other side of the fence waiting to find out if they were getting the day off. Thankfully, the state trooper was keeping them in an area away from the warehouse so as to not disturb the site any more than it already had been until the crime scene team arrived. Ben assumed the other PCPD officer must be keeping an eye on the skeleton inside.

After clocking everyone's position, Ben took the notebook that he always carried from his jacket pocket and turned back to LuCoco and the two workers.

"Mr. Warner, Mr. Haggerty, I'm Detective Ben Winters," he introduced himself as he flipped to a blank page in the notebook. "Can you tell me exactly what happened here this morning?"

The two construction workers looked at one another, each waiting for the other to speak first. Haggerty sighed in frustration, having already told his story three times. Clearly, Foreman Joe wanted to be involved as little as possible with all of this. He was too busy worrying about how long a delay this was going to cause in the demolition timeline.

"Come on. Just tell him exactly what you told me," LuCoco prodded as he wiped away the cascade of sweat pouring from his forehead with a wrinkled handkerchief he'd pulled from his pocket.

Haggerty once again explained how his morning began and the discovery he made while inspecting the site. Ben noted the salient points, then asked to be taken to the spot where the skeleton had been uncovered.

LuCoco and the foreman remained by the trailer as Haggerty led the way into the warehouse.

Stepping inside the cavernous space, Ben couldn't exactly describe the smell. Dust, dirt, and, no doubt, mold combined to give the stale air a thickness that made him feel as though after being there for only a few seconds he needed to take a shower. Debris from years of neglect scattered the floor, or what was left of the floor. There were vast expanses where the timbers were completely disintegrated revealing the dirt foundation. If it wasn't for the bright summer sun shining through the broken windows—and giant holes in the ceiling, Ben would have thought this was the perfect location for a horror movie. Looking at the beams that were supposedly supporting the structure, Ben started to wonder if he should be worrying about the place collapsing on top of them.

"It's a real mess," Haggarty said, seeing the look on the detective's face. "I'm surprised the place didn't fall down years ago. There's barely a foundation holding all this weight."

"Do you know anything about the owners of the property?" Ben asked.

"Nah," the construction worker shook his head. "Just some real estate firm from Jersey I think. I hear they own a bunch of shopping malls."

"Then I guess you don't know how long they've owned it?"

Haggarty snorted out a laugh. "You're asking the wrong

guy. That's way above my pay grade. I'm just here to tear this place down so a shiny new set of stores can take its place."

Ben hadn't expected to get too much more out of the guy. He'd be able to pull the property records later.

"In there," Haggarty pointed.

Ben could see the second patrolman standing just inside the doorway leading to a room off the main warehouse floor. As he got closer, Ben heard him talking to someone.

Please don't let him be talking to the skeleton, Ben thought as he got closer. One of the wooden boards under his foot cracked as he stepped through the door, causing the young patrolman to turn. At the same time, Ben saw that he hadn't been talking to the skeleton but another man in the room who was leaning precariously over the opening in the floor where Haggarty had fallen through.

"There is a whole skeleton buried under here," the guy said jumping to his feet with a big, child-like grin on his face.

More than a partner, more than a friend, Detective Thomas Mason was the brother Ben never had.

FIVE

TALL AND ATHLETIC, Tommy Mason always reminded Ben of Tom Selleck's *Magnum P.I.* character from television. Tommy always had that whole ruggedly handsome thing going for him. Mixed with a little bit of a "bad boy" vibe and he drove the women wild.

Next to Ben's clean-cut, buttoned-down appearance, their pairing caused many to do a doubletake. At first glance, they appeared to be complete opposites. But as one got to know them, they were very much alike. Each brought out the best in the other and at the end of the day, it was all about getting the job done. Sure, each had his own style, but that's what made them such a formidable team.

Tommy's apparent willingness to skirt the rules was always offset by Ben's ability to find ways to use the rules to their benefit. Just as Ben's refusal to play the internal politics game allowed Tommy to use his charm to keep too many feathers from getting ruffled amongst the powers-that-be. They each knew the other's strengths and weaknesses and how to adapt them to their own, which is why they'd been so impressive in getting the PCPD's Detective Squad off the ground.

"What are you doing here?" Ben asked, more than a little surprised to see his partner.

"Shirley from Dispatch called me. She thought I'd be

interested," Tommy explained. "And before you say anything about what I'm wearing, I just want to remind you, it is our day off, so I didn't think I needed to get dressed up to come to a potential crime scene. Especially when we don't actually know this is a crime scene yet."

He was referring to the fact he had on a T-shirt and comfortable pair of jeans, as opposed to the full suit and tie Ben was wearing.

"Besides, now you don't have to worry about getting your fancy suit muddy. I have no problems getting down there in the dirt." Tommy smiled, pointing at the fresh mud stains on his knees. With that, he knelt back down to take another look at the exposed skeletal remains under the floorboards.

"So, tell me. What do we have?" Ben asked, crouching next to Tommy so he could get a better look.

"You can see there's a pretty big cavity here under this part of the floor," Tommy pointed out. "It's got to be a good ten by ten area where the ground has been eaten away, even though it's not too deep, less than a foot in some places. It's definitely because of water…there's a lot of mud down there. As the earth under the floor eroded, it uncovered the skeleton. Partway, at least. Of course, no one could see what was happening under here until our friend Mr. Haggarty had the unfortunate experience of stepping on a board that was rotted through and it snapped, sending him falling through the floor. You can see where he landed in the mud.

"And right there," Tommy pointed, "you see the skull and top portion of the skeleton sticking out of the ground."

"You came face-to-face with that thing, man?" Tommy

looked over at the construction worker who was leaning against the wall. "Not a good way to start the day."

"Yeah. You're telling me," Haggarty answered.

Turning back to the skeleton, Tommy said, "I'm no expert, but that hole in the skull right there…see it, it looks like it could be a GSW from a pretty heavy caliber gun."

Leaning down and twisting his head so he could try and get a better look at the skull, Ben saw the hole and wondered if his partner was right. Finding a skeleton buried under the floor was one thing. Finding a skeleton buried under the floor with a bullet hole in its skull was something else. It took everything to a different level.

Standing and stretching their legs, Tommy said, "When Shirley first called me, I thought this was going to have been some kind of prank. Some kids snuck into the site on a dare and left a skeleton for the crew to find."

"You thought kids somehow buried a skeleton under this building in the hopes someone would fall through the floor and find it?" Ben asked, raising an eyebrow. "Not to mention having to figure out *how* to bury the thing under the floor?"

"In my defense," Tommy started, raising a finger and shaking it at his partner, "I didn't know the skeleton was buried *under* the warehouse. I just knew they'd found a skeleton *at* the warehouse."

The first thing that needed to happen was to get the skeleton out of the ground. That would be up to the crime scene techs. Even though he could easily reach in and pull the skull out to get a better look, Ben didn't want to disturb anything more than it already had been when Lance Haggarty crashed through the floor. Thankfully, he hadn't actually landed on the skull itself.

"So much for our day off," Ben said, looking at his watch, wondering where the crime scene guys were.

The unit that covered that part of the state was based out of the Parker City Barracks, less than ten minutes away. It was moments like this when Ben wished the PCPD was a bigger agency with its own crime scene unit. He understood that in the past, Parker didn't need a large police force. But since the flood, things had really started changing. Crime, not necessarily violent, was increasing in certain areas. And as it stood now, only thirty officers were responsible for keeping the entire city of roughly thirty thousand people safe. Though, under the new chief, that was changing. Brent had ramped up hiring, convincing the city council to approve at least ten more officers in the budget—if not more. He'd also begun looking at creating more specialized groups within the department. Now, along with the Detective Squad, which was designed to be the PCPD's criminal investigation division, there was also a small Drug Task Force working to fight the local war on drugs. Sadly, First Lady Nancy Reagan's "Just Say No" campaign wasn't working as well as some would like, so the police were being required to step in.

Even with the changes in the department, the PCPD still required and relied on state agencies for more technical services. Like CSU. That meant if the unit was already at one scene, they had to wait.

Jotting a few notes down in his notebook, Ben looked up when three men in jumpsuits with the Maryland State Police insignia emblazoned on them walked in behind Officer LuCoco and Chief Brent.

Ben couldn't help but notice the stark contrast between the two police veterans. LuCoco was disheveled, overweight, and always looked out of breath, while Brent was sharp, muscular, and commanded every room into which he set foot. Under Brent's leadership, Ben wasn't sure how much longer LuCoco would last.

Brent was really putting his stamp on the department. For years, he had been the PCPD's second in command, next to Chief Edgar Stanley, who'd been in charge for over thirty years. But while Stanley was the face of the PCPD, it was Brent who kept things running from behind the scenes. So, when Stanley died after suffering a massive, yet not altogether unexpected, heart attack the year before, Brent was his natural successor. A former Navy man, the new chief towered over everyone in size and presence.

"Ben, Tommy," Brent gave each of his detectives a quick nod as he scanned the room from behind his sunglasses. "I wanted to check this one out for myself."

At six foot four, Chief Brent and Tommy stood eye-to-eye, making Ben feel like he was standing between a pair of giants. He always wondered if the two realized they kept their mustaches trimmed in the same style. Though Brent's was a bright red.

Shaking off the completely irrelevant thought, Ben began to fill the chief in on what had been discovered as the CSU team went to work. Listening intently, Brent kept his eyes focused on the hole in the floor around which the techs were taking photos and beginning to pull up more boards so they could have access to the skeleton, which they were clearly excited to get their hands on and examine.

"Do you think there is any way the skeleton could

have been put there recently?" Brent asked, watching as the guys slowly began lifting the bones out of the muddied earth.

"I can't say it isn't *possible*," answered Ben, "but I would have to say it is highly unlikely. The thing was buried in the mud, under the floor. And it's not like it was a new section of flooring that someone had recently put down. These boards are falling apart. So, to pull them up, put a skeleton under them, then replace the floor… My gut says that isn't what happened here."

"Yeah, chief, those bones were pretty well sunk into the mud under there," added Tommy. "They've been there for a while."

"What's your next move, detectives?"

"Well, sir," Ben thought for a moment, "we need to see what the skeleton can tell us…age, sex…"

"…if that is a bullet hole in the skull," Tommy added.

"Then we'll look into open missing person cases, see if anything jumps out at us. And I want to pull the building's records and see when it was built, by whom, how many times it's been sold," Ben finished as he closed his notebook.

"Alright," Brent said with a quick nod. "Keep me posted and let me know if there's anything you need."

With another nod to the detectives, the chief turned and left them to their work.

"I like him so much more than Stanley," Tommy said as they watched the chief disappear through the warehouse's main entrance into the sunlight outside. "He never tells us 'don't fuck this up.' I really do appreciate that," he added with a wry smile.

SIX

THE HEADLINE IN the next morning's *Herald-Dispatch* announced the discovery of a skeleton under one of the buildings in the old Warehouse District.

Ben read the accompanying article while he ate a quick breakfast at the little deli around the corner from the station. Between bites of scrambled eggs and bacon, he was trying to figure out where the reporter had gotten his information. He certainly hadn't spoken with anyone. And to his knowledge, the department hadn't put out any information yet.

The whole thing brought up memories of a reporter Ben and Tommy dealt with during the Strangler case. Roger Benedict, a smart-mouthed journalist working for the *Herald-Dispatch*, always seemed to be one step ahead of them on the case. Mysteriously showing up at the crime scenes before anyone else and having information no one else knew. He'd been top on both detectives' lists as being the killer. Even after the case was closed, Tommy still thought Benedict was involved. It could have been the snot-nosed young reporter's arrogance that caused the investigators to want to throw him in a cell and lose the key; or the fact that there was more than enough circumstantial evidence to tie him to the murders. Either way, Ben and Tommy both wanted him behind bars.

Shortly after the Strangler case, Benedict moved on from Parker City, so this piece came from a different reporter. But as Ben got further into the article, it was obvious someone from the construction crew had been the one to tip off the paper.

Ben was hoping there'd be some actual facts waiting for him when he arrived at the office. The medical examiner had been as intrigued about the discovery as Ben, so he promised to deliver a preliminary report on the skeletal remains as quickly as possible.

The forensic techs had taken their time yesterday. Carefully pulling up enough of the floorboards so they had complete access to the area of muddied ground where the bones were buried took hours. After that, they methodically cleared away layers of grime and debris so as to not damage the remains anymore than nature had already done.

Once the full skeleton was uncovered, small fragments of material were found clinging to various pieces of bone. The chief crime scene tech thought they could have been pieces of clothing that hadn't fully deteriorated and survived being buried. There was a chance the remnants might be able to help provide an identity for the bones. There wasn't much to go on, so it was something.

Ben was turning everything over in his mind as he parked in the lot the Parker City Police Department shared with City Hall and headed into the station. A sturdy building, its classic design could easily have passed for a small school or library. Until one noticed the bars lining the basement windows where the holding cells were and the lot full of police cars in the rear.

The traditional brick and stone structure was over a hundred years old, Ben had learned. A post-Civil War project, however, it wasn't specifically built to house the city's police force. It was to match City Hall, which sat right next door. In comparison, though designed by the same person and constructed in a similar style, City Hall was a beautiful, white-columned, stone-carved palace beside its lucky-to-have-a-roof-that-didn't-leak little stepbrother.

Letting himself in through the parking lot entrance, Ben checked the bulletin board to see if there were any new notifications or announcements of which he needed to be aware. Seeing nothing new, he headed for the squad's office on the second floor. Passing a few of the night shift patrolmen heading home, Ben stopped to chat for a few minutes. He wasn't out on the street every day anymore but liked to keep up with whatever the latest might be. It also helped to prove to some of the uniformed officers that he was still one of them, just in a suit.

Heading up the warped stairs, Ben saw the building quickly coming to life. A skeleton crew kept the department going throughout the night, but come eight o'clock, Chief Brent wanted the day shift punched in and ready to go.

It wasn't uncommon to find the chief already at work when Ben arrived in the mornings. And Ben was usually an hour or so earlier than most. He liked the quiet time with fewer people running around to take care of the administrative side of his job and gear up for whatever might come his way throughout the rest of the day. Brent was very much the same. A far cry from the last chief who usually didn't stroll in until sometime around eleven—knowing full well that Brent, his right-hand man at the time, would always have everything under control. Now, there were many mornings when Ben and the chief would have a cup of coffee together in the second-floor breakroom before anyone else arrived. Between the two of them, they could finish off an entire pot of coffee before another soul stepped foot in the office. The frequent occurrence gave Ben and the chief a lot of time to get to know one another and become more friendly than simply commanding officer and detective.

When the Detective Squad was created, a small office space in the middle of the second floor was carved out for them. "Small" being an extreme understatement. What was once a storage closet, now had two desks side-by-side, a couple of file cabinets wedged into the corner, and exactly one trash can. It was better than nothing, Ben thought at the time. Since then, he and Tommy had gotten used to their quaint quarters and enjoyed the separation from the other sections of the department. A window and some natural light would have been nice, but they made do. And the ugly green linoleum floor was horrendous, worn, and in desperate need of being replaced. Like so much of the rest of the building though, it functioned, even if it needed updating.

Tucking his briefcase into a small nook between his and Tommy's desk, Ben was happy to find a file from the medical examiner waiting for him.

Tossing his jacket over the back of his chair, he quickly flipped open the folder and began reading the

M.E.'s initial report on the skeleton that had been recovered the morning before.

Running his finger down the lines on the report, he found the key pieces of information in which he was most interested. The remains were that of a male in his late forties to early fifties. The back of the skull was fractured, though the medical examiner could not with "certainty" declare whether it was post- or perimortem. What he could confirm was that the hole clearly visible in the skull was, in fact, a gunshot wound.

Ben leaned back in his chair. They had a homicide on their hands now. It was right there in black and white.

SEVEN

BEN WASN'T SURE what he'd been expecting. Clearly, finding a skeleton buried under the floor of a rundown building meant there had been some sort of foul play. And in all honesty, there were only so many ways that could have happened. So why did it make such a difference to have the fact that this was a murder confirmed? Ben couldn't answer that question. Nor was it important.

There was a job to do.

The first phone call he made after reading the M.E.'s report, was to the head of the state police's crime scene unit. He was going to need them to head back out to the construction site and pull up the rest of the floor around where the bones were found to see if there was anything else buried in the ground. If they were lucky, maybe the murder weapon with intact fingerprints was stuck in the mud somewhere. Or the victim's wallet with ID.

That was the first time Ben used the term "victim."

As he was hanging up the phone, Ben heard the unmistakable voice of his partner coming down the hallway. If there was one thing he could count on every morning, it was being able to hear Tommy coming. Whether he was singing a song—horribly out of tune—or greeting each and every person he passed on his way to the office, Tommy's gregarious nature always signaled his imminent arrival.

Practically skipping into the office, Ben was surprised to see Tommy was already wearing a tie. Normally he waited until the very last minute to put one on. Even then, it was because Ben forced him to do so.

"What's the occasion?" Ben asked while rereading the M.E.'s report.

"You mean the tie? Oh, I just knew we were going to have to do some detective work today and I know how much you like it when I dress up."

As usual, Tommy was being a smartass, but that didn't make what he said any less accurate. On all counts. Ben did like when he looked professional and they were going to need to do "some detective work."

Tommy dropped into his chair and swung his feet up on the desk. As he did, Ben tossed the medical examiner's report in his lap.

"And what do we have here?" Tommy asked flipping open the file.

"The M.E.'s initial report. You were right. That was a bullet hole in the skull. Read."

Tommy's eyes scanned back and forth across the page. The further into the report he got, the more his demeanor changed. Putting his feet on the floor and the report on his desk, he was now leaning over the paperwork completely engrossed by its findings.

After reading the report for a second time, he asked Ben, "Is the crime scene still locked down? The tech guys need to go rip up the rest of the floor and see if they can find anything else under there."

Ben smiled, then said, "Exactly what I thought. I just got off the phone with Sergeant Bradford over at the state police. The team is going back out to do just that.

In the meantime, you and I need to go through the missing persons files. We can at least narrow them down to males in their late forties to early fifties."

"Even if we don't know how long that skeleton has been buried?" Tommy asked.

"Even if we don't know how long that skeleton has been buried," repeated Ben. "I requested the files yesterday afternoon. I was hoping they'd have pulled them by now. Any chance you want to head down to the Records Room and work your charms to move things along a bit?"

A devilish grin slowly appeared on Tommy's lips. "Are you saying you think I can go downstairs and sweet talk little old Betty?"

"That's exactly what I'm saying."

"I know. I just like hearing you acknowledge my superpower," he said heading for the door.

"Being a shameless flirt is not a superpower!" Ben hollered after his partner.

"Yes, it is!" Tommy shouted back.

The man was unbelievable, Ben thought as he laughed to himself.

Picking up the M.E.'s report, Ben started toward the chief's office. Brent said he wanted to be kept updated. Now that it was a confirmed homicide, even though they didn't have a timeline or ID yet, he should still know.

Entering the chief's outer office, Ben found Mildred Greene sitting at her desk shuffling through a thick stack of papers. Chief Brent's secretary—and Chief Stanley's before him—Greene was jokingly referred to around the station as the longest employed staffer with the PCPD…having been hired around the time the police force was established back in the 1800s. Of course, this was not something that was ever said to her face, because everyone was afraid of the woman. It didn't matter that the men all carried guns, even the biggest and burliest of them was terrified of the wiry little woman with a seriously outdated beehive hairdo. As always, she was surrounded by a haze of swirling cigarette smoke wafting up from the Lucky Strike dangling from her lips.

"Is the chief free?" Ben asked, sounding almost sorry to be disturbing her.

Without looking up from her work, she gave the customary jerk of the head towards the door, letting him know it was alright to go through. Not wishing to disturb her any more than he already had, Ben nodded a quick thank you and let himself in to see the chief.

"I'm sorry, Mrs. Greene gave me the okay to come in," Ben said when he saw the chief wasn't alone.

"It's fine," Brent said, motioning for Ben to come in and take a seat. "Hank and I were just wrapping up."

Lieutenant Hank McMaster was the PCPD's new Field Services Commander. A twenty-five-year veteran of the force, he'd only recently assumed his position overseeing all patrol and policing operations, including the Detective Squad. As Ben's direct supervisor, he was the one supposed to read all of Ben's reports, but Ben doubted how much attention he paid to the two detectives under his command. McMaster was very much one of the old school members of the department. He liked the more traditional ways things had been done. But as long as Ben and Tommy didn't screw up and make him look bad, he didn't much care what they did, so he left them up to their own devices. He was much different than their former supervisor. Lieutenant James Dennis had been very hands-on and always wanted to know what Ben and Tommy were up to and the status of their cases. Earlier that year, Dennis took a job out west, and now McMaster was in charge.

Since the Spring Strangler case only three years earlier, the Parker City Police Department had gone through a number of changes. Not only in personnel but policy. For many of the old guard, it had been like whiplash. For Ben and Tommy, and the couple other younger officers walking the beat, it was a refreshing transformation. And with Brent in charge, Ben thought it was only the beginning.

"Sir," Ben began, placing the M.E.'s report on the chief's desk, "I thought you'd want to see this. It looks like we do have a homicide on our hands. We just don't know who the victim is or when it happened."

"The bones in the warehouse?" McMaster asked.

"Yes, sir," the detective nodded. "They belong to a male somewhere in his late forties to early fifties."

"And we don't know when he was buried?" the chief asked after reading the file.

"No. As you saw, initial findings are inconclusive."

Ben explained that he and Tommy were going to start the identification process by going through all the open missing persons cases to see if there was anyone who fit the very vague details they had. They were also going to check the records to see when the warehouse was built, by whom, and who owned it now. They were hoping then, they would have some pieces of information that would start to fit together.

The chief, as usual, said he wanted to be kept updated. To Ben's surprise, so did McMaster. Ben's face must have betrayed his surprise because, with a shrug, the lieutenant said that the case sounded interesting.

By the time Ben returned to his office, Tommy was seated at his desk behind a pile of old, beat-up folders.

"Betty gave me every file she had. Seriously, going back as far as she could find. I think one of the ones on the bottom is from the '30s. The *'30s*, Ben! That's over fifty years of files."

"I have to admit. I'm surprised the PCPD has records that actually go back that far."

Tommy gave his partner a cold stare.

"That isn't the part I wanted you to be focused on," he said dryly.

"Okay, how about I make a deal with you," Ben started, "I will go through all of these files and find anyone that fits the age we're talking about and you go over to the courthouse and pull the records on the warehouse. Find out who owned it, when it was built, all the details."

"Deal!" Tommy said jumping to his feet. "At the courthouse, the clerks will do the searching for me."

"We'll regroup over lunch," Ben said, watching his partner practically run out of the office.

EIGHT

1959...

"WHAT THE HELL are you doing in here? And what the fuck are you doing with a gun?" Billy Roscoe snapped. His cold, hard stare locked on the man sitting comfortably behind his desk as if it were his own. The undeserved confidence he saw in front of him reminded Billy just how much he hated the arrogant, young upstart and everyone like him who never had to work a day in their life. But right now, "the Kid"—as Billy referred to him—was a necessity, a means to an end. Which meant he was going to need to be tolerated.

"I thought I might need it for protection," he shrugged, not understanding why Billy sounded so irate. "You've got Freddy and all his guys watching your back. Who do I have watching mine?"

"Nobody's watching your back because no one knows you exist," Billy snarled, deliberately taking a shot at the younger man's over-inflated ego. It was like trying to get through to a little puppy. Roscoe couldn't understand how a guy in his thirties, not without a good deal of intelligence, could be so adolescent sometimes. Then he reminded himself again, it wasn't like he was ever forced to grow up. Which is exactly why Billy thought of him as a kid.

"I'm here because I own the place. Remember?" The young man was staying very cool even though he could tell Billy was looking for a fight.

"You own *part* of this hotel," Billy said, slamming the crystal tumbler down on the desk next to the gun. The last of the scotch in the glass shot up, performing an aerial ballet before splashing back down. "And you are a *silent* partner…at best. That was the deal. Now get out of my chair."

"What's gotten into you, Billy? You seem tense. Everything's going great. I saw the restaurant was full. Did you see the line outside to get in? All the rooms are booked and have you been upstairs yet? It's packed. We've got to be raking in the dough up there."

Roscoe's pulse was already racing after his encounter with Ramsburg, but now he felt his heart thundering in his chest. He needed some time to cool off. Instead, he had to deal with another unwanted visitor. Some days he felt like his life was charmed. Other days, like today, he was wondering what it would have been like to stay in Jersey and live out his life there as just an average Joe.

"I said, get out of my chair."

"Cool off," the Kid said, raising his hands defensively. "I'm not here to cause any problems. I'm just checking in on my investment."

"You mean your father's," Roscoe shot back. "And get this off my desk. Put it away."

Billy pushed the gun out of the way.

"The last thing I need right now is you walking around with a gun. You're going to shoot your foot off. Jesus Christ! What do you think, you're some big tough guy now? A gangster?"

Taking his rightful place behind the desk, Roscoe took a deep breath. He tried to clear his mind so he could focus. Ramsburg had been crawling all over him for months and hadn't come up with anything to pin on him or anyone in his company. And as far as the Kid went, he wasn't all that bad. He just had an unbelievable tendency to pop up at the worst possible moment and start pushing Billy's buttons. At least Freddy wasn't there to bring the room's IQ down.

There was a knock at the door.

Not needing to ask who it was, eyes closed as he massaged his temples, he said, "Come in, Freddy."

Slowly opening the door, the former boxer's large physique filled the doorway. "How'd ya know it was me?"

"Lucky guess," Billy said. "Come on in."

Freddy Quinn pushed his way into the room and took a quick look around. It was rare for Billy to invite him into the office. He could think of maybe a handful of times he'd been asked in. Even then, it wasn't for very long. Freddy didn't take it personally. Other than Marty, he couldn't think of anyone Billy let into the office.

Which is why Freddy was surprised to see the young, well-dressed guy standing next to his boss. He'd only seen him on a couple of occasions and didn't know much more than he was "the money" in the operation. Even though Freddy wasn't the brightest of bulbs, he knew not to ask too many questions about him. It was better for everyone that way.

"Everything okay in here, boss?" Freddy asked with a combination of curiosity and concern.

"I'm just hosting an investor's meeting," Billy answered, picking up the scotch glass and tossing back what little remained. "Could one of you refill this please?"

Hoping to get back on Billy's good side, the Kid quickly took the glass and crossed to the bar. Filling Billy's glass, he also poured himself a drink, then motioned to Freddy, asking if he wanted one. Never one to turn down good liquor, Freddy licked his lips. As happy as he would have been to accept the offer, it wasn't *Billy* making it. So, for the first time, he thought before answering and begrudgingly declined.

"You know you can talk to me," the Kid said, handing Billy his glass. "I want to be a part of this. I want to know what's going on. What has you so worked up?"

Roscoe swirled the dark liquid around, weighing whether it was worth discussing the matter with his not-so-silent partner. There was a chance he could end up being useful, Billy thought.

"Alright, fine. You want to know what's going on? I'll tell you." Billy paused long enough to empty his glass for the second time in a matter of minutes. Thankfully, the alcohol was starting to take the edge off. "There is a policeman who has decided I am the root of all evil in Parker City and he has been trying his damnedest to find something to prove I am involved in some sort of illegal activity so he can throw me in jail. That's the problem in a nutshell."

"I see. How concerned are you about this cop? Do you think he actually *knows* something?"

The Kid's careless, playboy demeanor disappeared. In just a few seconds he'd become all business, taking a much more serious tone. Billy wondered if his concern was for the operation with which he'd invested a good deal of money or if he was worried people would find out he'd gone into business with the notorious restaurateur who was so looked down upon by the influential members of Parker society. His father certainly wouldn't approve.

"I'm not sure what he knows. For the last year, he's been snooping around, but hasn't come up with anything."

"There you go. There's nothing to worry about."

"*Except*...he sounded a hell of a lot more confident just now."

The Kid frowned. "You don't think someone upstairs talked?"

"I hope they didn't for their sake," Freddy chimed in, his tone a little too menacing. "Our people know not to talk. They all know what would happen if they do."

Both Roscoe and the Kid stared at Freddy, not immediately sure how to respond to his ominous proclamation. Billy appreciated the sentiment but didn't care much for the dramatics.

He felt like he was surrounded by a wannabe cast of *Little Caesar*. The Kid, Freddy, Freddy's brother Jimmy, they all were walking around like they were a part of the mob. Billy was well aware of the fact they were breaking a number of laws on a daily basis, but gangsters they were not. And if people kept living in this film-noir fantasy, someone was going to screw up, and then everything was going to come crashing down.

"Can't Chief Stanley order this cop off your case?" the Kid asked, interrupting Billy's train of thought. "He's always real buddy-buddy with you when he's here eating dinner. Can't you just ask him to do you a favor?"

"Marty says we need to be careful. We don't want to apply so much pressure that we arouse any suspicion."

Billy once again leaned back in his chair and began massaging his temples. He was beyond ready to call it a day and head home. The sooner he could crawl into the giant bed in his suite on the third floor of the hotel and go to sleep, the better. Before he could do that though, he knew he needed to check in and see how things were going upstairs.

"Do you think we could just talk to this cop?"

"Talk to him?"

"Yeah. Talk to him. You said you've already got a guy on the inside. Maybe we offer him the same deal. Everyone has a price. My father taught me that years ago."

Freddy decided to throw in his two cents again. "Maybe it could work, boss. Just pay Ramsburg off."

"Enough!" Billy snapped. "We're not trying to pay him off. That little shit can't be bought. And we aren't going to try because then he'd be able to come at me for trying to bribe him! You two don't need to worry about doing any of the thinking. Leave that up to me. Jesus. I don't need this."

Billy stood up and straightened his tie. "I don't want either of you doing anything. Do you understand me? Do I make myself perfectly clear? Now, both of you, get out!"

NINE

BILLY'S MOOD SWINGS tonight were even taking him by surprise. Sure, he had his bad days like everyone else, but he just wanted today to be over with already.

After throwing Freddy and his wannabe protégé out of the office, he poured himself his final scotch of the day. Hoping this one would do the trick and help him relax enough to fall asleep. Not before making a stop on the fourth floor though. It was his evening ritual; the last thing he did before heading to his suite was check in upstairs. He needed to be seen there as much as he did working the Derby Room downstairs. He was the face of the company after all. His guests wanted to see the great Billy Roscoe in action and he wasn't going to disappoint any of them.

In the corner of his office, behind Billy's desk, was a door that most people would assume was a closet or private bathroom, a luxury for the owner of the building. In reality, the door opened onto a private elevator that could take Roscoe directly to his hotel suite on the third floor, or one floor further up to the fourth floor's surveillance room. Billy stepped in and pushed the button to take him all the way to the top.

The elevator cage rattled its way upward, climbing one floor after another until it came to a stop at its destination. Billy opened the door and stepped into a large, brightly lit room. At a long desk in the center of the space sat four men, each with a pair of telephones, a pushbutton control panel, and small joystick in front of them. Beyond the men was a wall, in which two dozen television screens were arranged. Each one connected to a closed-circuit camera, giving the men a view of the entire fourth floor from any angle. With the joystick and control buttons, the men could adjust the direction of the cameras, as well as zoom in and out making it possible for them to see everything happening in real time. It was the latest in surveillance technology. As with the air conditioning, this was another large investment Billy was all too happy to make.

Each man was responsible for keeping his eyes on six screens. Behind them was the supervisor who was responsible for watching the watchers. Arthur Donnelly had Freddy Quinn's build and Marty Schulman's brains, along with a pair of eagle eyes. He ran a tight ship and saw everything. Nothing could get by him. Donnelly was also one of Billy's most trusted employees, which is why he held such an important position in the company.

"How's everything going this evening, Arthur?" Billy asked, allowing his eyes to jump from screen to screen to catch as much action as possible.

"Pretty quiet night so far, Mr. Roscoe. All things considered. I think the heat outside's kept some people at home. Even so, all the tables have been full since we opened," Donnelly said as he flipped a gold casino chip back and forth across his knuckles. It was a simple trick Billy was never able to master. Whenever he'd try, the chip would always slip and go flying in one direction or the other. This minor shortcoming didn't bother him too much as he reminded himself he had a good number of other talents.

"No one up here that shouldn't be?"

"Not that we've seen." The watchman's brow furrowed. "Is there someone in particular you're worried about, boss?"

"Anyone in a police uniform, Arthur," Roscoe half-heartedly quipped. "Talk to Freddy. He'll give you the rundown. We're getting some heat from a pesky cop who won't mind his own business. I just want to make sure he doesn't get up here somehow."

Donnelly shook his head emphatically. "Our guys keep an eye on the door. There's only one way in and one way out. Anyone coming in must have the special key to show they belong. No one's getting in here that isn't supposed to be here. I promise you that, Mr. Roscoe."

"I trust you, Arthur. Just don't let me down."

"No, sir. Are you gonna take a walk around the floor?"

"Just a quick one tonight. It's been a long day. I want to turn in early."

Donnelly looked at his watch. Most nights, Roscoe would spend on the floor glad-handing until the wee hours of the morning. It wasn't even nine o'clock yet.

Straightening his tie and adjusting the cuffs of his shirt, Billy Roscoe took a deep breath before opening the door and making his entrance.

Stepping out of the silence of the surveillance room, he was immediately engulfed by the racket created by countless conversations all taking place at the same time, of electronic machines chirping various tunes as coins dropped into metal trays, and of little white balls bouncing around spinning wheels. As dice flew through the air and landed on the green felt of a table off to one side, the crowd cheered with excitement, while across the room a groan went up as the dealer busted all the Black Jack players at the table.

For all the success of his restaurants, the continuous full occupancy of the rooms downstairs, and the fleet of shipping trucks—which by themselves transported cargo that was twenty percent contraband—it was the casino hidden away on the fourth floor that was building Billy's fortune, increasing his bank account exponentially on a daily basis.

Roscoe scanned the room, absorbing the energy. He never felt as alive as he did when he was up here. The electricity in the air filled him with such excitement. It always felt like he was a kid on Christmas morning. Silly to think that way, maybe, but the glittering lights and shiny metallic slot machines paled in comparison to the gleam in his eyes when he was strolling the casino floor.

Before he had come along, the closest place for people in Maryland to place a bet and spin a Roulette wheel was in Las Vegas. And those places were all run by gangsters. Billy was just a businessman providing the good people of Parker City with a service. An outlet for some harmless vice. If he just so happened to make a profit off their weakness, so be it. After all, the house always wins in the end.

As soon as he stepped out of the secured surveillance room, Billy picked up a shadow. Whenever he was walking the casino floor, one of Freddy's guys was always a few steps behind him. He didn't know what the big deal was. This wasn't Vegas. He wasn't Bugsy Siegal. No one was going to try and bump him off. If they did, they better sure as hell not try it in his own place. Billy simply wouldn't allow that to happen.

Ignoring the goon trailing him, Billy went into his act, shaking hands and patting players on the back. A code had been worked out with the dealers and croupiers so they could casually signal to their boss whether a player was on a winning streak or losing their shirt so he knew how to talk to them. It made Billy appear clairvoyant to the guests playing his games. Unlike down in the restaurant, though, up here he never comped anything. People paid to play. Some nights, they paid big-time.

This was what Bert Ramsburg was snooping around looking for. If he could just get to the fourth floor, he'd have all the evidence he needed to lock Billy up. But the casino on the top of Billy's hotel was one of the most unbelievably well-kept secrets in the city. A person needed to know someone who knew someone just to find out about the extremely secretive gaming club. That's how it was sold to the outside world, as a private *club*. That way, if someone happened to find their way to the top floor of the hotel, standing in front of the oversized double doors outside the elevator, and didn't have a "club key" to show the "doorman," they were sent on their way with apologies.

If they did carry one of those special keys with the head of a lion embossed on it, they were granted access to a world very few people ever saw. It was a world with which the vast majority of Parkertons were completely unfamiliar.

The funny part was, all of Billy's guests at the casino

were simple working stiffs looking to blow off steam. None of the city's elite ever set foot there. Honestly, he didn't think any of those snobs even knew about it. If they did, he was sure they'd be raising holy hell about it and trying to run him out of town. Roscoe loved how he was so easily able to pull the wool over so many people's eyes. The mayor loved having a nice big dinner down-stairs and being seen in one of the most fashionable res-taurants in town. If only he knew how many laws were being broken, literally, over his head. What would he do, Billy wondered?

Satisfied that everything was as it should be, Roscoe was ready to turn in for the night. He was exhausted and couldn't wait to crawl into bed. The last thing he did before his private elevator carried him down to his suite was flash Arthur Donnelly a smile that showed off his sparkling, pearly white teeth and wish him a good night.

TEN

THOUGH BILLY'S MOOD had improved significantly after spending time amongst the spinning tumblers of the slot machines and rich green fields of gaming tables, he would not have gone to bed happy if he knew what Freddy and his partner were discussing when left on their own.

After being dismissed from the office, it was obvious to Freddy that the Kid was frustrated having been put in his place by Billy. Guys like him didn't like being talked down. Guys like him thought they were entitled to be treated better than everyone else because they had an important name and money. As for himself, Freddy understood that taking crap from his boss when he was in a bad mood was just another part of the job.

"I hope you don't mind me sayin'," Freddy said as the two men walked down the back hallways toward the rear parking lot, "but you can't let Billy bother you when he's like that. He's got a lot to think about and sometimes he just blows off steam. He knows what he's doin'. Why are you worried about running the hotel anyways? You've already got a job, don't ya? I saw you in that article in the paper the other day."

"Yeah. But that was because of my father. I want to prove to Billy that I can be an asset to him here…running the hotel and…. upstairs."

"Asset?" Freddy let out a laugh. "You're nothing but *assets*. You're the *money*, buddy. Trust me. Billy knows how important you are."

"That isn't what I mean."

Freddy stopped and stared at him. "I don't get why you're trying to expose yourself so much. I'd think you would wanna do everything in your power to keep from being associated with Billy. He don't seem to be too popular in your circle of friends. But here you are, tryin' to make a name for yourself. Maybe you should be thankin' Billy because he's trying to protect your name and reputation. Did you ever think about that? Nah. Of course not. You're used to snapping your fingers and always gettin' whatever you want. Well, guess what. That ain't how it always works. If Billy says to stay out of it, stay out of it. You're a businessman. As far as I can tell, this is just a business arrangement, you and Billy. He needed an investor and you fit the bill. He's makin' you money, so let him keep doin' that."

The little speech was the most articulate Freddy had ever been. It surprised both of them.

"Don't you want Billy to ever see you as anything more than just the hired muscle?"

Freddy was stunned by the Kid's nerve. He might have just been the "hired muscle," but he was just that— the *muscle*. And that meant very few people ever stood up to him. It looked like this spoiled rich kid might actually have a backbone, Freddy thought.

Laying his meaty hand on the younger man's shoulder, Freddy looked straight into his eyes. There was a fire in them he hadn't expected. If there was any chance he thought this kid could make it through a physical altercation, Freddy thought he might be useful. But one hit and he'd probably snap in half.

"You need to cool off or you're really gonna get yourself in trouble."

"Or, you and I work together and take care of Billy's problem for him. Show him what we can do. What was the name of the cop causing the problems?"

"You're way over your head here. Friggin' forget it." Freddy started down the hall again. While he would like nothing more than to throw Officer Bert Ramsburg in the Tasker River and get rid of the guy once and for all, he wasn't going to do it unless Billy told him to.

"Come on, Freddy!"

For the second time that evening, the tough guy made the smart decision and kept walking.

"Fine. I'll just ask your brother. He's always willing to talk."

Freddy stopped.

The Kid wasn't wrong. Jimmy had a way of saying things he wasn't supposed to without even realizing it. He wasn't the brightest, so a smart, college-educated guy like this would definitely get him to spill the beans.

Slowly turning back to face him, Freddy, in a tone that signaled his resignation, asked, "What exactly is your plan, smart guy?"

A smile appeared on the younger man's face. He knew he'd gotten to Freddy.

Taking a few quick steps to catch up, he said, "I'm a great negotiator. I just want to talk to the cop. That's all. Offer him some money to go away. Everyone has a price."

"I don't know why Billy hasn't tried to buy him off

already," Freddy admitted. "It ain't like we haven't done it with other cops before."

The wheels were slowly beginning to turn in Freddy's head. It was his job to protect Billy after all. And getting Ramsburg to back off would be doing just that. Maybe his initial thought to drop the whole thing and go home wasn't the right thing to do. He was beginning to second guess himself.

Frustrated with having to use so much of his limited mental capacity, Freddy pulled a pack of Pall Malls out of his pocket. Lighting up, he let the sharp intake of nicotine wash over him. Ironically, the smoke circling his head on the outside helped to lift the mental fog he was experiencing on the inside.

"But if Ramsburg says no to a bribe, then he could accuse Billy of trying to buy him off." Freddy was trying to reason his way through the conversation, not realizing he'd given up the name of the police officer in question.

"He's not going to turn down the money. We'll offer him more than he's ever seen before."

"We should talk to Marty about this," Freddy said. "He'll know what to do."

"Since when do you need to get Marty's permission to do things? I thought you were supposed to be Billy's right-hand man. You should be allowed to make decisions too."

He'd gotten off to a rough start, but the Kid was seeing progress. He knew he just needed to keep Freddy talking. The longer he could do that, the easier it became to manipulate him. A few more minutes and he'd have Freddy believe the whole thing was his own idea and he was just tagging along to help. If only everyone was as simple-minded as Freddy Quinn, he thought to himself.

Freddy remained silent. The wheels in his head were now spinning wildly. Weighing his options, trying to decide what was best for him, how angry Billy would be if he didn't follow his orders, what his reward could be if he was able to get Ramsburg off his boss's back. It was all too much to think about. He was starting to get a shooting pain behind his eyes. He could really use a drink.

Finishing his cigarette and immediately lighting another, Freddy said between puffs, "Let me figure out the best place to have a…meeting…with Ramsburg. Okay? Don't do anything until I can make some arrangements. Alright?"

The grin on the Kid's face gave Freddy an odd feeling inside. He'd take working with a hardened convicted felon over a Harvard-educated rich kid any day. They could both be just as crazy, but in his opinion, the Harvard guy was a hundred times more ruthless. With that thought rattling around in his head, he was wondering if he was making a big mistake.

ELEVEN

1984...

OFFICER JOE NOFFSINGER was beginning to see the light at the end of the tunnel. He'd worked every day for two and a half weeks straight and in just a few short hours, he'd be able to clock out for some much-needed time off. He was looking forward to working around the house and maybe, just maybe, sleeping in one morning—something he hadn't been able to do since being tapped by Chief Brent to head the PCPD's fledgling task force charged with taking on the rising drug epidemic.

Since First Lady Nancy Reagan had taken up the cause and brought national attention to the issue, Parker City had undertaken an effort to clean up the drug activity Downtown. It was all part of the mayor's master plan to revitalize the city. If they were able to rid the shady streets in the very heart of Parker of the illegal narcotics trade, it would go a long way in attracting new business and redevelopment.

Noffsinger was surprised the day the chief selected him and three other officers for the assignment. Even more so when he was made its commanding officer. As far as seniority went, there were a number of others who could have been chosen who'd been with the department much longer. But Brent made it clear to Noffsinger and his new team that to fight this battle, he wanted a fresh perspective and bold action. Something for which the more senior members of the force were not known. The unit had his full backing to do what was necessary— within the law—to start cleaning up the streets.

Taking the lead of the Drug Task Force on his 40th birthday, Joe Noffsinger hit the ground running. Sweeping through the streets, he and his team began to disrupt the drug business in some of the worst sections of the city. No matter how many arrests were made though, they still felt they were pushing against a powerful force far better equipped for this fight. They were only four police officers against countless lowlifes, gangbangers, and two-bit drug dealers. From the beginning, the odds were stacked against them. Yet, it never deterred Noffsinger. He never shrank from a challenge and this one was the biggest he'd ever faced.

He was a constant source of positive reinforcement for his men. Each knew just how difficult their jobs were. None of them were delusional enough to think their new assignment was going to be easy. In fact, a number of members of the force were thrilled when they'd been passed over for the post, giving those who had been chosen their condolences. But as the task force's commanding officer, Noffsinger knew he needed to keep the morale of his men up so they wouldn't get discouraged.

Until the PCPD's Detective Squad had been christened, specialized units within the department were unheard of. Parker wasn't a big city like New York or Los Angeles. It barely had enough officers to cover the city's roughly twenty square miles, let alone devote any of the department's resources to focusing solely on one type of crime in one specific area.

The job ahead was daunting, and at times, it did seem like for each step forward they made, it was followed by a step back. But the team kept going.

One of the task force's greatest achievements to date was that over the last several months, they had begun building a network of informants throughout the city. The small busts of street-corner dealers peddling their poison wasn't making a big enough impact. It was just the tip of the iceberg. The plan was to shut off the flow of drugs to the dealers. To do that, they needed to know who was bringing the drugs into Parker City and how.

It was for that reason Noffsinger was on his way to meet with someone who offered to share information about a shipment of drugs that was about to hit the streets. It was all about the supply. If the supply chain could be disrupted, it would be a big win. Something upon which they could continue to build.

Earlier in the day, the task force received a phone call from someone at the Ramshackle, one of the seedy bars that had taken the place of a once-popular restaurant downtown. The individual who, naturally, did not want to share his identity, said he was willing to share some information that might be helpful to the police... for the right price. Though it wasn't a popular method, paying for information was sometimes a necessary evil these days.

Noffsinger wanted the unknown caller to come into the station, but the informant was adamant about meeting one-on-one as far away from the PCPD as possible.

He'd agreed to meet behind the bar as long as Noffsinger came alone and *not* dressed like a cop.

The situation bore all the hallmarks of a setup, which is why Joe Noffsinger had no intention of showing up without having some sort of backup. He wasn't stupid. Or a cowboy. He played things smart.

The plan was, he would meet the informant while one of his men waited in a police cruiser up the street. Noffsinger would have a concealed radio on him and would be armed. If anything went wrong, his backup would be there in less than thirty seconds.

As his backup, he'd brought along Officer Ron Kramer, who could be said to be the "hotshot" of the Drug Task Force. Young and full of self-confidence, Noffsinger saw a lot of himself in Kramer. Which is why he was trying to mold the junior patrolman into the kind of officer Noffsinger knew he could be and Chief Brent wanted on the force. Kramer was showing a lot of promise, proving himself to be a good officer and hard worker. Even if his arrogance flared up from time to time.

"Keep the engine running," Noffsinger instructed as he tested his walkie-talkie, then clipped it to his belt, covering it with his jacket. "As soon as I have the info, I'll radio you and meet you back here."

"Are you sure you don't want me to come with you?" Kramer asked, showing an uncharacteristic amount of unease. Seeing the concern in his eyes, Noffsinger wondered if he should call this off. Police officers needed to trust their guts and maybe he should be listening to Kramer if something was bothering him.

"Look, I agreed to meet this guy alone. I don't want

to do anything to spook him. If we can find out about this shipment, we can really do some damage by getting to it before it goes into circulation. This could be a big break for us. Besides, you think he's going to shoot me in broad daylight?"

"I still don't understand why he wants to meet you *in* broad daylight to begin with."

Kramer made a good point. It was almost six-thirty. The sun was still going to be up for another couple of hours. There was a good chance they could be seen. Why didn't this guy want to meet somewhere completely out of the way? Somewhere there wasn't any chance they would be seen?

"Let alone," Kramer continued, "meeting so close to a known gang hangout. Isn't he worried about one of those guys in the Ramshackle catching him talking to you? Something about this just doesn't seem right to me."

"There's nothing that says this guy's all that smart. I'll be careful. I promise, Ron. You just wait for my call. And if you don't hear from me in fifteen minutes, you can do a drive-by. Just don't make it *look* like you're looking for me. Just be a cop on routine patrol. Got it? I'm gonna be fine."

Noffsinger gave him a wink, stepped away from the squad car, and started walking casually down the street toward the designated meeting place.

TWELVE

HALFWAY DOWN THE BLOCK, Joe Noffsinger could feel the sweat pouring down his back. The Metallica T-shirt he'd thrown on to try and look as unlike a cop as possible was clinging to every square inch of him. The temperature should have started going down by this point in the day, not up, he thought as he wiped his face with his sleeve. It didn't help matters that he was wearing a jacket—lightweight as it was. But the baggy, beat-up windbreaker was the only way he could conceal the radio and service revolver he had tucked into the waistband of his jeans.

He'd been pleased to see Kramer's concern over the meeting. The young officer had grown quite a bit in the last few months under Noffsinger's mentorship. There was a time he would have placed a cash bet on the fact Kramer would be one of those cops who ran headlong into a gunfight without any backup. It was good to think that today he'd lose that bet.

It was depressing that at six-thirty on a beautiful—albeit sweltering—summer afternoon, the street was completely empty. Except for a few cars parked along the side of the road, Noffsinger felt like he was walking through a ghost town. All the scene needed was a tumbleweed rolling down the middle of the road trailed by a cloud of dust.

Most of the storefronts he passed were boarded up. However, there was still a tattoo parlor open across the street and a few doors down, a grungy little pawnshop with a couple of guys lingering on the front stoop. They appeared to be wrapped up in some deep conversation. He doubted it was a philosophical debate of any kind.

No sooner had he finished chuckling to himself about the absurdity of the two derelicts discussing the theories of Hegel and Kant, a sudden feeling of unease surged through him. So strong, he paused for a moment, looking around to see if anyone was watching him. Something in his gut was telling him he should head back to Kramer and forget about the meeting.

Just as he was about to radio back to Kramer and call off the meet, a loud rumbling started behind the door of the building he was standing next to. Instinctively, Noffsinger reached for his weapon just as the rusted metal door flew open and a gang of teens came running out shouting back and forth to one another.

As the band of misfits disappeared around the corner, Noffsinger exhaled. Releasing the grip on his gun, he shook his head and silently chastised himself. He had a job to do. He needed to keep it together. Getting this information was very important.

More determined than ever to learn what the informant was offering, he continued on toward the Ramshackle with a new purpose in his step.

What he didn't realize was that he was being followed. A block behind him, staying as close to the buildings as possible and out of sight, was Officer Ron Kramer. He'd decided he couldn't just sit in the squad car and let his C.O. walk into this blind meeting alone.

Yes, he could have responded in less than a minute if Noffsinger called, but this way, he'd be even closer if something went wrong. Alternatively, if everything went as planned, then he figured there was no harm, no foul.

Kramer wished he'd changed into street clothes. Walking down the street in his uniform, he stood out like a sore thumb.

The closer the two police officers got to the Ramshackle, the louder the muffled music emanating from the bar became. An aggressive, thumping beat pulsated through the air. Kramer could feel the rhythm pounding in his chest, and he was close to three hundred feet away—almost two full blocks! If nothing else, maybe he and Noffsinger needed to site the place for disturbing the peace. Not that there was anyone around to bother, except the two guys across the street. Though they didn't seem to even notice the music.

After another second or two, Kramer watched as they disappeared inside the pawnshop. He figured their smoke break must be over and they needed to get back to work, or whatever it was they were doing in there. The young officer hated that he was suspicious of everyone in this part of town, but facts were facts. Illegal activity was the major source of income around these blocks.

THIRTEEN

THE ALLEY BEHIND the Ramshackle Bar was where the meet was supposed to take place. While it wasn't the most ideal location, there'd be at least a little cover so that anyone who may pass by wouldn't necessarily see Noffsinger and his new informant. If they did, they could have just been a couple of guys out back shooting the breeze while having a smoke.

Noffsinger was just coming up to the entrance of the alleyway on his right. A few more minutes and he'd have the information they were after. Then he could head back to the station with Kramer and debrief the team. He was starting to believe the anxiety he was feeling had more to do with the fact he was overdue for some time off than the situation itself.

Peering around the corning, he could see the backside of the rundown dive bar. Overflowing trash cans, broken crates piled a few feet high, and empty beer kegs lined the wall. A typical sight. At least it was all hidden away in the alley, Noffsinger thought. It was the piles of trash and garbage bags sitting on the sidewalk in front of buildings around this part of town that bothered him. It was going to be hard reviving Downtown if people didn't take pride in their own property.

But that wasn't something he needed to be thinking about right now.

He needed to stay focused.

That was the thought going through his head as he carefully stepped into the alley. Just before he saw the flash from the gun.

FOURTEEN

WITHIN MINUTES OF Ron Kramer's "Officer down!" call, the first squad car came to a screeching halt in front of the Ramshackle. Fifteen minutes later, half the PCPD units on patrol throughout the city had arrived on the scene. By dusk, as the sun was finally disappearing below the horizon after a long summer day, there were so many police vehicles lining the streets, the flashing lights lit up the neighborhood as if it were still the middle of the afternoon.

In addition to the city police, deputies from the Parker County Sheriff's Department and Maryland State Troopers responded, swarming the vicinity around the dive bar. As word spread that an officer was down, it was like a call to arms for everyone wearing a badge. On duty or off, officers were drawn to the scene.

As first on the scene, Kramer took the lead as uniforms began arriving. Even though he was still in a state of shock—the victim being his own commanding officer after all—he still found the wherewithal to remember the crime scene procedures he'd been taught in the Academy. Once the head Patrol arrived, Kramer gladly handed off control of the scene to his superior officer. Which in turn was then given to Lieutenant McMaster when he barreled into the alley. With the constant arrival of higher-ranking officers, as well as those from the state police and sheriff's department, the entire scene was becoming more and more chaotic. Everyone had the best intentions and wanted to assist, but there were now too many cooks in the kitchen and officers were literally beginning to step on one another's toes. It wasn't until Chief Brent marched into the melee that it became clear there was one man and one man alone in charge.

But as the mayhem was unfolding across town, Ben and Tommy purposely remained behind at the station. They'd heard about the shooting shortly after the call came in and while their desire and natural instinct was to follow everyone out the door, they knew how many people would be all over the scene and they didn't want to add to the confusion. When and *if* their services were required, they'd be called in. Neither Ben nor Tommy wanted to simply presume they were going to be assigned the case. Though it would only make sense for the detectives to be the ones investigating the shooting of a police officer, the chief might need to do some politicking to keep the various members of his command staff happy.

That's what the two were discussing when the phone on Ben's desk rang at seven-thirty.

Picking up the receiver, Ben answered, "This is Ben Winters."

It was Deborah, one of the department's dispatchers. "Ben, I have the chief for you."

There were a couple of clicks, followed by a momentary silence, then another click.

The next thing Ben heard was a loud commotion, various muffled voices shouting in the distance, then the booming voice of Nicholas Brent.

"Ben, you and Tommy need to get down here. I'm telling everyone this is your case. And if anyone gives you any trouble, I'll handle it. But I need you two down here right now."

Short and sweet. The chief had made his decision. Ben and Tommy were on the case. This would be their biggest assignment since the Spring Strangler three years ago.

Fifteen minutes after Brent's call, Ben squeezed the Crown Vic between the rows of police vehicles lining either side of the street.

"What the hell?" Tommy said, exhaling the final puff of smoke before putting out his cigarette. "This is insane. It's a madhouse."

"Yeah. And the chief wants us to take charge of this circus."

"Oh, no. Not *us*, buddy. *You're* the detective *sergeant*. I'm just a lowly detective," Tommy pointed out, only half-joking, as he debated lighting up another cigarette.

Stepping out of the car, Ben was practically blinded by the flashing red and blue emergency lights. The sight of it all took him back to his arrival at Beverly Baker's crime scene in '81. At the time, it was the most shocking crime that had occurred in Parker City in decades. Even then, he thought the number of police that showed up was a bit of an overreaction. But what he saw in front of him now put that to shame. Ben wondered if there were any police left anywhere else in the county at the moment.

Making their way through the crowd of uniforms, Ben needed to ask three different patrolmen where the chief was before someone was able to point him in the right direction. Even then, it took the detectives a few minutes to push their way through to the alley behind the bar.

"This is a mess," Tommy said to no one in particular.

Looking around, there were some who clearly had specific tasks on which they were focused. While at the same time, Tommy could see a bunch of guys just standing around talking and smoking.

Across the street, a small crowd of looky-loos had gathered, so a few uniforms were keeping them at bay. Another team of officers was already taking statements from the bar patrons, who weren't being allowed to leave, making them visibly frustrated.

"At least half of these guys need to be sent back to their actual duties," Tommy said to Ben as they came upon the alley which was at the center of all the activity.

It occurred to Ben that for the second time in two days, he was starting an investigation not fully knowing what he was *actually* walking into. The first report was that an officer was down. To this point, they didn't know who it was or if he was alive. Ben didn't like how fast things were moving. A hyper uncontrolled response like all of this only meant mistakes would be made. This once again proved to Ben that the PCPD still had a long way to go to catch up with other police departments. While an officer-involved shooting was something none of them ever wanted to deal with, there needed to be a set protocol as to how to handle things when there was.

As the entrance to the alley came into view, Ben was happy to see that crime scene tape had gone up and there didn't seem to be as many people randomly milling about on the other side. Ben's mood instantly changed when he and Tommy rounded the corner and looked into the confined space. Standing there, looming above everyone else as only he did, was the unmistakable figure of Chief Brent, alongside the sheriff, Hank McMaster, and a handful of other uniformed men. At their feet, being photographed by one of the crime scene technicians, lay the lifeless body of Officer Joe Noffsinger, the head, Ben knew, of the department's new Drug Task Force.

"Shit…" Ben heard his partner say under his breath.

FIFTEEN

It took another two hours before the sweltering heat that accompanied the day finally evaporated, leaving in its place an unseasonably cold summer evening. Much of the time since arriving at the Ramshackle had been spent by Ben handing out assignments and getting his bearings. Laying out a thoughtful, organized plan was one of Ben's talents. Not having all of the details as he walked into the alley behind the bar, the moment he saw that they were dealing with the murder of a police officer, it was as if a switch was suddenly flipped inside of him. His mind became instantly clear and he knew everything that needed to be done to begin the investigation.

For Tommy's part, he proved to be an invaluable enforcer, making certain his partner's orders were followed. Even though they were a team, Tommy respected Ben's stripes and recognized he was the commanding officer. Gone was the wisecracking, smartass most people were familiar with. He was all business. But that was Tommy. He knew when it was alright to joke around and not take things too seriously. Just as much as he knew when he needed to buckle down and get to work…and make sure everyone followed Ben's lead.

Knowing it was going to upset people, but not caring how many feathers he ruffled in light of the case at hand, Ben's first request was that the chief clear the scene of all nonessential personnel. Too many people milling about was going to do nothing but complicate the work that needed to be done. Ben completely understood where his fellow officers were coming from. An attack on one of them was an attack on all of them. They all wanted to do their part. But right now, the best way most of them could help the investigation was to go back to their actual duties and let the criminal investigation team do its job.

While Ben coordinated with the chief and crime scene technicians, Tommy organized the questioning of the dozen patrons who were drinking at the Ramshackle during the time of the shooting. As he expected, none of them claimed to know anything about what happened in the back alley. A few of the potential witnesses were so drunk they weren't even certain of their own names, let alone cognizant of anything that had gone on around them in the last few hours.

"The bar was cleared out shortly after the first officers responded," one of the patrolmen with Tommy said. "That was over two hours ago. I don't understand how some of these guys are still so loaded."

"I'm not sure what you expect me to say, Thompson. Some of these guys have nothing better to do than drink. They spend most of their day drunk. Obviously, as far as being a witness, they're not really going to be of help to us. We need to focus on the sober ones."

"Not that there're too many of those. And the ones who are aren't being all that cooperative," Officer Thompson pointed out.

Tommy couldn't argue. He expected that when they

ran the names of everyone in the bar with whom they'd spoken, each and every one would have a rap sheet as long as his arm. In general, these weren't the type of "upstanding citizens" that were going to be willing to assist the police in a criminal investigation.

Making certain they'd collected all the contact information for the bargoers, Tommy gave the word for them to be let go. No doubt there'd be some follow-ups that would need to take place but for now, he was alright to send them all home. Or at least off to another bar where they could continue drinking. Tommy did, however, leave the questioning of the Ramshackle's owner until the end.

The inside of the bar was exactly as he expected. Dark and dank. The air smelled of stale beer and peanuts, the shells of which crunched under his feet as he made his way over to the irritated woman standing behind the bar. The interruption to her business was clearly having a negative effect on her mood.

Tall and muscularly toned, her height was increased by the four-inch heels on her boots and oddly high ponytail on her head. Tommy couldn't quite pinpoint her age. The closer he got to her, the less sure he became. At first, he would have guessed early thirties but now, standing across the bar, maybe fifties. Her facial features showed signs of a tired, worn soul. Albeit buried under layers of garish makeup.

"I'm Detective Mason with the PCPD." Tommy showed her his badge as he introduced himself. "Do you mind if I ask you a few questions?"

"Not like I've got anything else to do since you sent my customers runnin'," she snapped.

"I'm sorry about that. But a police officer was shot to death behind your bar this evening. This whole area has been shut down."

"It figures it would take a cop gettin' popped to get you guys to come down here and do your job. Anything else happens down here we have to fend for ourselves."

"I'm not sure I understand," Tommy said wrinkling his forehead.

"I was broken into a couple a weeks ago and they got all the money in the register. I called the cops but nothin' came of it. The pisser they sent out to talk to me was here for all of five minutes. Basically said it was my own fault for having a business in this part of town. As if I have any other choice. Then something happens to one of you and all hell breaks loose and every cop in the state's outside my door!"

"I understand your frustration," Tommy said with all sincerity. "I wish I could say something that—"

"Save it," she cut him off. "I don't need to hear meaningless apologies from some suit. Just ask your questions so I can close up and go home. Might as well take the night off since there's no business to be had."

Calling him a "suit" stung. Tommy never really thought of himself as part of the establishment before.

Flipping to the next page in his notebook, he read the name Thompson had given him for the bar owner. Angel Sanders. Angel? He shook his head as he read the note.

"Now, Ms. Sanders, I know one of the other officers has already spoken with you, I just wanted to clear a few things up if I could. You say you didn't hear a gunshot earlier this evening and didn't know anything had happened behind your establishment until the police arrived."

Angel Sanders raised an eyebrow and sighed. Tommy wondered how many times she'd been forced to answer questions like this throughout the course of her life. He'd need to pull her sheet as well.

"If that's what you've got written down there, that's what I said then."

Tommy looked around the room. There were only a handful of tables with mixed-matched wooden chairs. The bar itself ran along one wall but only had a half dozen stools in front of it. None of which matched either. Overall, he figured the space to be thirty feet by thirty feet, so not that big.

"It seems odd you wouldn't hear a gun go off right behind these walls."

"It ain't that odd 'cause the music was up loud. When some of my boys get to playing that radio, you can't hear yourself think. Let alone a pop gun going off outside."

"Did you know everyone in the bar this evening? Were they all regulars?"

"Yes."

"Did you see anyone you didn't know in here tonight?"

"No."

"Did you know Officer Joe Noffsinger?"

"Who's he?"

This is going well, Tommy thought to himself.

Taking a slightly different approach, Tommy took it from the top, walking the bartender through the evening from when she first opened until the police arrived and started rounding everyone up. Until that point, it had just been like every other day. She hadn't seen or heard anything strange. Certainly, no one talking about wanting to kill a cop. She admitted her customers weren't the most innocent of Parkertons, but she didn't think any of them had the balls to actually kill a police officer. Most of them were a lot of talk, but that was about it.

She was specifically vague when Tommy began asking about illegal drug activity in the area. And again, she said she had no idea who Noffsinger was and claimed to have never had any dealings with the Drug Task Force or even knew one existed.

Other than her open hostility towards the questions, Tommy got the impression she was telling the truth. It didn't mean one of the guys in the bar couldn't have been involved in some way. If nobody was paying attention, it was possible someone could have slipped out back, shot Noffsinger, and returned without the barflies being any the wiser.

For the time being, Tommy thought he had everything he was going to get out of Angel Sanders. Though he had a suspicion he would be talking to her again in the future, once they put all the information they collected together back at the station and took a look at what the crime scene guys were able to find.

SIXTEEN

TENSIONS OUTSIDE THE Ramshackle were, understandably, running high. One of the PCPD's own had been gunned down in broad daylight. A fuse had been lit, leaving everyone on edge. Ben understood an overreaction could end up doing much more harm than good.

Which is why he had enlisted Chief Brent's assistance in sending away all unnecessary personnel. Only the individuals with a specific task to do at the crime scene were allowed to remain. The rest were ordered to return to their regular assignments. And if they weren't on duty, they were thanked for their show of support, but tactfully told to go home. Brent even managed to get Sheriff Woods to round up his men and clear out, leaving just a few deputies to assist with the residents of the neighborhood who had ventured out of their homes to see what all the fuss was about on the other side of the crime scene tape.

The difference in jurisdiction between the Parker City Police Department and the Parker County Sheriff's Department could be extremely confusing to the average Parkerton. Within the incorporated city limits, the PCPD was in charge. However, being a part of the county, they could request assistance from the sheriff if necessary. Outside of Parker City proper, throughout the rest of the county, unless another municipality had its own police force, the Parker County Sheriff's Department was the law enforcement agency calling the shots. If someone tried to explain the details and differences between the various organizations' charters and official duties, most people's eyes would glaze over. Only to be made more complicated if the Maryland State Troopers' piece of the law enforcement puzzle was added into the discussion.

The only thing that was perfectly clear was that Ben needed to negotiate his way through a figurative minefield. He needed to be careful and very diplomatic. He certainly didn't want to offend the sheriff by sending him on his way. And he knew he was going to require the resources of the state police, just not the small army of troopers who had amassed outside the Ramshackle.

There were times when Ben wished he could go back and tell his boyhood self that there was a lot of politicking that went along with being a detective. It wasn't always just about going out and solving cases. Like with every profession, egos were always a factor.

As the head of the department's Detective Squad, and having been called in to take command of the scene by the chief of police himself, Ben knew he had the authority to do what needed to be done to begin the investigation the right way. Even if it meant upsetting some people or appearing to step on some toes.

Once Ben, Tommy, and Chief Brent came up with their game plan, they all went to work. Tommy's main job was to handle the questioning of potential witnesses. The chief's was to organize the scene. And Ben was going to focus on working the alley—coordinating with the crime scene team, the M.E.'s people, and speaking with the members of the PCPD's Drug Task Force who were all huddled together in the far corner with Lieutenant McMaster.

The officers that made up the task force were some of the department's younger members. Officers Ron Kramer, Peter Vernon, and Brian Woods (no relation to the sheriff) were all in their early thirties, athletic, and, to be perfectly honest, very handsome. If the PCPD ever did a calendar like the New York City firefighters, these guys could divide up the entire year and take four months each, Ben thought as he approached the group.

"I'm so glad you're here, Ben." Officer Vernon was the first to speak. He'd joined the department the same year as Ben, though had served as a sheriff's deputy in a neighboring county for a few years prior. The two had always been friendly and, at the time, Vernon was one of the few officers who never gave Ben and Tommy a hard time about their promotion to detective.

"Peter, guys," Ben began, "I'm so sorry about Joe. He always spoke so highly about all of you and the work you were doing. I've read some of the reports and know you've all been making some big progress down here."

"Obviously, we've been making *too much* progress for someone to execute Joe like this," Kramer snapped without looking at Ben. Knowing he was the one who called in the shooting and was first on the scene, Ben understood why his nerves were still raw. But he needed everyone to keep a cool head.

"I know you've already answered a bunch of questions tonight and told the story a few times, but I have to ask it again," Ben said, sounding very apologetic. "Take me through it. What happened?"

Ben specifically left the question very open-ended.

"I took a call at about fourteen hundred hours today," Woods, a former army sergeant, was the first to speak. "The caller refused to give his name and asked to speak with Officer Noffsinger."

"He specifically asked for *Officer Noffsinger* by name?" Ben asked, jotting a note in his notebook.

"Yes, sir. He did. He asked for Officer Noffsinger and said it was regarding a drug shipment coming into the city."

"Do you receive many anonymous tips?" Something about the call was already bothering Ben.

"Not really," Peter Vernon answered, with a benign shrug of his shoulders. "The task force is pretty new, all things considered. And the people down here don't really trust the police to begin with so…"

"Right," Ben agreed. "So, did Joe wonder why this caller asked for him?"

"He never said anything about it," Kramer answered, still a little too much irritation in his tone for Ben's liking, his words now coming out in short puffs of steam as the temperature began to nosedive. "Joe'd been cultivating informants since day one. He said the more ears on the ground we had the better we'd do disrupting the drug trade. Those were almost his exact words. He wasn't interested in how many arrests we made, he wanted to stop the supply."

"Okay, so this guy calls and asks for Joe. It was a guy. Yes? Alright. He says he has information about a drug shipment. Then what?" Ben asked.

Woods picked up where he'd left off. "Officer Noffsinger asked the caller to come into the station to provide us with the information. The caller didn't want to be seen entering the police station so he requested that Officer Noffsinger meet him behind the Ramshackle at eighteen-thirty hours."

"Six-thirty?" Ben asked, making sure he'd converted the military time correctly.

"Correct," Woods said with a sharp nod of his head. "He was told to come alone and in civilian clothing."

"He was specifically told to come alone?" The entire thing sounded like a set-up to Ben.

"Yes, sir. I know. It didn't sound good to any of us. None of us wanted him to come down here by himself. But he didn't. He brought back-up."

"I came with Joe," Kramer said. This time, he sounded more defeated than anything. "I was supposed to wait up the street a couple of blocks out of sight and Joe was going to meet the informant right here. If anything went wrong, I would have been able to be here in less than a minute. Not that it would have mattered I guess."

"How do you mean?" Ben understood that under the circumstances, it was clear something *had* gone wrong. But there was something in the way Kramer said it. As if he'd failed in some way to protect his commanding officer.

"I didn't wait in the car," he said. "Like Brian said. None of us wanted him to go it alone. This had all the trademarks of a trap. So... I followed him about half a block back. He didn't even know. He told me to wait in the car."

"Did you see anything suspicious?" Ben was scribbling notes through the entire conversation. He wouldn't have everything they'd said verbatim, but it would be close enough if he needed to go back and revisit the conversation later. "Was there anyone on the street that looked like they could have been waiting for Joe? Anyone out of place at all?"

Kramer closed his eyes, having already gone through this, and thought back once again. "There were a couple of guys sitting outside the pawnshop over there. They didn't seem to be paying the least bit of attention. At one point, a gang of kids came out of the one apartment building up the street. Other than that, there was nothing. You know what it's like down here. It's not like it used to be. It would have been easy to see someone standing around on the street."

"What happened when Joe entered the alley?"

Kramer shook his head.

"That's just it. He walked around the corner and I heard the gunshot. Literally, the second he walked into the alley. Boom. The minute I heard the gun I took off running. I was there… I mean, here in seconds."

Ben bit his lower lip. The next question needed to be asked the right way. He didn't want to sound accusing, but genuinely interested.

"If you were here in a matter of seconds, as you say, why is the shooter not in custody? How did he get away?"

"That's just it. There wasn't anyone."

Ben raised an eyebrow. "What?"

"When I came around that corner," Kramer said, pointing back to the opening of the alleyway where two crime scene technicians were now standing, "there was no one here. The alley was *empty* and Joe was lying on the ground. He didn't even have time to pull his gun. He walked into the alley and was shot."

"I just have to ask so I can put it in the report," Ben began, "after you heard the gunshot, you didn't see anyone run out of the alley?"

"No. I would have run right into him, that's how fast I was here."

"And when you came around the corner…"

"There was no one."

"So he either ran into the bar to the left or this building here to the right? Did you check to see if either of the doors were open?" Ben said, eyeing the only two doors leading into the alley.

"After I radioed in, I checked Joe's pulse. He was… there wasn't…" Kramer took a deep breath and gritted his teeth. "He had to have run back into the bar. One of those gangbangers in there did this."

"There is a team out front right now talking to everyone who was in the bar," Ben said.

"They all need to be dragged down to the station. They're not gonna talk here," Kramer spat out, his frustration finally boiling over.

"I don't think taking them down to the station would make that much of a difference," Vernon offered. "Getting people like that to talk… Don't hold your breath, Ben."

"Detective Winters, can I speak to you privately for a minute." This was the first time Lieutenant McMaster had spoken. He'd been very convincingly playing the part of a shadow hovering in the background.

Stepping away from the other men, Ben could see the frown on McMaster's face.

"Ben, I think it's pretty clear what happened. Joe was targeted by someone in the bar. But they're right.

Getting anyone in there to talk is going to be difficult. What are you going to do?"

Hank McMaster was a beefy guy. Not overweight, but not exactly fit. And he was just enough taller than Ben to make it feel as though he was looming over him, expecting the detective to have the solution to all of this on the tip of his tongue. Looking into the lieutenant's eyes, Ben could see all the man's fifty-plus years wearing on him.

Unfortunately, it was far too early for Ben to have any answers yet.

SEVENTEEN

By the time they'd returned to the station, Ben felt as though he'd run a marathon wearing a pair of plastic sandals with a two hundred pound weight strapped to his back. Mentally, he was exhausted. Emotionally, he was drained. Physically, he was frozen to the bone. In the hours following the setting of the brutal summer sun, the temperature had plummeted, giving way to an equally brutal chill. That's just the way the weather worked in Maryland.

Dropping into his chair behind his desk, Tommy summed it up pretty well when he said, "I feel like I've been run over by a tractor-trailer."

Knowing they were going to need it, Ben walked down the hall to the breakroom to start a fresh pot of coffee. It didn't matter that it was closer to Midnight than eleven o'clock now, he and Tommy had a lot of work to do, and, speaking for himself, he needed the caffeine. Not to mention something hot to warm him up.

As late as it was, the station was still a beehive of activity. Not that Ben was surprised considering what had happened only a few short hours earlier. This was naturally a time when every member of the department would pull together because what had happened to Joe Noffsinger could happen to any one of them. It was a fear with which each of them, and their families, all lived.

Filling the coffee machine, Ben hit the button and waited for the stream of dark liquid to begin pouring into the pot. The smell of a freshly brewed pot of coffee was one of his favorites. Even the horribly cheap stuff the PCPD stocked. Listening to the sound of the machine gurgling, he paced back and forth across the greenish-yellow linoleum floor, deep in thought.

He wanted to check in with Natalie and let her know he had no idea when he'd be home but didn't want to call and wake her if she'd already gone to sleep. While he was still at the Ramshackle, he'd taken a few minutes to find a payphone and call his fiancée to let her know what was happening. As always, hearing her sweet, caring voice lifted his heart and reenergized him. Which was exactly what he needed to finish the initial sweep of the scene.

In their time together, Nat had never once complained about his job. Ben knew he'd gotten lucky. Though he could see it in her eyes from time to time, that she was afraid of what could happen to him while he was on duty, she knew being a detective was more than a job to him. She knew he had an almost unnatural desire to do right and protect the people of Parker City. Nat understood that about him. It was very much like her love of teaching. She was there for the students, to help them learn and achieve their goals.

"Dear, God. Are we a pair of idealistic saps or what?" Ben said reaching for an empty mug as he thought about what drove him and Natalie.

"I absolutely agree," said Tommy, standing in the

doorway. "I assume you're talking about you and Nat. Because I always picture you two as being like the husband and wife from that old show in the '50s. The perfect couple that always says and does the right thing. You wearing a full suit and tie around the house on the weekends, her with her white apron and Donna Reed bouffant. Just tell me. Does she wear anything under the apron?"

Ben raised an eyebrow and stared at his partner.

"What?" Tommy asked, playing with his mustache.

"I'm not sure what surprises me more. That you know who Donna Reed is or that you know what a bouffant hairstyle is."

"Very funny. After all these years, you should know I am a fountain of knowledge."

Ben sighed. "You are a *fount* of knowledge."

"Fine. That too. Is the coffee done? Splashing cold water on my face didn't do it. I need coffee. I don't suppose there are any donuts lying around here anywhere?"

Ben looked at his watch. "They're probably making them for the breakfast crowd around the corner at the diner right now."

Pouring them both a steaming cup of coffee, the detectives headed back to their office to start sorting through their respective notes from the evening's investigation.

Pointing at the stack of missing persons case files on Ben's desk, Tommy asked, "What do we do about the skeleton under the warehouse?"

"It goes on the back burner for now," Ben answered, picking up the folders and putting them on the floor next to his desk. He'd love to have more room to spread the files out, but up until now, they'd never had two major cases underway at the same time.

So they could both be on the same page, Ben started by walking Tommy through the timeline he'd been given by Noffsinger's men. Starting with the phone call earlier in the day, up until the moment he'd walked into the alley. Using the chalkboard he'd squeezed into the small office, Ben began listing out some of the more important details. Ending with…

"Kramer said Joe walked into the alley and bang, the gun went off. It took him a matter of seconds to get there and when he did, the alley was empty." Ben closed his notebook and laid it on his desk.

"Did anyone else see Joe go into the alley?" Tommy asked.

"Ron says there were two guys across the street outside the pawnshop. Though, he didn't think they were paying them any attention."

"So, those guys didn't see Ron following behind Joe either? We're going to need to try and find them and talk to 'em."

Ben's brow wrinkled. "I agree. But I have a feeling we're thinking two different things."

Tommy leaned forward and looked at the chalkboard.

"All's I'm saying is, as of this moment, the only person that saw…or heard the gunshot was Kramer. No one I talked to inside the bar heard anything. I would just like to confirm things happened like Ron said they did."

"Tommy, you're not saying you think Ron did this?"

"No. I am definitely not. But I want to make sure. We're dealing with a cop killing here. We need to think about every angle. You always say we need to cover all the bases."

"I do. It's nice to know you've been listening all these years. You're becoming a first-rate investigator, Detective Mason," Ben said with a smile.

Returning the smile, Tommy said, "Well, I have learned from the best. Those guys on *Hill Street Blues* are great!"

"Oh, you're so funny."

"The ladies think so."

Even with the pressure on, the two longtime friends could still find a moment to give each other a few friendly jabs. Or, maybe because of the pressure, they knew they needed to laugh.

Ben started sketching a layout of the crime scene on the board. "A shell casing was found in the alley right here. They found it next to a trash can. For the casing to be there, the shooter would have had to be standing somewhere around here, in front of Joe. Which fits with Ron's account of what happened. Joe turns the corner, the shooter is standing there, bang."

"A shell casing is good. Maybe it will match up with something or someone else. And as long as those two guys saw Ron go into the alley after the gunshot, then we're good on that count."

"There could be a problem though," Ben pointed out. "Ron thought the two guys went back inside the store before the shooting took place. They wouldn't be able to say what happened."

"Like I said," Tommy began, scratching the Midnight shadow now peppering his chin, "I just want to ask these two what they remember. Just so we know. Plus, they may have heard the shot and come out to see what was going on. Maybe they saw someone running away."

"That's another thing. Ron said no one came *out* of the alley. He got there too quick. Whoever did the shooting must have run into the bar."

Tommy sighed, flipping through his notes, he said, "And of course, no one inside the bar saw anything. No one came running in waving a gun around, shouting about how they just offed a cop."

"Even if they had, do you think anyone would say that's what happened?" Thinking for a moment, Ben said, "Since they were there before Noffsinger and Kramer arrived, maybe those two guys across the street might have seen someone go *into* the alley. We can hope."

Tommy's mind had rewound to the part of the conversation about the shell casing.

"You said there was one shell casing found?" he asked. "How many times was Joe shot?"

"Just once," Ben answered with a frown.

"A single shot? And it hit him where exactly?"

"Square in the chest," Ben said referring to his notes to see what he'd written down after talking to the M.E. "Right through the heart. He would have been dead before he hit the ground."

"One shot…" Tommy said under his breath. "Lucky shot? Or did this guy know what he was doing?"

The detectives sat in silence for a few moments as they each studied the notes on the chalkboard.

"Do we start by assuming Joe was targeted?" Tommy said, not sure if he was asking himself or his partner. "If he was targeted, was it *Joe* that was the target, or anyone in a uniform?"

"We have to assume Joe *was* the target. The anonymous caller specifically asked to meet *him* in that alley at that time. Joe was lured there and shot. He *was* the target. That's where we start," Ben answered.

EIGHTEEN

IN THE ROLE of Field Services Commander of the Parker City Police Department, Hank McMaster oversaw all the uniformed officers who patrolled the streets, as well as the Detective Squad. Basically, he supervised all policing activities that took place outside of the station. In the short time he'd held the post, his greatest accomplishment had been the initial success of the force's new Drug Task Force. Though he was a very hands-off commanding officer, when good things happened, he made sure he was there to share in the credit. With Joe Noffsinger—the head of the task force, nonetheless—being shot down in broad daylight, McMaster wasn't sure what that meant for the small team going forward. Or how it would reflect on him.

He'd joined the PCPD back in the '50s when life was much simpler and the city was going through an extremely prosperous period. Walking the beat in those days, wearing the uniform, he was like a superhero. Children would stop him on the street and talk to him in awe as their parents paid him the due respect and reverence he believed he deserved. And as for crime... a few parking tickets here and there, kids loitering out front of May's Menswear, it was nothing.

For the most part, the '60s were the same. For the first ten years on the job, he'd never been forced to pull his gun. Even when students from Hammermill College, just north of Parker City, took to the streets to protest the Vietnam War and damaged several buildings, the use of force was minimal.

If he needed to put his finger on it though, that was when things began to change. Though Parker never saw a civil rights movement like other parts of the country, McMaster started to see feelings of unrest begin to emerge. People didn't seem as happy as they once were. The shopkeepers and other business owners he'd speak with while walking his streets were all becoming more anxious. Even kids stopped being as friendly to him.

Then in the '70s, everything changed. The bottom fell out of Parker's economy and the entire city went crazy. Most of the population fled as more and more buildings, which once housed popular restaurants and shops, began to sit empty and boarded up. Downtown crumbled, literally and figuratively. Then came the flood. What hadn't already fallen into ruin was ravaged when the waters of the Tasker River overflowed and surged through the streets.

McMaster had reached the rank of sergeant by the time of the Great Flood and was head of the department's Patrol Division, which put him directly in command of all the officers on the street working non-stop as the waters rose over the course of days. He'd figured once he might have gotten a total of five hours of sleep during that entire week in '78. With all hands on deck, the small police force was stretched to its breaking point, even with the assistance of the county's sheriff and state police.

When the floodwater finally receded, it left in its wake complete devastation.

After that, Parker City's Downtown had become a crime-ridden breeding ground for derelicts and druggies. Even with the mayor's plan to rebuild, they were fighting an uphill battle. Six years since the flood and they were only barely beginning to scratch the surface of returning the area to what it had once been. A large part of the plan was to curb the drug activity, which is why the success of the PCPD's Drug Task Force was so important. Now, its commanding officer's body was lying in a van on the way to the Chief Medical Examiner's Officer in Baltimore.

McMaster stamped out his cigarette as he watched the last cruiser pull away from the Ramshackle. It had been a long night. Looking at his watch, he saw it was nearly midnight. He was exhausted and every muscle in his entire body ached. Thankful for the fact most of his days were now spent sitting behind a desk, he couldn't even imagine having to be out patrolling the streets anymore. Spending the last several hours at the crime scene was more than enough fieldwork for him. But if he wanted the promotion to captain to fill the chief's old position, he needed to be there and act like he had things under control. Fortunately, when Brent called in the detectives, he was able to step back and let Winters and Mason take the lead. It was the best of both worlds for him. He was there to look like a leader while letting someone else worry about the details and actually do the work.

With Chief Brent on his way back to the station to work on a statement for the press in the morning, and

Detectives Winters and Mason officially running the investigation, he felt everything was in hand so he could head home. Someone was going to need to be rested and fresh in the morning.

Hauling his large frame into his unmarked police cruiser, he tossed his hat on the passenger seat and loosened his tie. All things considered, with the way things had changed so drastically over the last several years, McMaster started to wonder if it might be time to put in his papers and sail off into the sunset. Was sticking around to be captain really worth it? When Nicholas Brent was captain, he was really the one that ran the PCPD. Everyone knew old Chief Stanley relied completely on his number two. McMaster didn't know if he wanted the headache. He already had a nice pension coming to him when he retired, even though going out as a captain would add a few more dollars. But he'd already built himself a pretty nice nest egg over the years through some investments he'd been able to make and side jobs he'd taken on when he was younger.

"Dammit," he said, putting the car in gear. He remembered he'd promised his wife he'd stop and get milk on his way home.

He'd have to stop at the 24-hour High's on the other side of town. Completely in the opposite direction from his home. Letting out a long string of obscenities, he switched the direction of his turn signal and headed for the all-night convenience store.

At least there was no traffic to deal with. Otherwise, he would have considered using the lights and siren to get him there faster.

Listening to the weather report on the radio as he

sped through the deserted streets, the forecaster was predicting a much cooler day ahead. The recent heat-wave was on its way out. McMaster was happy to hear that. It wasn't that he was out of shape, but as a big guy, he wasn't a fan of the heat. He'd sweat right through his uniform this afternoon, then when the temperature dropped, nearly froze. He wouldn't be surprised if he woke up with a cold.

The thought of getting sick just gave him something else to grumble about as he pulled into the parking lot of the High's. Two dim lamps, one on either side of the lot, cast a faint glow over the pavement. There was more light coming from the windows in the front of the store than the streetlights. McMaster made a mental note for when he got to the office in the morning. He wanted to see if this place had ever been robbed. If it hadn't, he'd be shocked.

His mission clear, he was in and out of the store in three minutes. It would have been less if the cashier hadn't taken so long giving him his change.

Still tucking his wallet into his back pocket as he walked outside, milk carton in hand, he never saw the dark figure standing in front of him. If he even had time to register what was happening before the two shots ripped through the air, Hank McMaster would never be able to tell anyone.

NINETEEN

1959...

THE CONVERSATION LEFT Freddy Quinn craving a drink. That's what happened when he got stressed. He was a tough guy. No one would argue that. But even a tough guy like him needed to take the edge off from time to time. And when cigarettes didn't help, he headed for the bottle.

He and his brother Jimmy watched their father drink himself to death when they were teenagers. Which would lead some to swear off the stuff altogether, using their past as a cautionary tale. Not the Quinn boys. They knew the drink was in their blood so neither ever tried to fight it. Though neither ever became as beholden to the booze as their old man either.

Knocking back his double whiskey, Freddy was finally able to put the conversation with the Kid out of his mind. He'd worry about it tomorrow, he kept telling himself. There was nothing more he was going to do, or could do for that matter, tonight.

The Kid was heading upstairs to play some poker, so that would keep him out of trouble for a while.

The music coming from the jazz band on the stage was happily filling Freddy's head as the liquor began to relax his muscles. Quite often, he'd stop by the hotel's lounge to grab a drink and listen to some music before heading home at night if he didn't have any other plans.

Staring at the empty tumbler in his hand, Freddy was debating whether he should order another or call it quits and head home. Just as he was about to signal to the pretty little brunette waitress to bring him another, an anxious-looking Jimmy appeared in the doorway to the lounge. His brother was clearly looking for someone and needed to find them in a hurry. As their eyes met, Freddy knew he's who Jimmy was trying to find.

Pushing himself up from the cocktail table he'd been sitting at in the corner of the room, he met Jimmy halfway to the entrance.

"What's wrong?" Freddy asked, hoping it was nothing serious.

"I'm glad you're still here. I didn't think you'd left yet," his brother said, a little out of breath.

"Man, you've got to lose some weight, Jimmy. I swear. If you're winded just from coming in here lookin' for me..."

"Freddy," his younger brother, cut him off. "The cop's back. One of the guys saw him parked around the corner. They thought he might be tryin' to sneak in through the basement entrance."

"*Droch chrích ort,*" Freddy muttered under his breath, repeating an Irish curse his grandmother brought with her from the old country. "Where is he?"

Following Jimmy out of the lounge, he found himself once again in the hotel's back hallway. The two goons thundered down the corridor like a pair of charging rhinoceroses. Between them, their bulk filled the hall from wall to wall and would have rolled over anyone who got in their way like a tidal wave. Thankfully, they had a clear shot to the door leading into the back alley where a number of the staff, the Quinn brothers included, parked their own cars.

Pushing through the double doors at the end of the corridor, the brothers stepped out into the damp air. The recent heatwave brought with it humidity that made everything feel soggy. Just walking outside felt like walking through thick wet rags.

"Where is he?" Freddy asked, scanning the parking lot.

"Around the corner, just up the street." Jimmy pointed, starting in the direction he'd indicated.

Freddy was only a step behind his brother when he walked out of the parking lot onto the sidewalk next to the hotel. Just as Jimmy'd said, up the street, Freddy could see a police car parked along the side of the road. The glow of the streetlamps wasn't nearly bright enough for him to see clearly but he didn't think Ramsburg was alone. Freddy thought he saw two figures silhouetted in the light.

Motioning for his brother to stay where he was, Freddy decided to have a word with Officer Ramsburg. They'd already warned him away once today. Now, he was back. Had he even left? Should he go wake Billy and let him deal with this? Was Marty still at the hotel?

Close enough now to see who Ramsburg was talking to, in an instant, Freddy's mind went blank. He stopped dead in his tracks.

"Fuck."

It was the Kid.

He and Ramsburg were having what looked to be a heated discussion.

"Dammit," Freddy said, clenching his fists.

Moving twice as fast as before, he was only a few steps away when he saw Billy's partner pull the gun he'd been carrying around from inside his jacket. Brandishing it in front of the cop's face, he was trying his best to come off as intimidating. Freddy could tell by Ramsburg's reaction that it wasn't working. For his part, the officer was remaining extremely calm, except his hand was now wrapped firmly around the handle of his own gun, still in its holster. He'd be able to draw his revolver and get off a shot before the Kid even knew what hit him.

Two more giant steps and Freddy inserted himself between the two men. With one hand, he pushed Ramsburg back against the police car. With the other, he grabbed for the Kid's gun, which was still flailing around.

"What's going on here, boys?" Freddy asked, trying to sound as calm and collected as possible. Like this was all routine to him.

"You better get your hands off of me, Quinn," the cop barked.

"I'm just tryin' to do my civic duty and help out a cop who looked like he was in trouble."

Releasing Ramsburg, Freddy squared himself with the wiry police office, completely blocking his view of the Kid. "Billy told you to stop snoopin' around here. You might get yourself hurt if you don't listen."

"Are you threatening me now, too?" Ramsburg's anger seemed to be making him grow right before Freddy's eyes. He didn't look so weak and frail at the moment. "Your boy here made a big mistake just now. Trying to threaten me. Trying to get me to take money to go away. Billy's done. Bribing an officer of the law is all I need to get the warrants to search this property and every other one your boss owns. He's done."

Freddy's mind was racing. He didn't know what he wanted to do more, kill the cop standing in front of him or the spoiled little rich kid behind him. He needed to do something and do it fast. Thoughts, one after another, flew through his mind but strategizing wasn't his thing. Let alone coming up with a plan in a matter of seconds. But if he didn't do something, all hell was going to break loose tomorrow. At least that's what he thought just before the Kid swung around from behind him and smashed the butt of his gun into Ramsburg's face.

TWENTY

FREDDY WATCHED AS the situation went from bad to worse.

It all happened so fast. Out of the corner of his eye, he saw the Kid come around his shoulder. He didn't see the gun in his hand until it cracked into Ramsburg's cheekbone with a sickening crunch. The force of the blow knocked the officer back against his car as a spray of blood spurted from the gash on his face. Before Freddy could move, the Kid struck him again, sending Ramsburg crumbling to the pavement.

Only then was Freddy able to blink through what he'd just witnessed and spring into action. He heaved the cop up and tossed his limp body into the backseat of his own patrol car. They couldn't be seen standing on the street with a bloody police officer lying at their feet. There'd be no explaining away that one.

Quickly looking up and down the street, he didn't think anyone had seen what happened. Except his brother, who was now huffing and puffing his way toward them. At this time of night, there wouldn't be too many people out and about.

"What the hell happened, Freddy?" Jimmy asked, leaning against the hood of the police car as he gasped for air after his short run. As a big guy, he could act as a great barrier, but speed was not one of his skills.

Freddy didn't answer. He was too busy trying not to

lash out in anger and frustration. Knowing Ramsburg was safely out of sight, he turned on the Kid, fighting every urge within him not to pummel him right then and there.

He knew, there was no way this was going to end well. No matter what happened next.

Surprisingly, Freddy wasn't sure how to read the expression on the face of the newest tough guy in town. It was blank. He wasn't scared and he wasn't excited. His eyes showed no sign of emotion. He just stared at Freddy stone-faced, the gun with a smudge of blood on its butt dangling from his hand.

"What do we do now?" the Kid asked, his voice hollow and unfeeling.

Freddy wondered if he was in shock. For all he knew, this was the most physically aggressive the little snob had ever been. Kids who grew up on Grandview Avenue along Jefferson Park weren't exactly known for being versed in street fighting.

Thinking quickly—which wasn't something he was comfortable with—Freddy knew they needed to get Ramsburg somewhere they could control the situation. And, if nothing else, away from the hotel…and Billy.

"Get in the car," Freddy barked the order with such ferocity, the Kid didn't even think to question it.

Easing into the front seat of the patrol car, he watched as the Quinn brothers huddled under the streetlamp. The amber light cascading down upon them accentuated their rougher physical traits, making them look like ogres out of a fairytale. The Kid never realized how big these guys were until now.

For the very first time since he'd met Billy Roscoe

and decided to do business with the charming scoundrel, he wondered if he was in over his head.

There was no question Freddy Quinn was not happy. His already beady little eyes had completely disappeared into the scowl that was now plastered on his face. Getting behind the wheel of the police car, he slammed the door and gunned the engine without saying a word. As the car eased away from the curb, the Kid watched as Jimmy began shuffling back to the hotel.

"Where are we going?" he asked Freddy, without looking at him.

The question was met with a deafening silence.

After a few blocks, in a tone so flat the lack of emotion scared the hell out of the Kid, Freddy finally said, "Unless we can figure something out, Billy is going to kill you. Then he is going to kill me for letting this happen. And I really don't wanna be dead right now, you little fuck up."

Not another word was spoken as the car carefully crossed out of Parker's bustling downtown retail district into the city's industrial sector. Small manufacturing plants and warehouses lined the streets in this part of town. Well after normal working hours, the streets were deserted. Which is exactly what Freddy was counting on. Turning onto Antietam, their destination was just a couple blocks ahead.

An area the Kid had never spent time in, he was feeling extremely uncomfortable as Freddy pulled the car into a small alley behind one of the big, brick warehouses. With strange shadows cast on the walls and hardly any light with which to see more than a couple feet in front of you, the dark alley, with its wooden crates and barrels stacked along the outside wall, looked like something right out of an old detective movie. It looked like the kind of place where the hero would show up for the final confrontation with the crime boss he'd been after.

"What is this place?" he asked Freddy.

"It's a warehouse Billy owns."

"Figures," he said under his breath.

"Let's go. Help me carry the cop inside."

Doing as instructed, he grabbed Ramsburg's feet as Freddy heaved him out of the backseat by his shoulders. The little cop wasn't heavy, just cumbersome. Especially for someone not used to dragging bodies around in the dark of night.

After placing Ramsburg's unconscious body on a table in the middle of the small room, Freddy sat down in a rickety wooden chair next to an old beat-up desk set up along one wall. Slowly tracing the scrapes and scars along the golden oak surface, Freddy watched as the Kid circled the room inspecting the sparse furniture. Obviously, he didn't want to touch anything for fear of coming down with the Poor Disease. Freddy could kill him and bury him under the floorboards. No one would ever know and the world would probably be a better place. He'd deserve a plaque or some other sort of recognition. One less spoiled brat in the world wouldn't be missed.

"So…this is Billy's warehouse? What does he keep here?"

"Things for the hotel. And the shipments from the trucking company."

"What are we doing here?"

"We're waiting. You're not all that smart, are you?"

"For what? What are we waiting for?"

"I sent Jimmy to go get someone who's gonna help us with the situation you put us in. And if he can't help, then we're in trouble. So you better start prayin' to your rich-people gods that this all works out."

"Rich-people gods? You think there are…" He stopped before saying another word. The look on Freddy's face told him this wasn't a time to try and pick a fight with him.

"I was bein' fasequess," Freddy said, in a sarcastic tone.

"Fasequess isn't…" Again, the Kid stopped before saying anything else. It was probably better to let it go.

The staring contest was interrupted by a low groan from Ramsburg. Both men's heads instantly snapped in the direction of the sound.

Freddy was on his feet and standing next to the table before he realized it. His movements were all instinct. No thought behind any of them at this point. Seeing the cop was starting to come to, he carefully removed Ramsburg's service revolver from its holster so he didn't wake up and try to shoot them. Freddy realized he should have taken the Kid's gun away from him and given it to Jimmy, but it was too late for that.

Slowly, Ramsburg's eyelids began to flutter as another groan filled the dimly lit room.

"What? Where am I?" the officer asked, carefully reaching up and touching the now horribly swollen side of his face. "Ow!"

The surge of pain jolted Ramsburg upright, obviously helping to clear the post-blackout cobwebs from his head. As Freddy predicted, he instinctively reached for his gun.

"Now just relax," Freddy said, in what he thought was a soothing tone. To anyone else, it would have sounded anything but. "You had a little accident. You're alright. No need to get worked up."

Blinking through the confusion, Ramsburg tried to remember what had happened. The searing pain was making it difficult to collect his thoughts, as was the ringing in his ears. Swinging his legs over the side of the table, he leaned forward, a wave of nausea sweeping over him. He thought for a moment he was going to be sick. But slowly the bleariness began to fade.

Remembering everything, his mind once again clear, the adrenaline began surging through his body. Scrambling off the table, he looked for anything he could use to defend himself.

Being put in the position of being the levelheaded one in the room, Freddy raised his hands in a show of nonaggression. He needed everyone to stay calm until Jimmy arrived with help.

"Look, Officer Ramsburg, everything that happened was an accident."

"An accident! Are you kidding me, Quinn? First, your friend there offers me a bribe to leave your boss alone, then he attacks me. You're under arrest," Ramsburg said, reaching for his handcuffs and advancing on the Kid, who was trying to make himself disappear into the shadows.

"Come on," Freddy protested. "You misunderstood. He wasn't tryin' to bribe you. This whole thing has been blown out of proportion. You gotta let us…"

"I don't have to do anything. I'm taking him down to the station then I am calling a judge and getting a warrant to search the hotel. Billy Roscoe will be behind bars before the sun comes up."

"You can't do that," the Kid said, putting himself nose-to-nose with Ramsburg.

All of a sudden, Ramsburg's expression changed. Anger and vindication, knowing he was now going to be able to arrest Billy Roscoe, was replaced by confusion.

"Wait a minute," he said. "I know you. *You're* mixed up with Roscoe? Oh, this is going to be big."

"Wait! No! You can't..." The Kid was becoming flustered.

Freddy was watching the entire thing like it was a picture show. The Kid didn't think there would be a problem by attacking a police office. That he was fine with. But the idea of his name—his father's really—being associated with someone like Billy Roscoe was what was the most upsetting to him. Again, Freddy thought how he'd never understand people with money.

"Listen, officer. You can make this whole thing go away. I mean, I can make it worth your while to just forget about everything. Please, you don't understand. This is all just a mistake. A misunderstanding."

Ramsburg raised an eyebrow.

"Kid, you have no idea how much trouble you're in."

As Ramsburg grabbed for a wrist to slap the cuffs on, the Kid—whether he realized or not—pulled the gun from under his jacket.

"Put it down," both Freddy and Ramsburg said in unison.

"You have to listen to me. No one needs to know about any of this. I can't let anyone know."

"You should have thought about that before you got mixed up with people like this," Ramsburg said taking another step forward, not worried about the gun pointed in his direction. From the way it was shaking in the younger man's hand, he obviously didn't know what he was doing. The gun probably wasn't even loaded.

Grabbing the gun with one hand, Ramsburg pulled the Kid toward him. Freddy was amazed at how nothing ever deterred this cop. He was fearless. He actually admired the guy for that. The thought was short-lived as he saw the two men beginning to wrestle for the gun.

"No! Stop!" he shouted before he was able to move his feet.

One step closer and Freddy might have been able to pull the two apart like he'd done outside the hotel. But this time, he was too late.

With two sets of hands jostling for the weapon, someone had gotten their finger on the trigger.

The small room amplified the sound, making the detonation of gunpower sound like a bomb going off, the explosion resonating around the tiny space.

In horror, Freddy watched as the Kid and Officer Bert Ramsburg fell to the floor.

TWENTY-ONE

STANDING OVER THE two men now lying on the floor, Freddy saw a pool of blood spreading out beneath them. Both bodies remained motionless and for a split second, he wondered if they could both be dead.

The Kid was face down on top of Ramsburg. Slowly, Freddy reached down and grabbed his shoulders, ready to roll him over and see the damage. To his surprise, at his touch, the Kid flinched and quickly rolled to the side under his own power, quickly curling into a fetal position. In doing so, he revealed Ramsburg's lifeless body.

Freddy knelt down next to the officer, trying his best to avoid the sticky gore creating a crimson halo around the dead man's head. The struggle for the gun had caused it to go off, projecting the round up through Ramsburg's chin and out the top of his head, leaving a gaping hole just above his forehead. Staring down at the injury, Freddy felt a tightening in his chest as his anger began to grow. Things could not have gone any worse. And it was all because of the little shit curled up on the floor like a whiny baby.

Freddy thought about putting a bullet in the Kid's head as well and walking away. He'd be happy to let someone else deal with the mess. But the thought was fleeting. He didn't want any of this to blow back on Billy, so he was going to have to take care of everything himself.

Turning his attention back to the younger man who'd caused the problem, Freddy yanked him to his feet.

"I didn't mean to," he sputtered. "It just went off. He should have taken the money. I didn't mean to."

"Yeah, well, it's too late now," Freddy growled, his voice barely audible.

"What are we going to do? I can't… I can't…"

"Enough! We're going to deal with this." Freddy gave him a good, hard shake to snap him out of his daze. "Now pull yourself together."

It was bad enough there was a dead body to deal with—a police officer's dead body, nonetheless—but Freddy couldn't have the Kid completely freaking out as well. They both needed to be very careful. They couldn't make any mistakes. Well, *any more* mistakes, Freddy thought to himself.

Freddy began looking around the room, an idea beginning to take shape in the recesses of his mind. Bert Ramsburg's body needed to disappear. One would think there would be many ways to get rid of a body, but it wasn't always as easy as in the movies. Especially when there wasn't a plan and everything had to be done on the fly. Options were limited. But Freddy knew he was better in these types of situations. Planning wasn't his strong suit. But taking care of business in the heat of the moment, that was where his particular skills shined.

Sizing up Ramsburg's motionless body, Freddy was beginning to circle the floor. He thought he'd figured out the perfect place to dispose of the corpse.

"I need you to remove his badge, his name tag, holster…take everything out of his pockets. Anything that could possibly identify him."

Freddy wasn't sure if the Kid had heard him. He was just standing in the middle of the room, his eyes fixed on the body, showing no signs of emotion whatsoever. Freddy wondered if that's how rich people handled stressful situations. They allowed themselves a few minutes to lose control, then the cold, hard façade went up once more.

Now wasn't the time to be considering the differences between the socio-economic classes—they had a body to get rid of. And Freddy didn't know how long they had. The bulk of the warehouse workers wouldn't be back until the next morning, but there were a couple of night watchmen that could complicate matters. Even though Freddy knew the guys and was confident they'd look the other way, the fewer people that knew what happened, the better.

"This isn't what I intended to happen," the Kid said, his eyes still on Ramsburg. "If he had just taken the money and walked away…none of this would have happened."

"Well, maybe this'll teach you a lesson. There are actually people in this world that can't be bought off. They're rare birds, but they exist."

"What about you?"

"What? What about me?"

"Are you someone that can be bought off? No one can know about this. Not even Billy."

"Oh, don't worry. You're gonna pay. I thought a smart guy like you would have already figur'd that out. Now stop talking and strip the body of anything that could identify him."

Resigned to the horrific reality in front of him, the

Kid slowly knelt down and even more slowly began to reach for Ramsburg's badge. Once shiny silver, there was now a streak of blood smeared across it. The clasp on the back of the badge didn't want to give way. Struggling, the Kid didn't want to turn to Freddy for assistance. Finally, fed up with the piece of stubborn metal in his hand, he just tore it away from the shirt, taking a small swatch of uniform with it. It was a small victory of sorts. But it was what he needed to motivate him. He quickly emptied Ramsburg's pockets, removed his police gear, and was just about to hand everything over to Freddy when the outside door swung open. Both men turned to see the tall figure of a Parker City Police officer standing in the doorway, framed by the dim twilight beyond.

Everything in the Kid's hands crashed to the floor as he froze, wondering if there was any way to reach his gun—lying on the floor next to Ramsburg's body—before this cop was able to pull his own.

TWENTY-TWO

Officer Hank McMaster took in the whole scene from the doorway. When Jimmy Quinn had come to find him, telling him there was a problem they needed his help with, he hadn't expected it to be anything like this. Quinn had been fortunate to find him still at the station so late, having been forced to pull a double shift. Front desk duty, nonetheless! When he'd seen Jimmy lumbering in, wheezing and out of breath, McMaster thought he should have ducked into the back right then and there. If he had, he wouldn't be standing on the edge of a scene that could in no way turn out good for anyone involved.

Squeezing passed McMaster, the first words out of Jimmy's mouth when he saw Ramsburg lying on the floor with his brains blown out was "Jesus Christ, Freddy! What the hell happened?"

"What does it look like?" Freddy snapped. "Things didn't go exactly as planned."

"You can sure say that again," his brother said, walking over and taking a good look at the body. "But at least he won't give Billy no more trouble."

"But now we have to get rid of the body and make sure no one can tie any of this back to us." Turning back to the Kid, Freddy continued, "You can pick all that up. This is Officer McMaster. He's one of our guys."

Still a little shaken by what he was seeing, the policeman gave a slight nod.

"I was hoping you would be able to help us convince Ramsburg to back off," Freddy said to him. "But boy, you're going to earn your money tonight, Hank."

"I don't understand," Jimmy said. "I thought you just wanted to talk to him. What happened?"

"That's a real funny story," Freddy said, his voice thick with sarcasm. Trying not to waste too much time, he quickly caught everyone up on the events which had transpired over the last half hour. Expectedly, Jimmy listened slack-jawed as McMaster quietly leaned against the doorframe, still not ready to cross the threshold into the small warehouse office. As if by staying outside, he was somehow not already involved.

When Freddy was finished, a silence fell over the group as each man worked through what needed to happen next. After a moment, Freddy pulled his brother aside, giving him some orders, then sending him into the warehouse to find some equipment to assist with the task at hand.

As Jimmy exited through one door, McMaster finally stepped into the room. The policeman took a long hard look at the Kid. "Don't I know you? Isn't your father…"

"Whoever you think he is, Hank, I'm sure you're wrong," Freddy said, sending a clear message. "He's nobody. But he's a nobody who's gonna show his appreciation for your help."

"As long as this is never talked about again," the Kid said, sounding like a petulant child. "I can't be…no one can ever know I was here. People can't know I've been spending time… I can't have people…"

"Not as articulate as I expected him to be," McMaster said to the Quinn brothers, happy to take a dig at the young man who was obviously out of his element.

"Alright," Freddy snapped. "This isn't how any of us thought our night was gonna go. But it is what it is. We've gotta make this whole thing go away. And no one can ever know what happened. Especially Billy."

"You don't wanna tell Billy?" Jimmy asked, confusion in his voice. Though he often didn't understand the plan, this truly perplexed him. "Billy will know what to do about all this. We can't keep it from him."

Freddy's frustration quickly turned to anger. He didn't like it when any of his men questioned him. Particularly his baby brother. His wicked temper, something for which he was known, began to erupt.

"Don't question me! I told you. We're gonna take care of this and Billy never has to know. Understood?"

"Yeah. Okay, Freddy. Take it easy," Jimmy said, keeping his eyes fixed on his shoes.

"Anything you wanna say, college boy?" Freddy asked, glaring at the man responsible for the current crisis.

The Kid took a silent step backward, crumbling under Freddy's hard gaze.

Before Freddy could turn his harsh attention to McMaster, the officer asked, "What do you need me to do?"

TWENTY-THREE

1984...

TOMMY HAD LEFT a few minutes earlier. Leaving Ben to close up the office after the two put together the beginning of a game plan for the next day. It was late and they were both exhausted. At this hour, there was nothing more that could be accomplished except to get a few hours of sleep before the investigation into Joe Noffsinger's murder could begin in earnest in the morning.

The shock felt over losing one of their own had not subsided. On any normal night, the PCPD would be virtually empty by now. Only a handful of staff worked the overnight shift, but this evening was different. Even as Ben and Tommy were winding down, the station was still buzzing with subdued activity.

The telephone on Ben's desk began ringing just as he was about to turn off the lights. He knew it had to be important. If someone was calling his office phone after midnight, there was a good reason.

Grabbing the receiver, a paralyzing feeling of dread washed over him. Whether it was his detective's instinct or simply common sense, deep down, he knew this wasn't going to be a good phone call.

After a deep breath, Ben slowly answered, "Detective Winters."

What he heard made his entire body go numb. With just a few sentences, the entire world was turned upside down. Frozen in place, the receiver still held in his clenched fist, Ben was stunned. He'd just received a verbal sucker punch to the gut.

The young detective now felt himself being gripped by a combination of rage and abject terror. Ben stood frozen in his office, phone receiver still in hand. He hadn't heard Tommy reenter behind him.

"Hey, what's going on?" he asked. "I thought you were right behind me."

Seeing the expression on his partner's face, Tommy didn't need to be a detective to know something was wrong.

"The day's not over," Ben said, finally replacing the receiver. "There's been another shooting. Lieutenant McMaster was shot outside the High's over on West Lincoln. We've got to go."

With the bubble light spinning wildly on the roof of the car, Ben and Tommy raced through the streets of Parker with ease; the flashing ruby light reflected off the darkened buildings. At the early morning hour, with the streets empty, Ben felt the addition of the siren would be overkill.

"The call came in at twelve-fifteen," Ben explained. "A state trooper was first on the scene. Chief Brent has already been notified and is on his way."

One ear tuned to the scanner on the dashboard, Ben was listening as other units on duty responded to the shooting. He was silently praying it wouldn't be as chaotic as it was outside the Ramshackle. Too many bodies showing up, even with the best of intentions, could compromise the scene. Which could prove devastating to the investigation.

The section of Lincoln Avenue where the pair was heading was a commercial corridor on the western side of the city. One of the newer developed areas, strip malls, fast-food restaurants, and gas stations lined the street. During the day, traffic was heavy, Lincoln being a new thoroughfare in and out of Parker City to all points west. At the current hour, however, only a couple of cars passed the detectives' unmarked police cruiser. With the shops and eateries closed, the only establishments with their signs still alight were the Amoco and Mobil stations and the High's, in front of which now sat nearly a dozen police vehicles.

For the second time in less than twelve hours, members of the PCPD, Maryland State Troopers, and Parker County Sheriff's Department had descended upon one location. Until today, Ben couldn't remember ever seeing such a response to any call throughout his entire time on the force. Of course, the circumstances were extraordinary.

Though the sign atop the convenience store usually cast a bright neon glow over the parking lot, it now paled in comparison to the emergency lights flooding the area with flashing red and blue streaks.

The convergence of vehicles forced Ben to park across the street in front of the new Roy Rogers, along with two state police cars.

"They didn't even save us a parking space," Tommy said, trying to inject a brief moment of levity, as the two detectives crossed the street toward the commotion. It was a halfhearted attempt on his part, but Ben appreciated the effort. Being that their chosen profession afforded them a front-row seat to see the worst of humanity from time-to-time, they needed to remember the world wasn't all bad, and a laugh every now and again—even when walking into a serious situation— could help keep them grounded. They could never allow themselves to spiral too far into the darkness.

Neither said it out loud, but both men shared the same horrifying thought. In a span of just a few hours, Parker City had seen two of its police officers shot down in what appeared to be cold blood. There was no way these two shootings were a coincidence. The odds of that were astronomical. That left only one alternative. Someone was out there targeting police officers.

TWENTY-FOUR

Ducking under the bright yellow police tape that now circled the parking lot in front of the convenience store, Ben hoped he would never get used to the feeling of walking into a crime scene. He never wanted to feel desensitized to any of it. He needed to be angry, sad, uncomfortable. His thoughts and feelings were what he knew made him a good detective. Sure, there were some who said a police detective needed to remain detached so they could look at everything objectively, but Ben thought there needed to be a compromise between completely walling off one's emotions and entirely giving in to them.

The overarching feeling he had as his shoes scraped the pavement walking toward the epicenter of activity was curiosity. What had happened? Two police officers were killed within hours of each other. Why?

The flash of a camera caught Ben's attention. He'd missed seeing the CSU van parked off to the side behind a couple of PCPD cruisers, but the technicians were already on-site and at work. The photographer was taking pictures of the area around Lieutenant McMaster's body while a couple of other techs were working their way around the parking lot collecting evidence.

"You got here fast," Ben said to the head of the tech team.

After seeing him at three crime scenes over the

course of as many days, he felt they were getting to know each other. A tall, gangly fellow with slicked-back hair and a pair of oversized tortoiseshell glasses, he was congenial but very matter of fact.

"We were just finishing logging in the evidence collected at this evening's scene when this call came in," the sergeant responded, not looking up from his clipboard. "The van's engine was still warm."

"What have you found so far?" Ben asked.

"Have you found *anything* yet?" Tommy asked at the same time.

"We're still working," he said, his eyes darting back and forth between the two detectives, "but the first thing we found, which was pretty easy actually because they were just lying right there, were two shell casings. I'm not the medical examiner, but I did take a look at the body. Two GSWs to the chest. Two shell casings, two bullet holes. The math adds up. Oh, speaking of which. When we went back and took another look around the warehouse this morning…you've kept us very busy today…we found a round in one of the ceiling panels."

Watching the CSU guys pull the skeleton out of the dirt seemed like a lifetime ago, Ben thought. But as he'd told Tommy, that case would have to be put on ice for a while. Although, a bullet in the ceiling *was* interesting. It sounded like the kind of clue that would end up unraveling one of Agatha Christie's elaborate yarns.

"That's going to have to remain an unsolved mystery for a while," Ben said. "Two dead police officers takes precedence."

"I understand completely. I promise, I'll make sure we analyze everything as quickly as possible. Word came down from the top that we need to give these shootings priority. Just keep in mind, we can only work so fast. But we'll make sure you get everything you need from us."

After Ben thanked the CSU chief for his assistance and let him get back to work, he and Tommy went in search of the trooper who was the first to arrive after the shooting. With the help of another trooper, the pair of detectives found Trooper First Class Len Glendale huddled in a corner of the lot with Chief Brent. Glendale was the poster boy for what a police officer should look like, Ben thought. Or at least what Hollywood would think one should look like. He was tall and clean-cut, handsome with an athletic build, yet an approachable air.

"It looks like we have a supermodel with a badge," Tommy said just loud enough for his partner to hear.

"Don't be jealous just because he looks better than you in a uniform," Ben responded.

"Wow. That was unnecessary," Tommy said, his voice filled with mock indignation. "Is it because his eyes are so dreamy?"

"Trooper Glendale, I'm Detective Sergeant Winters. This is my partner Detective Mason," Ben said, extending his hand to the state policeman, ending his and Tommy's banter.

"Sir," the young trooper answered, along with a handshake and a quick nod of the head.

"Chief," Ben acknowledged Brent, who also gave a quick nod. "Do you mind if I ask Trooper Glendale some questions?"

"I just got here myself. I was waiting until you arrived to start asking questions," Brent said. His voice sounded hoarse and he looked tired. Ben couldn't imagine what he'd been going through all evening. He'd heard that the chief left the earlier crime scene to personally speak with Joe Noffsinger's family. After that, it appeared Brent had gone home, because he was now wearing jeans and a simple polo shirt under a PCPD windbreaker. It was disconcerting to see Nick Brent out of uniform. However, even dressed casually, he still possessed the most commanding presence of anyone Ben knew.

"Trooper Glendale," Ben began, flipping through his notebook to a clean page, "you were the first officer on the scene? Can you just walk me through what happened when you arrived?"

"I was set up out on 70 at the junction with Lincoln watching for any late-night speeders when the dispatcher reported an officer down here at High's. I was only a couple minutes away. When I arrived, I found a Parker City officer lying on the ground. He was nonresponsive, no pulse."

"You said you were here within minutes?" Tommy asked. "Did you see anyone fleeing the scene? A car driving away? Someone on foot?"

Glendale thought for a moment.

"No. Actually, I didn't. I was traveling east. They must have gone in the opposite direction because no one passed me that way. By car or on foot. And there was no one here in the parking lot except the clerk."

"Thank you, trooper. If you could stick around for a bit longer. I want to go talk to the person who called it in. Do you know, was that the clerk?"

"Yes, sir. They have him inside the store," the trooper motioned.

Ben, Tommy, and the chief left Trooper Glendale with another patrolman as the three entered the store in search of the young man who'd witnessed the shooting. And he *was* young. Possibly a student from one of the city's two high schools, he looked like he might not even be old enough to drive.

Tommy wondered if there was some law being broken by leaving a kid like this alone on the night shift at a convenience store. His next thought was more concerning. If he was a minor, they'd need to wait to speak with him until one of his parents was on hand.

No sooner had the thought crossed Tommy's mind, Ben said, "Crap. He's what, twelve? We shouldn't talk to him until he has a parent present."

"I knew that one," Tommy said, proud of himself. "Excuse me, Eddie, is it?" He read the nametag on the guy's shirt. "My name is Detective Mason. How old are you?"

In a rather squeaky voice, Eddie the Clerk answered, "I'm twenty."

"Seriously?" Tommy and Ben said in unison.

"I know. I get it. I look like I'm a little kid. But I'm in college. I'm just home for the summer."

Tommy still didn't believe him, so asked if he could see some identification under the guise of obtaining his full name and address for their report. But when the young man handed over his driver's license, it confirmed he was in fact Edward O'Donnell, age twenty.

"Thank you, Eddie," Tommy said. "You just have a very youthful appearance."

The clerk shrugged as if it was a problem with which he was all too familiar.

Overcoming the first potential hurdle, Ben was happy they wouldn't need to wait to question him. He just hoped the kid...*young man* had some useful information.

"How are you doing, Eddie?" Ben asked, genuinely concerned. The vast majority of people could go through their entire lives without finding themselves in a situation like this. Those that did reacted to it in different ways. There was no way of guessing how individual people would handle the shock of witnessing a murder. For his part, Eddie didn't seem overly excited or agitated. Ben noticed he couldn't stop fidgeting with the watch on his wrist though.

"I didn't expect my night to turn out like this," Eddie said, without making eye contact.

"I'm Detective Sergeant Ben Winters. Would it be alright if I asked you a couple of questions, Eddie?"

"Sure. I guess."

"The person who was shot outside, did he come into the store this evening?"

"The cop? Yeah. He came in and bought some milk."

"Okay. That's good. Was anyone else in the store at that time?"

"No. The place has been dead all night." Eddie froze, a look of terror on his face as he realized what he'd just said. "I didn't mean it that way."

"Don't worry. I know you didn't. You're doing good. So, there was no one else in the store when the officer came in. Did anyone follow him into the store?"

"Nope. He came in, went back to the refrigerators, and came back with a carton of milk."

Ben was making some notes. "Did he buy anything else?"

"Just the milk. He was looking at the candy bars by the register," Eddie shrugged.

"How did the officer seem when he spoke to you?"

"Whadyou mean?" Eddie asked, a look of confusion passing across his face.

"Did he appear agitated? Calm? Did it look like he was looking for anyone? How was he acting when he came in?" Ben was trying to be as vague as possible, while still explaining what he was looking for. He didn't want anyone to say he tried to put words in a witness's mouth.

"Oh." After thinking for a moment, Eddie said, "He actually looked tired. Like my dad does when he gets home from a double shift. But he seemed alright. He might have been whistling when he came in. Or humming something."

"Did he say anything to you?"

"Just asked how much he owed me when he brought the milk up. If he wasn't a cop...and this hadn't happened," he said motioning out the glass doors, "I wouldn't even remember him."

It sounded pretty routine. If McMaster thought someone was following him, Ben would have thought he would have asked to use the phone or stayed in his car and radioed back to the station.

"Okay," Ben continued. "What happened after he paid?"

It was still fresh in Eddie's mind because he didn't need to think about it. He said, "He put his change in his pocket. Took the milk and walked out the door. The minute he walked outside I heard two bangs. One right after the other. Bang! Bang! Like that."

"What did you do then?"

"I jumped. The noise scared me."

"That's understandable," Ben said.

"Then I ran over to the door to see what the hell it was. I saw the cop lying on the ground. I ran out, saw blood on his shirt, then called 911."

"You did good, Eddie." Tommy spoke for the first time since Ben had begun with the questions. They hadn't needed to discuss it, but they both knew it would be better if only one of them did most of the talking. Even if he was twenty years old, they didn't want to come on too strong.

"Did you see anyone when you went outside? Other than the police officer that is."

This time Eddie did pause to think about his answer. Finally saying, "No. There wasn't anyone out there."

"Did you see or hear a car drive off?"

"No. Nothin' like that. There was nobody."

"I didn't see any security cameras outside. But the ones in the store here, do they work?"

"Yeah. I think so. I don't know how they work. You'll have to ask my manager."

"I'd like to take a look at those tapes. I think we should give your manager a call."

"I did. Right after I called 911. I'm surprised he isn't here yet. He was freaking out when I told him what happened."

Ben looked at the chief then back at Tommy.

"Alright, Eddie. Thank you for your help. Detective Mason is going to stay with you and ask you a few more questions until your boss gets here. Chief Brent and I are going to go take a look around."

When they'd reached the back of the store and were out of earshot, the chief turned to Ben.

"What the hell, Ben? Two of our men gunned down in a matter of hours. Are we being targeted?"

Ben honestly didn't know. And that's what he told Brent. "If the shootings are a coincidence, I can't even imagine what the odds are. But until we look into what could tie Joe and the lieutenant together…other than being PCPD… I can't say it's connected either."

The pain and frustration on both men's faces reflected back at them from the refrigerator cases in front of which they were standing. If this was just the beginning, how bad was it going to get? Was every member of law enforcement a target for some crazed shooter? Was it just the city police with targets on their backs? Was this going to turn into a spree? Each passing moment brought more and more questions. Ben just hoped to God he and Tommy would start to be able to come up with some answers.

TWENTY-FIVE

THE ANNOYING ELECTRONIC bleeping of his alarm clock jarred Ben awake. Through red, bleary eyes, he saw the six-three-zero staring back at him. Ben had given himself an extra thirty minutes this morning due to the fact he'd gotten in so late—or early, depending on how one looked at it—after leaving the crime scene. Even with the added minutes, he'd still only managed to get a little over two hours of sleep.

There was no chance of hitting the Snooze button this morning. He couldn't waste time, even if his body was telling him that it wasn't ready to leave the comfortable bed and soft sheets wrapped around him. Two police officers had been gunned down in the city in less than twenty-four hours. There was a lot of ground that needed to be covered, so lounging in bed was not an option.

Finally summing up the strength to swing his legs over the edge of the bed, he moved as quietly as possible so as not to disturb Natalie. Though, once out of bed, he realized waking her wasn't going to be a problem because she wasn't there. It was at that same moment a familiar smell caught his attention and drew him out of the bedroom toward the kitchen. It was the unmistakable aroma of bacon.

Ben stood in the living room of the apartment and

watched as his adorable fiancée whisked her way around the apartment's small kitchen. Who knows how long before him she'd gotten up? But it was enough time to start the coffee and get some bacon in the oven.

Without taking her eyes off the peppers she was expertly chopping, she said to him, "The bacon and omelets will be finished by the time you get out of the shower. I figured you were going to have a rough day, so you needed a good breakfast to get you going."

Ben couldn't help but smile, fully realizing how lucky he was that he'd found Natalie Kirkpatrick. "You're the best fiancée ever."

"I know," she said, looking up from the cutting board with a sly smile.

By the time Ben emerged from the bedroom a second time, he was showered and dressed, but only slightly more awake. He'd skipped shaving because he didn't want to spend too much time getting ready and he was afraid he might fall asleep halfway through and end up doing some serious damage to himself. He didn't need to permanently scar himself when he could go two or three days without shaving and you'd hardly notice. He had light hair and a baby face—though he preferred the term "youthful."

Sitting down at their small dining table, Ben saw the fruits of Natalie's labor. At this Godawful hour of the morning, she'd gotten up early to make him a Western omelet, bacon, toast, coffee, and orange juice. Though he highly doubted she'd squeezed the oranges herself. She liked to throw things together in the kitchen, but she didn't go that far when you could just buy a carton of juice at the grocery store.

Ben was famished. Taking the first bite of the omelet, it dawned on him, because of how busy they'd been yesterday, he'd skipped dinner.

Nat was engrossed in the front page of the newspaper, which she had laid out in front of her while she drank her coffee. From his side of the table, Ben could see the entire top half of the front page was an article under the headline *COP KILLER!* Once again, the *Herald-Dispatch* was showing its penchant for splashy headlines to catch readers' attention. As much as he would like not to, he knew he needed to read the article to see what the press was able to find out. Neither he nor the chief made any official comments at the scene. The plan was for the department to make a statement about Officer Noffsinger's murder first thing this morning, after there had been some time to evaluate what they'd been able to learn at the scene. That was the plan.

Now with a second member of the PCPD lying in the morgue, Ben wasn't exactly sure what Brent was going to want to say. Not to mention, there was no doubt the mayor was going to want to weigh in. Ben was a little surprised he hadn't already heard from City Hall yet.

"This doesn't say anything about last night's shooting," Natalie said when she'd come to the end of the article. "I guess that happened after the paper's deadline. How's the omelet?"

"This breakfast will probably be the highlight of my day. Thank you. And yes, according to the timeline we have for last night, Lieutenant McMaster would have been shot after the paper went to press."

"So that means tomorrow…"

"There will be another article about a second police officer being shot in the city," Ben finished her thought.

Natalie quietly drank the last of her coffee then went to the kitchen for a refill. As she was putting the pot back on the burner, the telephone rang. She picked up after the second ring.

"Hello." She listened for a moment. "Yes. He is." Another pause.

Ben wiped the bacon grease from his fingers, preparing to take the phone.

Then she said, "I will. Yes. Goodbye."

Ben raised an eyebrow as Natalie returned to her seat.

"That was the chief's secretary," she said. "She's very to-the-point, isn't she?"

"To say the least," Ben answered.

"Mayor Oland wants to see you and the chief in his office in twenty minutes. She wanted me to tell you."

TWENTY-SIX

CITY HALL WAS another of the city's historic structures built around the time of the Civil War. Though plans for the building had been completed before the war between the states broke out, the fighting forced the project to be put on hold. The delay proved to be a positive development because as soldiers returned home from battle, there was a large government project underway where they were able to find work. It had been one of the major reasons Parker City's residents fared so well in the years immediately after the war. With enough work for everyone, the city's economy kept churning along.

Ben always admired the building, with its giant white columns and elaborately sculpted stone parapets. A stately structure, it commanded respect. The building's shadow, however, loomed large—both literally and figuratively—over the police station next door.

As head of the department's Detective Squad, Ben did not like that politics sometimes dictated police policies and procedures. If the City Council needed to find ways to cut the budget and show the voters of Parker they were acting prudently with their money, a red line was drawn through building repairs for police headquarters or funding to hire additional officers. Yet, that didn't stop the politicians from demanding more and more of the already strapped police force. Though he didn't care much for politicians as a "species," Ben knew they were a necessary evil. And not all of them were bad.

In fact, he'd grown to like the current mayor, Charlie Oland. If ever one was in search of a dynamic figure, there was no need to look beyond the handsome, energetic, forward-thinking chief executive of Parker City. Some argued that he was singlehandedly trying to drag Parker into the modern era. At the very least, he was the individual spearheading the effort to revitalize the city after the devastating flood. Following the days of rain and destruction, Oland was there calling for the rebuilding of Downtown Parker; promising it would be the main focus of his administration. That was followed by countless hours of personally lobbying government officials at all levels for the funds needed to bring the heart of the city back to life. Though great strides had been made, and other areas of the city were beginning to blossom into thriving commercial and industrial corridors, Downtown's rebirth was still a work in progress.

As Ben climbed the steps toward the main entrance, he noticed a couple of news vans parked in front of the building. Both were from local network affiliates out of Baltimore. Passing through the set of sturdy wooden doors with their intricately etched glass windows, Ben wondered how long before more news crews showed up. Usually what went on in a small city in Western Maryland didn't interest the news outlets in Baltimore and Washington. But the cold-blooded murder of two police officers in the span of only a few hours was exactly the kind of item that caught the attention of news producers. Especially when the murders occurred in the same place that had found itself at the mercy of a serial killer just a few years earlier.

There was no question the *Herald-Dispatch* was going to feature the murders as much as they possibly could, using the nightmare to drive up readership, but Ben had hoped not too many others would pick up the story. The last thing his investigation needed was a press spotlight shining on it. How to handle the press and what to say was probably what this early morning meeting was all about, Ben thought to himself as he started up the grand staircase toward the mayor's office.

During his time on the force, there had only been one other occasion when Ben had visited the office. That was shortly after he and Tommy were promoted and Oland was looking to get a photo with the two new detectives. Ben assumed that meeting would be nothing more than a publicity stunt so the mayor could get his name in the paper and claim he was being tough on crime by ordering then-Chief Stanley to create a Detective Squad. To his surprise, after the photographer took the obligatory picture of the men all shaking hands, Oland asked the young detectives to sit down and talk for a while. He genuinely wanted to hear their views on the direction the department was headed and anything else for which he could advocate that would assist the PCPD. Both Tommy and he walked out of their private meeting with Charlie Oland impressed.

Shortly after, they found themselves speaking with Oland again. This time it was in his home, along with his wife and twin boys. One of Oland's sons had been dating a victim of the Spring Strangler. To cover all the bases, they needed to speak with the boy. Charlie Oland was surprised when they showed up at his doorstep, but understood they had a job to do.

Ben entered the mayor's suite of offices to find Chief Brent already seated in the reception area. Last night, he'd been dressed more casually than Ben had ever seen him. This morning, he was back in his crisp white shirt and blue trousers with the gold shield on his chest and stars on his collar shining bright. His hat sat next to him on the leather sofa, along with a file folder which Ben guessed contained copies of all the information they'd collected so far on the shootings.

"Morning, Chief," Ben said, taking a seat in the chair opposite the sofa. "Were you able to get any sleep last night?"

"I fell asleep on the couch for about an hour," he said with a sigh. Then he reached into the folder and passed a sheet of paper to Ben. "This is the official statement for this morning. At least it is if the mayor doesn't make any changes. I sent a copy over to him first thing. I have calls from the *Herald-Dispatch*, the *Register* from over in Harrison County, *The Washington Post*, *The Baltimore Sun*, all three networks out of Baltimore, one from DC—did you see the two outside? They all want an interview. I'm sure the mayor is going to insist on holding a full press conference. Because that's going to be the best way to spend our time," he said, shaking his head.

Brent was frustrated by something that hadn't even happened yet. Though Ben agreed. Mayor Oland would probably think it best to hold a press conference so the story could be "controlled." At least, *controlled* as best as they could. There was no way the mayor was going to want the public thinking a second serial killer was loose in Parker City.

Before Ben was able to weigh in with his thoughts, the door to Charlie Oland's office swung open and two men strolled out. The mayor, on the younger side, was athletic with chiseled facial features and the thick head of hair that central casting demanded of a political figure. The other man was older, slightly rounding at the middle, but very distinguished.

Howard Worthington, in addition to being the patriarch of the Worthington clan—one of the city's founding families—was the president of South Mountain Bank & Trust and a major player in the happenings of Parker. It was no surprise that he'd have the ear of the mayor, but an early morning meeting must mean it was something important. Ben knew a little about Worthington from some personal interaction but mostly through stories. Though he worked to build up his family's bank through the years, he was still known to enjoy himself. He was always seen around town in the fanciest new sports car or spending the afternoon on the golf course. Howard Worthington liked to play as much as he liked to work. But rumor was, he didn't like doing either before ten in the morning.

"Chief! Detective Winters!" Oland said with an enormous grin on his face. "You both know Howard, I assume."

The group exchanged greetings and quick pleasantries. All four were busy men and small talk was something none of them were looking for this morning.

Following the departure of the banker, Oland escorted Ben and Chief Brent into his office as he was handed a stack of papers by his secretary who sat dutifully outside his office watching everything that went on.

"Can I offer either of you anything? Coffee?" Oland asked.

Both officers gratefully accepted a cup of coffee, which the mayor poured himself from an expensive-looking urn sitting on a service trolly set up in the corner. The much-needed caffeine was delivered to them in delicate china cups, along with a silver container full of sugar and another with milk. Charlie Oland was the perfect host.

Finally taking his seat behind the antique desk, Oland leaned back, steepling his hands in front of him, and said, "I can't imagine what you two have been through. I am so sorry for the loss of your colleagues. I was sick when I heard the news. Two such good men. Officer Noffsinger then Lieutenant McMaster... I just don't know what to think."

Ben was always impressed at the mayor's ability to remember names. He had no idea if Oland had ever actually met either of them, but he knew who they were today. It was another reason why Oland always came off as being so genuine. If he asked you a detail about your life, somehow he remembered it the next time you spoke. It wasn't an easy feat. It was a skill that would make him one hell of a detective though.

"Thank you, Mr. Mayor," Brent began. "I brought copies of everything we have so far. It's still very early so we don't have reports back from the State's forensic team yet or official M.E. reports. These are just the initial notes and reports from both scenes."

Taking the file from the police chief, Oland laid it to one side of his desk.

"I also had a copy of the department's official statement sent over to you this morning. In case you wanted to see that."

From another folder lying on the desk, Oland pulled out a copy of the statement and began rereading it.

"This looks good. But the office has been getting calls all morning from the press. The killing of two police officers, especially when one of them was part of the department's command staff, requires more than a written statement. This isn't going to answer all the reporters' questions. I'd like to call a press conference for this afternoon so we can address everyone at the same time. This is just too big."

Neither Ben nor the chief were fans of public speaking, preferring to leave that up to others while they kept their heads down and focused on the job at hand. But they couldn't argue with the mayor's reasoning.

Before Ben began walking the mayor through the file and recounting events from both crime scenes, the mayor asked his secretary to have the staff schedule the press conference. He wanted to give reporters time to prepare and producers from the television stations the ability to slot in a segment on their evening news broadcasts. After that, he sat quietly as Ben briefed him on everything they knew. Which wasn't very much.

Forty-five minutes and several more cups of coffee later, Ben and the chief were leaving the mayor's office. They'd brought the mayor up to speed and discussed what they'd each say at the press conference. Now, with the hours they had before having to go before the microphones, the two wanted to get back to the station.

As he was turning to head back into his office, Oland stopped, turned around, and called after Ben.

"Detective Winters, have you learned anything about that skeleton you found?"

"No, sir. Actually, my partner and I were just beginning our investigation when we received the call about Officer Noffsinger. Under the circumstances, we're putting the skeleton case on hold."

"That makes sense," the mayor agreed. "No one knew it was there in the first place. I guess you've had to shut down the construction site."

"State CSU went through and collected as much evidence as they think they are going to get. But, no, I haven't officially released the scene just yet," Ben said, wondering when he was going to make that decision. Knowing the longer he waited, the longer the site would be shut down. Probably pissing off a lot of people in the process.

The mayor shook his head and said, "I guess Howard got lucky then."

Ben didn't understand. "I'm sorry. I don't know what you mean."

Oland leaned on the doorframe and crossed his arms.

"After the warehouse was condemned a few years back, the city took over the property," Oland began. "Since there was no way we'd be able to redevelop the site, we basically auctioned it off. It came down to two bidders. Howard and South Mountain against an out-of-state developer. I would have much preferred for Howard to have gotten the property, being local, but the guys from Jersey came in with a full plan that couldn't be beat. At the end of the day, I couldn't convince the City Council to stick with Howard no matter how hard I tried. Now, if he *had* gotten the property, it would be his project that would be tied up with this skeleton mystery."

"If I could ask," Ben thought for a moment, "do you know how long the city owned the property?"

"I'd have to go back and look to double-check the exact date, but it's been since sometime in the '70s."

"Thank you, sir. I'll see you at the press conference."

As Ben followed the chief out of the office and back down the winding staircase, he couldn't help but start mapping out a timeline for who owned the warehouse property. It was owned by an out-of-state company now, who had purchased the site from the city. The city condemned the property in the '70s. Who owned it then, he wondered. He knew that figuring out the line of owners for the building was going to lead them to figuring out the identity of the skeleton. Unfortunately, that wasn't the case to which he could devote any time. Though it seemed like the kind of mystery you would find in a classic whodunnit, *The Skeleton in the Warehouse*, he needed to devote all of this attention to catching a cop killer.

Assuming Noffsinger and McMaster were shot by the same person.

TWENTY-SEVEN

1959...

FREDDY QUINN WAS sitting across the street from the hotel in a coffee shop he frequented when Marty Schulman pushed his way through the door. Scanning the room, Marty found Freddy tucked away in a booth toward the back. Weaving his way through the crowd of morning diners and waitresses, the lawyer slid into the seat opposite Quinn.

There were no pleasantries. No greetings.

Marty locked eyes with Freddy and said, "Bert Ramsburg is missing."

Without breaking eye contact, Freddy took a long sip of coffee and casually replied, "So?"

"*'So?'* A police officer from the Parker City Police Department seems to have disappeared off the face of the earth. He hasn't been seen for a week."

"Maybe he was abducted by some little green men from outer space."

"Freddy!"

"What? What's the big deal? Maybe the guy decided to take a vacation. Wha' do I care where he is? He's been up Billy's ass for so long, why is him being gone such a problem?"

The attorney rested his elbows on the table and put

his head in his hands. "*Because* he's been on Billy for so long and is now missing *is exactly* the problem. There are people in the PCPD who think Billy had enough and finally decided to get rid of him. I've spoken to Billy and he said he has no idea what happened to Ramsburg. He specifically told you to leave the cop alone after the last time he showed up at the hotel. That's the very last time anyone saw him. *At the hotel!* Do you see why this looks so bad?"

Freddy didn't say anything. He sat nonchalantly eating his pancakes.

"Freddy!" Marty exploded, while still trying to keep his voice down. "The state's attorney is talking about bringing Billy in for questioning!"

"What if there was a witness that says they saw him leave the hotel that night?"

"You're Billy's bodyman. No one is going to take your word for it. They'll assume you're just saying what he wants you to say."

"Not me, you shyster," Freddy shot back. "One of the girls in the kitchen. She saw him leave that night. Around seven-thirty."

Marty's brow furrowed. "How do you know that's what she saw?"

"Because it's what I'm going to tell her she saw."

"Dammit! Freddy! What did you do?"

Marty threw himself against the back of the booth in exasperation.

Not sure how much he should tell the lawyer, Freddy's mind was racing. Between him and the Kid, and Jimmy and McMaster, they'd cleaned up the warehouse and hidden the body where no one was ever going to look. Since then, the Kid had stayed gone. He hadn't stopped by to pester Billy like he usually did every few days, sneaking in through the back of the hotel so no one saw him. Freddy just figured he'd gone back to his fancy house and upper-crust lifestyle.

McMaster had taken the police car back to the station and promised to report back if anyone started asking questions about that night. It looked like they were going to need him again.

Freddy pulled a clean napkin out of the silver container on the table and asked Marty for a pen. On the napkin, he scribbled a name, then slid it across the table to the lawyer.

"Give this to our guy McMaster. Tell him to question her about what she saw that night. Can you get him to be the one to look into this?"

Marty Schulman couldn't believe how stupid some people could be.

"Don't you think it would be a little odd for an attorney to request a specific officer to look into the disappearance of another officer? Especially when it is that attorney's client who is accused of doing something to said officer."

"I've seen you perform miracles before." Freddy's tone was as cold as ice. "Like Billy says, what does he pay you for?"

TWENTY-EIGHT

A FEW DAYS LATER, Billy Roscoe sat reading the *Herald-Dispatch*, as he found time to do every day. He never thought of himself as a news junkie, he just wanted to know what was happening in case there was a situation which he might be able to use to his advantage. Plus, it helped him keep up with the movers and shakers in town so when they walked into the Derby Restaurant, he'd have something to discuss with them.

Billy was reading the same article for the third time that day. He'd first seen it while he was having breakfast. After which he immediately summoned both Freddy Quinn and Marty Schulman to his office. As he'd waited for them to arrive, he reread the piece.

Now, as the two men watched him reading it again, they could see the tension in their boss's expression.

The front-page headline declared for all to see that one of Parker City's finest was missing. Until now, Billy had been oblivious to the absence of the scrawny little policeman who'd been giving him such a headache. He'd been so wrapped up in the business of running the hotel and casino upstairs, and the increased shipments that had been running up and down the east coast, that he simply hadn't noticed. And neither Freddy nor Marty had wanted to bring it up.

Folding the paper and laying it on his desk, Roscoe

leaned back in his chair and stared up at the ceiling. This went on for several minutes. Billy's mind was spinning, doing its best to digest everything he'd learned and calculating what it all meant. The man who'd become a thorn in his side for the better of a year had suddenly gone missing and there were people in Parker City that thought he was behind the disappearance. This was not the way he liked to see his name in the press. The reason he'd been so successful with his not-so-legal enterprises was *because* he'd been able to keep the spotlight off them. Now, there were questions lingering out there in the public. Unfortunately, and troublingly, he didn't have all the answers this time.

When the silence in the office finally reached a crescendo, he snapped forward and caught his two top men in a steely gaze.

Opening his mouth to speak, for the first time, Billy Roscoe found himself at a loss for words. He had too many conflicting thoughts fighting to be foremost in his mind. So many questions he wanted to ask. So many foul words he wanted to shout. So many items on his desk he wanted to throw across the room.

"I'm just going to assume that both of you were aware that Bert Ramsburg has gone missing." Billy didn't give Freddy or Marty a chance to respond. "I will also assume neither of you told me because you had good intentions. Would either of you care to share those intentions with me?"

"Yes, Billy, I knew Ramsburg had gone missing," the attorney said, sticking his head directly into the lion's mouth. "I started hearing things about a week ago. But I didn't bring it to you because it has nothing to do with you. I figured if he's been giving you so much trouble, there were bound to be others in Parker he was bothering. Who knows who he might have gotten on the bad side of?"

"That might all be true, but *I* seem to be the only one the police are looking at! And what's this horseshit about the state's attorney bringing me in for questioning? I gave specific instructions *not* to do anything to that cop. I gave them to you!"

Billy pointed a finger directly at Freddy. If it had been the barrel of a gun, the thug wouldn't have been surprised to see a bullet explode from it in the very next second. Freddy couldn't help but feel his temperature rise, a faint line of sweat beginning to form on his forehead.

"You made yourself clear, Billy. I swear. But we got lucky. Doesn't that article say McMaster is the one leading the investigation? Even if there was something to tie this to you, he's not stupid enough to come after you. Not after how much money you've paid him to keep lookin' the other way."

Roscoe bolted out of his chair, sending it crashing to the floor behind him.

"That isn't the point! *I* know I had nothing to do with this. *You* know I had nothing to do with this. But now there will always be this goddam cloud hanging over my head unless they can figure out what happened to that little sonofabitch!"

Marty cleared his throat and said, "The police have a witness that saw Bert Ramsburg drive away from the hotel on the night the police say he disappeared. They also have his police car being checked back in that night. Which means, he wasn't here. Anyone could have grabbed him after he left the station that night."

"What witness?"

"One of the girls who works down in the kitchen. She was out back having a smoke." Schulman shot Freddy a quick glance. "I was there when McMaster spoke to her."

"Then why isn't that in the article?" Billy picked up the paper and threw it at his lawyer.

"That part hasn't been released yet. Billy, I have been managing this. It's going to be fine. McMaster has already told me what he's going to put in his report. Ramsburg left the hotel on the night in question and returned to the police station. After that, they can't figure out what happened to him but there is no, I repeat, there is *no* evidence tying you to his disappearance."

Silence once again enveloped the room.

Turning to look out the window at the people on the sidewalk below, just loud enough for the other two men to hear, Billy asked, "Do I even want to know what happened to him? Where he is?"

Marty leaned forward in his chair, shaking his head, and said, "Billy, I swear to you on my granddaughter. I have no idea where Bert Ramsburg is."

Freddy Quinn didn't say a word.

TWENTY-NINE

1984...

THE PRESS CONFERENCE drew more reporters than Ben
was anticipating. It was a hot summer with not a lot of
news, so he shouldn't have been surprised that a larger
number of media outlets from the tri-state region would
show up to cover the mysterious and brutal murders of
two police officers. All of the local television affiliates
were accounted for, as well as radio stations and daily
papers. Because of the interest and unexpected turn-
out, the briefing was moved from its original location
in one of the building's conference rooms to the City
Council meeting room, which could accommodate a
larger audience.

Entering the room behind the mayor and chief, Ben
was momentarily blinded by the barrage of camera
flashes going off as they took their places behind the
podium. Ben's hope was that he wouldn't have to say
too much because, quite honestly, he didn't have very
much to say. He hadn't had a chance to really dig into
the investigation, most of his time since the second
shooting being taken up preparing for this briefing.
Valuable time that he felt could have been better spent.

While he was reviewing the facts they did have, he'd
asked Tommy to sit down with each of the members of

the PCPD's Drug Task Force and go through their statements once more just to make sure they hadn't forgotten anything. The best place for them to begin was with the first shooting since in that case, Officer Joe Noffsinger had received a call drawing him to his own execution. It was as good a place to start as any.

Ben had been lost in his own thoughts for several minutes when he realized he wasn't paying attention to what was going on right in front of him. The mayor was still standing at the podium speaking to the reporters. The detective had no idea what the mayor was saying. Hopefully, no one else picked up on the fact his mind had carried him off in another direction. Forcing himself to focus, Ben was pleased when the mayor turned the briefing over to Chief Brent who would walk the gathering through the timeline of events. After meeting with the mayor, he and the chief had discussed and decided exactly what the press was going to be told. They were going to be given the bare-bone facts and nothing else. There would be no speculation or theorizing because there wasn't enough information to work with at this point. They didn't even have the reports back from the state's forensic team or the medical examiner to share.

Following the events several years earlier, Ben and Tommy had gained a slight notoriety, having solved the case of the Spring Strangler. Though neither detective was comfortable with the outcome or the resulting media attention, for a short time, they were the flavor of the month, so-to-speak. How couldn't they be? A serial killer had strangled three women in Parker City. For a sleepy little city on the edge of the Blue Ridge

Mountains, it was a huge story. And for whatever reason—as sad as it was, Ben said—the press was fascinated with serial killers.

After their fifteen minutes of fame were over, Ben and Tommy were more than happy to return to being unknowns. They could both have gone for the rest of their careers without having to handle another murder investigation. Unfortunately, they were now faced with another set of crimes that naturally attracted the attention of the media.

When Chief Brent finished detailing the information the PCPD had collected, the mayor opened the floor to questions. Ben was more than happy he had not been expected to have a prepared statement, instead leaving that up to the mayor and chief. He was there more as a prop for the moment. Until the investigation was able to bear any fruit, there was not much more he could share.

The first question came from a reporter Ben recognized from one of the local evening news broadcasts out of Baltimore. A crime reporter who had tried to score an interview with Ben and Tommy after the Strangler case.

"Detective Winters," he began, focusing all eyes on Ben. "Do you believe Parker City has another serial killer on the loose like the Spring Strangler three years ago?"

THIRTY

"How did it go?" Tommy asked as Ben walked into the pair's office.

Slumping into his chair, Ben sighed. "Fine. Until the reporters started asking questions."

"Let me guess. They wanted to know if Parker City had another serial killer."

"That did seem to be the ten thousand dollar question. No matter how many times I said we don't have enough information yet to say one way or another, they kept asking. Mind you, they did try asking in different ways."

"Those reporters are sneaky that way."

"Oland kept things under control. That was nice."

"You really like him, don't you?"

Ben thought for a moment. He'd never really thought about it in the sense of liking or disliking the mayor. He just thought he was good at his job. Which is the best way he could explain it to his partner. For Tommy's part, he couldn't say he disliked Charlie Oland. But he was always wary of politicians in general.

Rubbing his tired eyes, Ben asked, "Did you talk with the task force guys again? Anything new come up?"

"Not really. At least, none of them recalled anything they hadn't already told us. Kramer is still pretty upset.

I mean, they're all upset, but Ron is blaming himself for not getting there in time to catch the guy."

Changing gears, Tommy opened his notebook and went on.

"I did talk to one of the guys on the street I have gotten to know a bit."

"One of '*the guys on the street*'?" Ben asked, raising an eyebrow.

"Let's just say, he isn't the most savory character. He never really gets into too much trouble, but he knows the people who do."

"And what did this character of yours have to say?" Ben leaned forward, his interest beginning to pique.

"Turns out, the task force has been making more headway than they realized. A lot of the dealers on the street are finding it more difficult to do their jobs. Before Noffsinger and his boys came along, no one was paying any attention to the drug trade Downtown. But now, they've made enough arrests and scared enough dealers to disrupt the natural order. And not everyone is happy about this."

"So Noffsinger's shooting could be revenge?" Ben asked.

"That could be one theory. Especially since the shooter called him specifically to set up a meet."

"That doesn't explain McMaster though. Sure, Joe reported to the lieutenant, but it would be the members of the task force themselves who should be the targets in this scenario."

"Yeah," Tommy sighed, leaning back in his chair and kicking his feet up on his desk. "I couldn't come up with a good enough reason to think McMaster was tied in to some retaliation plot that also involved Noffsinger. Which leaves scenario number two. This is a shooter who is just going after the police."

"But why did he call Noffsinger?" Ben asked, though it was more to point out the glaring flaw in the theory than anything else.

"Right… Okay, how about this? The target was actually McMaster," Tommy said, pointing to the photo of Lieutenant Hank McMaster that Ben had tacked to the chalkboard. "The suspect knew if he shot a cop, the odds were pretty good the brass would turn up at the crime scene. When McMaster left the scene, the killer followed him and took his shot. It was the only way he'd know where McMaster would be."

As far a theory went, it wasn't outside the realm of possibility, Ben thought. Except for the fact the shooter called and asked for Joe Noffsinger by name. If he just wanted to shoot a cop to draw out McMaster—hoping he would show up at the scene—he could have picked any random officer out on patrol. There was something to the fact that he wanted Noffsinger to be the first target.

Batting the idea around for a few more minutes, Ben finally said, "There's also scenario number three. The two shootings have nothing to do with one another. And we actually have two suspects to be looking for."

"We aren't going to know that until we get the ballistic reports and see if the shell casings we found at the two scenes match," said Tommy, reaching for his telephone. "I'll just give the guys over at CSU a quick call to…check in…and see how they're doing."

Listening to Tommy in the background, Ben walked

over to the board where they'd written down all of the facts they'd been able to accumulate. The timeline was clear; there was definitely no question as to when anything happened. And there was more than enough time for one person to do both shootings. It was the disappearing act *after* each of the shootings that Ben was thinking about.

Within moments of each incident, someone was there. Kramer after Noffsinger was shot, the store clerk after McMaster went down. Yet, neither witness saw anyone running away. Knowing the killer, or killers, couldn't be ghosts, Ben started wondering how they could have gotten away so quickly. If these were premeditated murders, they would have had a chance to plan an escape route.

The area around the High's convenience store was pretty open, so someone could run off in a number of different directions and not be seen because of one of the other fast-food restaurants along the road or other buildings behind it. The alleyway behind the bar was something completely different. Kramer said no one came out of the alley. Which meant, the shooter either went into the bar or the other building.

Ben went back to his desk and flipped through the files until he came to the one with the diagram of the Noffsinger scene. Mentally putting himself at the opening to the alley, to his left was the Ramshackle. To his right was an old abandoned building. Straight ahead was the brick wall of a third building. There were only two doors leading into the alley. One belonged to the bar, the other to the broken-down building.

Quickly scanning all of the notes, Ben found the

lines he was looking for. The door to the abandoned building was locked, cutting off any possible escape in that direction. That left only one way out of the alley. Through the Ramshackle. Someone in that bar had to have seen something.

THIRTY-ONE

NOT TOO MANY blocks from the Ramshackle sat what once was the city's pride and joy, the Harlequin Theatre. The largest building most of the residents had ever seen when it was built, its construction altered the city's skyline forever, remaining the tallest building in Parker City for decades.

Along with the opening of the theater came a cultural awakening. Parker City was no longer just a small farming town.

The Harlequin was creation of Bernard Parker Moss, a descendant of not just one but two of the city's original founding families. A powerful and exceedingly successful businessman, he wanted to bring "big city" entertainment to western Maryland. By the time all the bills were paid, construction of the performance venue exceeded $400,000. It was an unheard-of sum at the time. Millions upon millions of dollars in the modern equivalent, it was a mere drop in the bucket for a man who had amassed his wealth through manufacturing and coal mining not too far across the border in West Virginia. That fortune was in addition to his family's already considerable means, rumored in part to have come from the slave trade half a century earlier.

Parker Moss's desire was to introduce culture to the rural community. A gambler and all-around risk-taker, he was willing to challenge the status quo even though he was very much a part of the establishment. When the project was announced in the *Parker Chronicle Dispatch*, the paper questioned whether a grand showplace was something the city needed or if it was just another attempt by the Parker family to maintain its oppressive hold on Parker City and the lives of its citizens. Needless to say, the *Dispatch* was not very friendly to the upper classes during the early part of the 1900s.

When the Harlequin Theatre held its opening night performance, the doors were opened on the most spectacular elegance Parker City had ever seen. Polished marble floors and fresco covered walls welcomed guests as they walked through the bronze doors. Crystal chandeliers lit the way through the ornately decorated lobby full of gold trim to the 1,650 seat auditorium where ticketholders were escorted by uniformed ushers ready and willing to show them to their velvet-covered seats.

While the *Dispatch* did its part excoriating Parker Moss, the *Blue Ridge Herald*—a rival news outfit—was his defender. Its editor was the first to call the Harlequin "the Crown Jewel of Parker City," a nickname that had lasted for close to a century.

The *Herald*'s editor happened to be Parker Moss's uncle.

As for the Harlequin, it became an entertainment spot for the rich, poor, and everyone in between. For a few hours every evening, everyone was equal. The theater's staff treated the factory worker just as well and with as much respect as the factory owner. It was exactly the opposite of what the *Dispatch* predicted. The theater brought the community together.

Years passed, the popularity of vaudeville declined and the Harlequin, like many vaudeville houses in the country, transitioned into a movie palace. The cinema had become king. For a quarter, theatergoers were whisked away to a world created by Hollywood. During the bleak days of the Great Depression, while sitting in the darkened theater, the difficulties of everyday life would fade away and Parkertons could imagine what it was like to be Cary Grant, Joan Crawford, or any of the other larger-than-life movie stars projected on the screen. The Depression hit Parker hard, but the Golden Age of Hollywood helped to make it, if not better, tolerable.

The rise of television was the beginning of the end for the Harlequin. More and more, families would finish dinner then gather in the den to watch their favorite programs. Staying home to watch *M*A*S*H*, *Happy Days*, or *All in the Family* became much more economical for larger families. Not that movies like *The Godfather*, *The Exorcist*, and *Jaws* didn't bring out the audiences. By the late '70s, the final nail in the Harlequin's coffin came with the opening of the new suburban movie-plexes. The aging showplace just couldn't compete. Local dance companies and community theater groups would still use the theater, and on occasion, a third-rate tour or comedian might be brought in, but the once-grand venue had fallen into disrepair.

Photos of the various headliners still hung in the lobby along with vintage posters advertising their acts. The oldest piece: a signed show poster from Fatty Arbuckle's early appearance at the theatre. However, few had seen the historic treasures in recent years. As with so many of the buildings in the heart of Downtown, the Harlequin was devastated by the Great Flood. The once shiny marble floors now sat covered with a layer of filth left behind by the surging waters.

Even though Mayor Oland promised to return the Harlequin Theatre to its former glory, using it as a centerpiece of his campaign to revive and revitalize the city, there had not been much forward progress. Cleaning and refurbishing the theater would take millions of dollars. And as hard as he tried, the money just wasn't there. So, it sat, like so many other buildings on the street, boarded up, waiting to one-day welcome guests through its shimmering bronze doors.

Seeing the once pristine building in such decay was heartbreaking to anyone who remembered it from its heyday.

Sitting in front of the theater in his squad car, Officer Peter Vernon had a hazy memory of his grandparents taking him to the Harlequin once when he was just a young boy to see a showing of *Miracle on 34th Street*. That was only about twenty years ago. But it seemed more like a lifetime.

After graduating from the police academy, he'd been sworn as a sheriff's deputy in Harrison County, just to the west of Parker. It had been a very uneventful few years. When the opportunity arose to join the Parker City Police, he gladly made the transfer. When he was tapped by Chief Brent to join the Drug Task Force, he felt his years of loyal service were finally paying off.

Things with the new unit were going better than anyone expected until yesterday when their commanding officer was shot down in the line of duty. Like the other two members of the task force, Vernon felt angry. Though the entire department was mourning the loss, not surprisingly, he, Ron Kramer, and Brian Woods were taking it particularly hard. The foursome had become so close working together day-in and day-out over the last several months.

When the chief suggested the team take the day off, all three politely declined, insisting they report to work as usual. They knew full well it would have been what Joe Noffsinger would have wanted. He was always the first to say how important their current assignment was. If their work really was making a difference and it was hurting the city's drug trade, then they couldn't back off now.

After the events of the previous day, the order went out that every officer on the street needed to be extra vigilant. With two officers dead, until they had a better idea of what they were dealing with, everyone needed to be on their guard. If resources weren't an issue, Chief Brent would have insisted on officers partnering up for their shifts. Unfortunately, the manpower simply did not exist.

Which is why Peter Vernon sat on patrol alone Downtown. As the task force's assignment specifically focused on this particular section of the city, it was not uncommon for members of the unit to make regular patrols through the streets. Drug deals on the corner did not happen solely at night around here. So the more visible the police presence, the fewer deals were conducted. At least out in the open.

Thankfully, the stifling heatwave that lingered over the city for the better part of the last week had broken overnight. This was the first truly pleasant summer afternoon Vernon could remember in a while. The bright blue sky and fluffy white clouds floating overhead helped to lift his mood ever so slightly. On a day like this, he much preferred to be out on the street than back at the station behind a desk.

Making a pass down High Street, something caught Vernon's attention. He thought he saw a figure quickly duck into the narrow alley between the Harlequin Theatre and the rundown former appliance store next to it. In this part of town, it wasn't unusual for people to turn and head in the opposite direction when they saw the police coming.

But there was something different about the way this individual waited for the patrol car to pull up in front of him before darting off. Like he was waiting to be noticed. The young officer wasn't able to get a good look at the man's face though. He was wearing a baseball cap pulled down low along with a pair of sunglasses. He just looked suspicious.

Stepping from the car, Vernon saw a few people hanging around on the sidewalk several blocks down near a set of apartment buildings. From somewhere in the opposite direction, he thought he could hear the sound of construction equipment. Overhead, a passenger jet flew by on its route to BWI Airport. It was all very picturesque, if you ignored the fact most of the buildings were boarded up and covered with graffiti.

Placing his hand on his holstered weapon, more for a small sense of security than anything else, Vernon approached the front entrance of the Harlequin. Doing his best to peer through the grime-covered windows, the little he could see seemed to be as it had been for years. Checking to make sure the tarnished bronze doors were locked, he decided before he went any further to radio in his position.

After a quick call into Dispatch, Vernon slowly walked toward the opening between the two buildings where he'd seen the man disappear. Before turning the corner, he paused. An image of the last sight Joe Noffsinger saw when he turned into the alley behind the Ramshackle flashed in Vernon's mind, sending a cold chill down his spine. Trying to shake off the thought, it was too late. The tiny hairs on the back of his neck were already anxiously standing at attention.

Unholstering his gun, Vernon cautiously peeked around the corner.

The alleyway was empty.

A flood of embarrassment washed over him. Understandably, everything that had happened had him on edge. But if he was going to be worried about turning every corner from now on, it was seriously going to affect his ability to do his job.

Looking down at the gun in his hand, deciding whether he was just working himself up, he chose to err on the side of caution. Leveling the piece in front of him, he stepped into the alley and the shadows created by the buildings on either side of him. Maybe if the slightest bit of sunlight had been able to make it into the narrow corridor, he wouldn't feel so anxious. Sweeping his eyes from side to side as he went, Vernon involuntarily shuddered as another chill ran through him. His senses were starting to play games with him.

So far, he'd found nothing of note in the alleyway

except piles of garbage and a side door leading into the Harlequin that was sealed with an industrial-sized padlock. A few more feet and he would be at the rear of the theater. Closing the distance in a few quick steps, he once again assumed a secure position against the wall so he could peer around the corner of the building.

Not being a regular theater-goer himself, the one thing he did know was there was always a stage door. About ten feet from where he stood was a large metal door with those exact words stenciled on them: "Stage Door." The problem was that the rusted door sat wide open revealing a black emptiness leading into the theater.

"Shit," Vernon sighed.

Until yesterday, he wouldn't have thought twice about heading into the theater to make sure something wasn't happening inside that shouldn't. Today, seeing a door that should be bolted shut sitting wide open, inviting him into a building that was all but condemned, was not sitting well with him. He wasn't going to go charging in by himself.

Pulling the walkie-talkie from his belt, Vernon tapped the button.

"Dispatch, this is Vernon. I'm requesting additional units at the Harlequin Theatre. There's an open back entry door. We may need to go in and clear the building. You may want to track down the property owners and have them come down too."

"Copy," answered the sharp voice. "Will send additional units. Stay put until they get there, Pete."

Now all he had to do was wait.

THIRTY-TWO

BEN LOOKED UP from his desk when he heard someone calling "Sarge" from the doorway. Very few people ever referred to him in that manner, which is why he wasn't used to it when they did. It *sounded* wrong to him. He'd prefer if people just called him by name. But in a police station, rank was important.

The person standing outside Ben's office happened to be a sergeant himself, which accounted for the friendly greeting. Al Shepard was a round, happy fellow. Quick with a smile and slap on the back, he was one of the friendlier members of the department's old guard. He was also the desk sergeant on duty that afternoon.

"What can I do for you, Al?" Ben asked, tossing his pen on the desk and flexing his aching fingers.

"It's what I can do for you," the sergeant replied, handing over a manilla envelope with the seal of the Maryland State Troopers emblazoned on the front. "This was just delivered for you."

Ben quickly took the envelope. Tommy had spoken with the CSU supervising officer earlier and had been promised the preliminary results on the shell casing by that afternoon. Hopefully, this was that report.

Thanking Shepard for the personal delivery, Ben tore open the envelope and withdrew the pages it contained. There was more information than he'd expected.

He knew he was going to have to go back and read everything very carefully. But right now, he was looking for one thing. Flipping back and forth between the first two pages, then turning to the third, he found exactly what he was looking for.

Seeing it in black and white, he realized he wasn't sure if this was good news or bad news. It all depended on the way one looked at it. If nothing else though, they finally had a lead. Of sorts. But right now, he'd take whatever he could get.

CSU report in hand, Ben took off down the hall to the breakroom where Tommy was making a fresh pot of coffee.

"Preliminary ballistics just came in!" Ben said excitedly.

Tommy put his empty mug down and reached for the papers in his partner's hand. "And?"

"They're a match," Ben answered, then began reading a brief excerpt from the report's summary. "Examination of the evidence found at the two crime scenes shows a specific and identifiable indentation on each of the three shell cases that can be attributed to the gun's ejector mechanism. It can therefore be presumed the same weapon was used in both shootings. A more conclusive examination will be conducted once the bullets themselves are delivered following the medical examiner's pending autopsies."

Tommy leaned back against the counter as he scanned the report for himself. His first thought was the same as Ben's. Was this a good thing or a bad thing? Two guns meant two killers. Two killers meant two cases that could have nothing to do with one another, which required a division of their time. However, one gun meant there was a single killer. One person out there killing police officers.

"Nine millimeter rounds…" Tommy said, only reading small portions of the report out loud. "Ninety percent certainty…high powered…matching unique scratches. Okay, now what? They compare these to other gun deaths? Not that we've had any in Parker for… I honestly don't know how long."

Ben shook his head. "I don't think those shell casings will match anything else on file anywhere. Think about it. If those bullets could lead us—the police—back to the shooter, would he have left them lying around?"

"So it could be a new gun the shooter got especially for his little spree," Tommy theorized.

"Or," Ben offered, "a gun that's never been used in the commission of a crime. Either way, my gut tells me we won't be able to find the killer through the gun alone."

The coffee machine broke the silence by emitting one last hiss of steam as the pot Tommy was waiting for finished brewing.

"I'm going to go show this to the chief," Ben was saying as Tommy turned to pour himself a fresh cup of coffee. "Mind pouring me one of those too?"

"Your wish is my com…" Tommy was interrupted by a commotion in the hallway.

Turning, he saw Ben stick his head out the door to see what was happening. In doing so, Chief Brent nearly took Ben out as he was charging past the break room, two other uniforms only steps behind. Tommy took his hand off the coffee pot's handle. He had the sink-ing feeling he wasn't going to have time for coffee right now. The deathlike pallor of the chief's face said it all. Something bad had happened…again.

"I was just coming to find you two," Brent huffed. "There's been another shooting."

THIRTY-THREE

Fall 1959...

FOLLOWING AN INVESTIGATION lasting some two months, the *Blue Ridge Herald* declared on its front page that the Parker City Police Department was unable to locate the whereabouts of its missing officer, one Bertram Ford Ramsburg. The article went on to recap the details of his disappearance stating that the last time anyone had seen the policeman was one summer evening when he was leaving Billy Roscoe's ParkMar Hotel. After that, he simply vanished. Though, it was determined he had returned to the police station because his patrol car was found returned that evening. And there were several witnesses claiming to have seen him at various locations throughout the city in the following days. However, Hank McMaster, the officer leading the investigation into the disappearance of his colleague, was unable to verify those accounts.

Early in the investigation, suspicion had fallen upon Billy Roscoe, as it was reported that Ramsburg held a grudge against the popular businessman and was inquiring into his enterprises. Theories tying Roscoe to the disappearance were quickly dispelled by McMaster and the state's attorney, following the complete lack of evidence connecting him in any way to the disappearance.

As it stood, the investigation was stalled. Officer Bert Ramsburg would remain an official missing person.

Billy tossed the newspaper onto the seat next to him as he stretched his legs in the back of his spacious Cadillac Fleetwood. With Jimmy Quinn behind the wheel and Freddy in the passenger seat, the limo wheeled its way through the streets on a cool, crisp autumn morning.

"I told you you'd be happy to see that article, Billy," Freddy said over his shoulder.

"Why? It says exactly what we already knew. Bert Ramsburg is missing."

Craning around in his seat, Freddy pointed out, "It also says the police are closing the investigation."

"No. They aren't *closing* it. They just have nowhere else to go with it. It's still an open case."

"It's the same thing." Freddy shrugged. "I talked to McMaster personally. He says he doubts he's ever gonna be able to figure out what happened to Ramsburg. And between me and you, it doesn't sound like he's gonna be spendin' too much of his time looking for him."

"It doesn't matter. There is always going to be a cloud hanging over *my* head. People will always be wondering what *I* did to that little pissant. I've done things in my life that I could easily go down for. Believe me. The ironic thing, this *isn't* one of them."

"Yeah. But McMaster says there's no evidence you had anything to do with this. And you didn't even have to pay him to say that," Freddy offered.

"There are still going to be people who think I was involved. It could hurt business. Chief Stanley hasn't been at the restaurant in weeks! I haven't heard from the mayor, except to say he doesn't believe anything the paper said about me. And that sonofabitch is a terrible liar. Do you know, I went so far as to tell Marty to hire some private investigators to see if they could dig anything up."

The turn of phrase instantly caused a line of sweat to form on Freddy's forehead.

"But Marty said they didn't find anything either," Roscoe said, picking up the paper again and tapping it on his knee.

His anxiety level was higher than normal. He was frustrated by the implication he was the one responsible for the cop's disappearance. Even though he'd specifically ordered his "head of security" *not* to do anything to him. Hank McMaster being the one leading the investigation was a stroke of luck. Even though Billy knew he was innocent, there was no way his guy on the inside would ever try and pin the disappearance on him. Marty would surely take care of that.

But it was still damn curious what actually happened to Ramsburg. He'd been so deadset on bringing Billy down. Then he just up and vanished. There had to be more to the story that someone wasn't telling him, Billy thought.

"Like I've said before," Freddy began, trying to interject a bit of humor into the conversation, "maybe it was aliens."

Jimmy chuckled. "He always looked like one to me."

Rubbing his eyes with his free hand, Billy said, "I'm going to need both of you to be quiet now."

THIRTY-FOUR

FREDDY QUINN HADN'T seen much of the Kid since that fateful night back in the middle of the summer when everything went to hell. He'd stopped showing up at the hotel unannounced and pestering Billy at every turn. He'd fallen into the role he'd been meant to play. That of a *silent* partner. The couple of times he did visit the property, his cocksure swagger was nowhere to be seen. Whether he still acted as though he was something special when he was around his own kind, Freddy did not know. That was a circle in which he certainly did not run.

If it wasn't an urgent matter, Freddy wouldn't be on his way to the Kid's office. But a development necessitated the unexpected visit.

The brisk walk through the cool fall air was invigorating. With a bright blue sky overhead, Parker seemed to shine around him. Maybe another day he'd have been able to enjoy the afternoon out, but he was on a mission and couldn't waste time. Billy might need him and he'd already made up an excuse why he wasn't going to be available for an hour or so.

Keeping the details of what had actually happened to Bert Ramsburg from Billy was not as difficult as he'd expected. In part because Marty was now a willing accomplice to keeping the secret. Whenever an article appeared in the paper about the mysterious disappearance, Billy would fume and fuss but he never asked too many questions. Which always led Freddy to wonder if he knew what they'd done.

Stepping into the building's lobby, Freddy found a convenient office directory hanging on the wall. Running his finger along the names, he found the location for which he was looking. It figured. The Kid's family's company had an entire floor to themselves. They probably owned the whole damn building, Freddy grumbled to himself as he headed for the elevator.

Thankfully, the lobby was empty. There would be no one able to say they saw him. Even if they had, would anyone know who he was? He wasn't like Billy, who was used to having his picture in the paper. But still, the fewer people he came across, the better. Keeping his head down and his eyes fixed on the floor, he waited for the elevator door to open.

Patience was not one of his virtues, so standing there with his hands in his pocket was making the tough guy extremely antsy. Not to mention, he hadn't figured out how he was going to explain who he was to whoever inevitably greeted him when he reached the top floor and asked how to find the Kid. Each passing second made him more frustrated.

Finally, there was a chime signaling the arrival of the elevator.

When the door swished open, Freddy couldn't believe his luck. Standing there was none other than the Kid himself. Even better, he was all alone.

As their eyes met, the younger man's grew to the size of billiard balls.

"What the hell are you doing here? You can't be here. I can't be seen with you!" He started quickly walking to the front entrance, leaving Freddy behind.

"We need to talk," Freddy said, raising his voice. Because when Freddy Quinn told someone they needed to talk, they listened for fear of what he might do to them.

Two men dressed in practically matching business suits entered the building as Freddy was closing the gap between himself and his quarry. The Kid stiffened upon seeing them. The men worked for him, well, his father. He couldn't afford to be seen with someone the likes of Freddy Quinn. How would he ever explain how they knew one another? What would he say to his father? What would his father say to him?

"Frank, I left the Riggler's account file sitting on your desk. They're asking about a possible extension," he said, hoping to distract them from noticing the brute following behind him. "Sam, you need to get the signed Mercantile documents to Bob before the meeting tomorrow morning. I'll check in with both of you when I get back."

The trick seemed to work. They'd kept their eyes on the boss's son the entire time he was talking and didn't even glance at Freddy. Two more steps and the Kid was outside on the sidewalk.

Before he was able to make his next move, Freddy's enormous hand grabbed his arm. A former boxer, his hands were like concrete. One hit could easily put someone down. And his grip was like a vise.

The Kid finally, though not willingly, turned to look into the big man's steel-gray eyes.

"What do you want?"

"It's not what I want. It's what our friend McMaster wants. Remember him? The nice policeman that helped take care of your little accident a few months ago?"

"The paper said…," the Kid lowered his voice and looked around. "The paper said the investigation didn't find anything. It's over. He did his job. I *paid him* to do his job. What more does he want?"

"He said that was just a down payment. Now the job's done, he wants the balance. Twenty-five thousand dollars will take care of it and settle the account."

Freddy liked seeing the college-educated rich kid on edge. He needed to learn life wasn't always going to be easy for him. Sure, he grew up with a silver spoon in his mouth, but he'd ventured out and gotten himself involved with things way over his head. Now, he needed to pay.

"Twenty-five thous…twenty-five *thousand* dollars?" the Kid stammered. "You've got to be kidding me! Where am I supposed to come up with that kind of money? I already paid him to take care of this."

"Yeah. And he wants more. It wasn't easy he says. Do you realize what will happen to you if any of this comes out? You should be grateful for everything he's done for you. Hell, you should be grateful for everything *I've* done for you. And I'm not even askin' for money. Not one red cent. I just know when I need your help, you'll be there for an old friend like me. Just like I've been there for you."

"I know, Freddy. I know. I will. Whatever you need. But twenty-five thousand is a lot of money."

"Is it worth more than your reputation?" Freddy allowed the question to sink in before continuing. "Is it worth more than your freedom?" Again, another pause.

"What about your father? Is twenty-five large worth more than *his* reputation?"

"I promise, I'll get the money. Tell him he'll get the money. I just need a few days. That's all…a few days."

Freddy's smile was anything but friendly. A lion in the wild preparing to pounce on an unexpecting elk would have been seen to be more congenial.

"Good," he finally said. "Because I'd hate to see your very…very comfortable lifestyle turned upside down because of an unfortunate mistake."

THIRTY-FIVE

1984...

DETECTIVE BEN WINTERS wanted nothing more than for the nightmare that now surrounded him to be over. Three members of the Parker City Police Department had been shot dead while on duty over the course of just two days. Two officers being victims could have arguably been a tragic coincidence. Three officers made it clear there was someone hunting the police. That, and the fact they'd already learned that the first two murders were committed with the same weapon.

Officer Peter Vernon was the latest to fall prey to the unknown killer. He was also the second member of the PCPD's new Drug Task Force to be gunned down. That could not be by chance, Ben thought standing amongst the frenzied activity behind the venerable Harlequin Theatre. Vernon was only a couple of years older than Ben. A thought that only tightened the knot already in the detective's stomach. He was too young to have been cut down like this. He was a good, solid officer who should have served out many, many more years on the force.

Upon his arrival, Ben learned that Ron Kramer and another patrol officer were the first on the scene. Initially, they were responding to a request by Vernon for backup after he reported seeing a suspicious individual. Tommy was speaking with them now.

Like the others, Vernon had been shot. A single GSW to the chest. The medical examiner's assistant said, after a brief examination, he would have died instantly. From the visible location of the wound, the bullet would have struck the heart almost dead center. It would need to be confirmed with a full autopsy, but that was the working theory.

It was the same for both of the other victims as well. The shooter knew how to handle a gun. Though, he did fire two rounds into McMaster. Ben wondered if there was any significance to that detail.

The same forensics team from the previous day was also hard at work collecting whatever they were able to find that appeared out of place or might be useful in identifying the killer.

"Detective Winters," the CSU sergeant said, taking Ben away from his thoughts, "we found a shell casing just inside the door to the theatre. It looks like the shooter could have stood there in the dark and taken his shot."

He handed Ben a small plastic bag so he could examine the spent shell inside.

"Nine millimeter," Ben said, eyeing the small piece of metal. "Same as the other two shootings."

"We'll test it back at the lab to make sure it matches, but, yes, it's definitely the same caliber."

In the back of Ben's mind, the pieces of the puzzle were slowly fitting into their proper place. He was nowhere close to figuring out who was behind the spate of shootings, but an idea was beginning to form about how they could proceed. Vernon's death could be a very important clue in and of itself. He and Tommy might now have a new avenue to pursue.

Ben slowly walked the scene, trying to take it all in from as many different angles as possible. He wanted to make sure not to miss even the smallest detail. He'd done the same at the previous crime scenes, cataloguing everything in his memory. All three were similar… to a point. They could all be considered "public," being as they were outside and anyone could have happened upon them. All three victims appeared to have been taken by surprise and may not have even known what was happening. And, in each instance, it only took one shot—two in the case of McMaster—to do the deed. It was all so clean, Ben realized. But the killer left behind the shell casings. That was puzzling, though Ben had already guessed it was because the gun being used couldn't be tied back to the shooter in any way. They would need to work under the assumption that the gun was "clean" and wasn't going to be able to help them with their investigation.

Tapping the corner of his notebook against his chin, Ben watched as his partner weaved through the assembled men, each focusing on his own specific task. Ben thought about how different crime scenes must have been a hundred years ago, before all the scientific advancements they'd made and were now able to take advantage of in the 1980s to help solve a murder. He wondered what it was going to be like a hundred years in the future.

"I don't like coincidences," were the first words out

of Tommy's mouth. "Kramer being first on the scene twice bothers me."

"But he wasn't at the McMaster scene," Ben pointed out.

"I know."

"Do you think he's the one behind the shootings?"

"No." Tommy didn't even have to pause to think about it. "Ron is no actor. Seeing him at Noffsinger's crime scene and now… He's not taking any of this well."

"I'd be more concerned if he was," Ben said. "What did you find out?"

"Kramer and Grassman were responding to Vernon's request for backup. Ron was coming from the west side of town. Andrew was several blocks south. They were both here within a few minutes of Dispatch putting out the call."

"Who was *actually* the first one on the scene?" Ben asked.

"Kramer. When he arrived, he found Peter. Checked for a pulse, didn't find one. That's when Grassman got here. And before you ask. No, neither of them saw anyone. Or anything out of the ordinary."

"Why was Vernon here?"

Tommy flipped backward a couple of pages in his notebook before answering, "His first call to Dispatch put him in front of the Harlequin. He said he saw a suspicious person lurking around the building. A couple of minutes later, he reported an open door and requested backup. Kramer got here a few minutes later. Basically, leaving a window of about five minutes for the shooting to occur and the suspect to get away."

"But why was Peter here at the Harlequin at all? What was he doing Downtown?"

"Well, according to Kramer, the task force would regularly patrol down here just to have a visible presence on the street. Whatever they could do to deter drug deals. That's what Kramer was doing too."

"Hmmm."

Tommy wasn't sure if Ben was about to say something or if he was just thinking. For his part, he was still trying to make sense of what had transpired over the last forty-eight hours. Taking the Strangler case out of the equation, this wasn't the sort of thing that happened in Parker City. Crimes like this were unthinkable in such a tight-knit community.

"We need to check all of the task force's reports for the last few months. Maybe as far back as when they got started," Ben finally said, breaking his silence. "Especially the arrests they've made."

"Are we looking for something in particular?" Tommy asked, running his hand through his hair, then scratching the back of his head.

"Yes. We are."

"Any interest in sharing what that might be?"

THIRTY-SIX

THERE WAS NO question that the PCPD's Drug Task Force had been hard at work. According to the team's reports, they'd made a number of inroads when it came to disrupting the flow of drugs into the city. But even with those accomplishments, there'd been setbacks. No one thought fighting the war on drugs was going to be easy. But for every step forward, there seemed to be two steps backward.

"I don't understand this," Tommy said, staring at the large stack of files in front of him. "The task force hasn't been around long enough for them to have filed this many reports. Look at this. I mean, how did they have time to fight crime *and* fill out all these forms?"

Ben, sitting behind a stack of files equally large, laughed.

Before the detectives returned to the station after leaving the Harlequin, they'd grabbed some sandwiches to take back for dinner. It was going to be a long night.

As evening settled over the city, Ben and Tommy weren't even halfway through their review of all the reports Noffsinger and his men had filed. The detectives had requested to see all of the team's reports, arrest records, files—anything and everything that might shed light on the recent shootings. The only thing Ben and

Tommy didn't have now was help combing through the mountain of documents.

It was the task force itself that was the key, Ben felt. That's what tied two of the three victims together. If the third officer shot had been a patrolman making a random traffic stop, then Ben wouldn't have been able to make any connection between the victims except that they all wore the uniform. But since two of the three worked in the same unit, one that had gained a little attention over recent months, it wasn't hard to think someone was specifically going after the members of the task force. That just left one question. How was Lieutenant Hank McMaster connected to them in the killer's mind?

Within the department, everyone knew the task force reported to McMaster. But outside the PCPD, when it came to the average Parkerton, they had no idea what the actual command structure of the police was. Ben wondered how many people even knew who the chief of police was these days, let alone one of the department's lieutenants. So there needed to be something obvious connecting McMaster to the PCPD's Drug Task Force that would have made his involvement in their oversight public.

Ben lost track of how many reports he'd already read. They were all starting to blur together. He told himself, if he didn't find anything in the next set of reports, he was going to take a break for a few minutes. He needed to clear his head and grab a candy bar from the vending machine downstairs.

Opening the next folder, he promised himself this would be the last thing he read before stretching his legs. This particular file was different from the many others he'd already read because it was the dossier of a single individual. Flipping back to the front cover, he saw the name "Dunn, Franklin Joseph" scrawled on the tab. It appeared as though Ben had gotten to the files the guys were putting together on individuals they were keeping an eye on. Any details they collected that might assist in a future investigation was included, whether it was a handwritten note or a copy of an old arrest record.

Sorting through some scribbled comments about restaurants Dunn frequented and the name of his latest girlfriend, Ben found an article from the *Herald-Dispatch* from not too long ago. The piece reported the recent arrest of Frank Dunn. The newspaper clipping was followed by a couple of PCPD arrest reports, Dunn's full rap sheet, and a few pages of biographical notes.

Ben quickly skimmed his criminal record. Dunn had an impressively felonious career. The file only listed crimes for which he'd been arrested after his eighteenth birthday, but Ben suspected his juvenile record was just as long. Several armed robberies, assault charges, drug possession, battery, the list went on.

The handwritten notes about Dunn that were included throughout the file painted the picture of a street thug who had gotten into the drug trade. If the information was to be believed, and Ben had no reason to doubt the work of the Drug Task Force, Frank Dunn was one of the biggest players in the Parker City drug world. He'd become a main target of Noffsinger and his team.

Looking at Dunn's most recent mug shot, Ben could tell just by looking at him that this guy was trouble. He

hated to make an assumption like that, just by looking at a photo. But in this case, there was a rap sheet
to back it up.

Dunn had the thickest neck of any man Ben had ever
seen. And a pair of jet black eyes that, even in a picture,
looked threatening. Unkept curly hair and a thick five
o'clock shadow completed the rough, "I-don't-take-shit-
from-no-one" look.

Clearing a place on his desk, Ben spread the contents
of Dunn's file out so he could start at the beginning. He
thought he might have found something to justify putting his trip down to the vending machine on hold for a
bit longer. If someone was targeting the members of the
PCPD's Drug Task Force, Dunn was a prime suspect.
Ben realized that even before reading the entire file.

The article which had first caught Ben's eye, reported
the task force's first big drug bust. In it, Lieutenant Mc-
Master, during an interview, said he personally gave the
go-ahead for the team to arrest Dunn. Reading the line
a second time, Ben sat up a little straighter in his chair.
McMaster took credit for the arrest? Well, at least ordering it. Ben was sure the lieutenant had very little to
do with it, but when it came to taking credit for things,
he'd always been the first in line.

Ben sorted through the papers until he came to the
arrest report and court papers specific to the article.
He remembered when the bust had been made several
months back. There'd been a lot of celebrating after
Dunn was arrested but something went wrong. Reading through the documents, it all started to come back
to him. After his arraignment, Dunn was held at the
county lockup awaiting trial. The dealer's lawyer man-

aged to get an expedited special hearing and the arrest was thrown out on a technicality. At the time, Dunn made a lot of threats about getting even with "the pigs" who arrested him. Ben wondered if he stood in the middle of the courtroom swearing to get his revenge on those who wronged him.

Whether or not it was like a scene from a movie, he threatened the members of the task force and now two of them were dead. And if he thought McMaster was the one calling the shots, that would put the lieutenant in the crosshairs as well.

This information could be exactly what he and Tommy were looking for. It was a connection between the three victims. It was the best lead so far. Ben wondered if it would be so easy though. He liked to think he might have just cracked the case. His more rational side, on the other hand, told him there would be more to it. But for the time being, Frank Dunn was their prime suspect and someone who the detectives needed to locate.

THIRTY-SEVEN

KNOWING FULL WELL time wasn't on their side, but not wanting to miss anything, Ben reread every piece of paper in Frank Dunn's file. He wanted to familiarize himself with one of the city's most dangerous criminals. At least, that was the picture painted by the documents that had been collected.

When he was finished, Ben handed everything over to Tommy to get his reaction. As he read, Tommy found himself coming to the same conclusion as his partner. Dunn was definitely someone with whom they needed to speak. He was an individual who certainly checked off all the boxes when it came to being a suspect...if not more.

Finding him was going to be the difficult part. But Tommy had a good idea where to begin. Plus, it would help answer a question they were going to need to ask anyway. They might as well kill two birds with one stone, he thought.

Which is why the two detectives found themselves standing outside of the Ramshackle shortly after ten o'clock that evening.

Twenty-four hours earlier, the entire area had been blocked off and was crawling with police as they investigated the first shooting. Now, a day later, things had returned to normal. It was as if the events of yesterday never happened.

The loud music pulsing from the dingy building drowned out all other sounds along the street. Occasionally, a voice could just barely be heard shouting over the blaring songs. Ben didn't understand how anyone could stand to be inside. The noise was loud enough on the street, and that was with a brick wall between him and the sound system.

"Are you ready for this?" Tommy raised his voice to ask.

"What do you think?" Ben responded.

Pushing through the door, the detectives were instantly assaulted by the thumping sound waves and a wall of cigarette smoke.

He'd been inside for less than two seconds and already Ben had a headache. Scanning the room, he saw only a dozen or so patrons scattered about. One was passed out at the bar. A few were toward the back playing pool on what looked like a billiard table ready to collapse at any moment. Behind the bar, Tommy pointed to an extremely tall woman with a strange hairdo.

Approaching Angel Sanders, the bartender, and owner of the Ramshackle, Tommy flashed her his brightest smile.

"Ms. Sanders, I'm Detective Mason from last evening. You remember our chat?"

"What?" she shouted over the music.

Ben tried his hardest not to roll his eyes.

Tommy flashed his badge and said, "We spoke last night. My partner and I need to ask you a couple questions."

"I know who you are. We talked last night," Angel shouted back.

Now Ben was getting frustrated. He'd hardly slept in the last two days. His head was throbbing. And there were three dead police officers lying in the morgue. He didn't have the time or patience for this.

Raising his voice so there was no way she wouldn't be able to hear him, Ben showed his badge and said, "Ms. Sanders, we have questions for you. Let's go somewhere a little quieter. Now."

Even Tommy was surprised by the forcefulness of his partner. If he was taken aback, he couldn't imagine what Angel Sanders was thinking. Looking at Ben Winters, not many people would think he could pull off the "bad cop" routine. But he was in no mood to be dicked around with tonight.

Angel motioned for the waitress roaming the bar to keep an eye on things while she escorted Ben and Tommy to a backroom that served as an office and storage area. Once the door was closed, the music still vibrated in the air, but it was a little better. Ben could at least hear himself think.

Once again producing his badge for the bar owner to see, he said, "My name is Detective Sergeant Ben Winters. You met my partner, Detective Mason, last night. We were hoping you might be able to help us. Have you ever seen this man?"

Ben handed her a copy of Frank Dunn's mug shot.

Looking at it for a second, she answered, "He looks like a bunch of the guys that come in here."

"Look closer," Tommy said. "His name is Frank Dunn."

"Yeah. Okay. He might have come in a time or two."

"Was he here last night?" Tommy followed up. "Around six o'clock?"

"I don't know," Angel said, handing the photo back to Ben. "He's come in before. He orders a beer. He leaves. I don't clock the people who come into my bar. They want a drink, I serve 'em a drink. I don't get into their business."

"What business is that, Ms. Sanders?" Ben asked quickly. "Does Dunn sell drugs here out of the Ramshackle? I realize we spent a lot of time looking around outside last night but maybe I should have CSU come and look around inside."

Angel Sanders realized what she said. "I didn't mean it like that. I meant, I don't pay attention to when they come and go."

"Did you see Frank Dunn here yesterday? It wasn't that long ago?" Tommy pressed.

"Maybe. Look, I don't remember. I wasn't feelin' good yesterday."

"But he has come in here before?" Ben wanted to clarify.

"Yeah. At least once a week," Angel said, giving up the defensive act. "He comes in and drinks. He has nothin' to do with me or my bar. And I don't have anything to do with whatever he's into. He ain't a nice guy, I can tell."

Tommy looked toward the closed door leading back out into the bar, "If we asked that waitress of yours if Dunn was here yesterday afternoon before the shooting, what would she say?"

"She wouldn't say anything. She wasn't here. It was just me last night."

Tommy mentally ran through the list of people he and Officer Thompson spoke with the previous evening. She was right. There'd been no waitress. And no Frank Dunn.

"Do you happen to know where Dunn lives?" Ben asked.

"I told you! I don't have nothin' to do with him. I serve him beer. That's all. We're not friends. I don't go over to his house for dinner parties."

After a few more minutes of the same around and around, Ben and Tommy left Angel sitting in her make-shift office as they headed back to their car. They hadn't learned much other than Dunn drank at the bar on occasion, though Angel wasn't sure if he'd been there the day before.

"Do you believe her?" Ben asked his partner. "That she can't remember if she saw Dunn yesterday?"

"For all we know, she was high as a kite yesterday afternoon."

"How did she seem when you questioned her?"

"Pissed."

Ben laughed.

He'd been hoping Angel Sanders would have been able to confirm Frank Dunn was drinking in the bar the previous day. It could go a long way to proving he was involved in the shootings, by being seen at the first crime scene.

Looking at his watch, Ben knew there wasn't much more they'd be able to accomplish at this hour. Plus, they could both use some sleep. It had been a very long forty-eight hours. And tomorrow, while he had some uniform officers speak with the victims' families and neighbors to see if anything out of the ordinary had occurred in recent days, he and Tommy would begin the hunt for Frank Dunn.

THIRTY-EIGHT

BEN'S NIGHT WAS not nearly as restful as he'd hoped. Though he'd fallen asleep the minute his head hit the pillow, he found himself waking up every hour or so with a cascade of different thoughts running through his head, making it more and more difficult to fall back asleep each time.

His exhaustion finally won out and he fell into a deep sleep around five-thirty. Only to be awoken a half an hour later by his alarm clock. The incessant bleeping jarred him out of a vivid dream in which he was the starting pitcher for the Baltimore Orioles, playing in a championship game against a team of gorillas. Rubbing the sleep from his eyes, Ben couldn't begin to imagine what his dream meant. But he had to admit, he made a pretty good left-handed pitcher.

Once again, Ben found Natalie in the kitchen with breakfast waiting for him. Though her first words were slightly different this morning.

"You better solve this case soon," she said, looking over her second cup of coffee. "This is my summer vacation and I don't want to have to keep getting up early to make sure you eat a good breakfast every morning. I'm giving you forty-eight hours to solve the case."

"Well, that's twenty-four more than the mayor and chief gave me. So… I'll take it."

Ben was still thinking about how unbelievably lucky he was to have Natalie in his life when he walked into his office and found a telegram sitting on his desk. Upon seeing the name of the sender, Ben's muscles tensed involuntarily. The message was from Roger Benedict, the smart-ass reporter who'd been a thorn in his and Tommy's side during the Strangler investigation.

The note was simple and cutting, just as Benedict intended.

"Another serial killer? Looks like Parker City really isn't a sleepy little town anymore."

Ben should have let Tommy shoot the guy when he'd asked three years ago. It would have done the entire human race a favor. But Benedict wasn't his problem anymore. According to the return address, the reporter was somewhere in Philadelphia now. The City of Brotherly Love could have him, Ben thought as he tore up the telegram and threw it in the trash.

Taking his jacket off and rolling up his sleeves, Ben was just sitting down at his desk when Chief Brent walked in. Seeing the bear of a man filling the doorway, Ben immediately stood at attention.

"Good morning, sir."

"Ben. You can relax. When it's just me and you, you don't need to stand."

That was the biggest difference between Nick Brent and his predecessor. He didn't stand on ceremony. He didn't need his ego stroked. Doing the job was what mattered. Not the stars on his collar.

Running a hand through his short hair, the chief said, "I've just finished another morning meeting with the mayor. To say he's unhappy would be an understatement."

"I can imagine," Ben answered. "But we do have a lead. We're looking into a drug dealer named Frank Dunn."

Taking the file from his desk, Ben handed it to Brent. As succinctly as possible, Ben explained why Dunn had rocketed to the top of the list of suspects. Albeit he was the *only* suspect they had so far. And in his and Tommy's first attempt to connect the drug dealer to the murders, they were unable to confirm he'd been at the Ramshackle the afternoon of the first shooting.

"It's a start. It's better than nothing," Brent said, reading Dunn's rap sheet. "It's possible this guy could have graduated to murder. He's certainly no choir boy."

"Tommy and I are going to try and track him down today."

Closing the file and handing it back to his senior detective, the chief instructed, "Put out a county-wide APB. Consider this guy armed and dangerous. If he's already shot three of our men, he won't come in quietly."

"I was thinking about that too," Ben admitted. "I'll speak with Officers Kramer and Woods and see if they have any more information on him that didn't make it into the file. They may know where he likes to have lunch every Wednesday."

"We could only be so lucky. When you do find him, make sure you have backup. I don't want any cavalier detective bullshit."

"You have my word, sir," Ben promised.

"I wasn't talking about you, Winters. I meant your partner."

With a smile, the chief headed for his own office. Ben knew Brent was only half-joking about Tommy. Though he'd have to admit, Tommy was getting much better at understanding the need to follow procedure. And he only complained about it half as much as he used to.

As if on cue, Tommy walked through the door.

"Good morning, partner," he said, sounding a lot more enthusiastic than Ben would have expected.

"You should have been here a few minutes ago. The chief and I were just talking about you."

"Singing my praises, I imagine."

"Yes. That's exactly what we were doing. He specifically pointed out that he thought Chief Stanley had made a terrible mistake by making me the sergeant when clearly you should be the lead detective. In fact, the investigation of the three murders we're working on right now is on hold while he decides if he should promote you and kick me back to foot patrol."

What impressed Tommy, more than the fact Ben was able to come up with such a sarcastic response in a matter of seconds, was that he was able to do so while typing something into the computer at the same time.

"You don't have to worry," Tommy said with a smile. "I would never take your job."

"Too much paperwork?" Ben guessed. And in an instant change of subject, he asked after looking at him for the first time that morning, "Are you wearing the same suit as yesterday?"

Tommy's smile grew wider.

"This is why *you* are the detective *sergeant*. I can't

get anything by you. I went over to Mary's last night after we were finished at the bar."

"Wait," Ben thought for a moment. "You spent the night at Mary's? You're wearing the same suit as yesterday, but that's a different color shirt. Did you have a clean shirt at her place? This sounds serious. Next, you're going to tell me you have a toothbrush there too."

"For your information," Tommy began, watching his partner's eyebrows raise nearly to his hairline, "I keep a spare toothbrush in the glove box of my truck."

Ben shook his head and laughed. After a few more keystrokes on the machine Tommy despised and avoided using at all costs, Ben was finished.

"I just put out an APB on Dunn," he said. "Between the PCPD, sheriff, and state troopers, I'm hoping someone comes across him today. I think we should also talk to the guys in the task force and see if they might have an idea how we could go about finding him."

"He doesn't seem like the kind of guy who's going to be too eager to talk to the police," Tommy pointed out.

"Which is why we need to be careful. If he is the killer, I don't think he'll hesitate to take a few more shots if given the opportunity."

"Do you think Kramer and Woods will want to help us track him down?" Tommy asked flipping through the Dunn file one more time.

"I'm sure they would. But I don't know if that's the best idea. First of all, they could be targets themselves. It may be better for them to stay off the street for the time being. Plus, we think Dunn took out two of their guys. They're too close to this. I don't want to take the chance of one of them possibly…" Ben trailed off, not wanting to think a member of the PCPD would ever overstep or act out of revenge.

"See?" Tommy said, from behind his trademark smile. "*This* is exactly why you're the head detective around here. I'd just let them kill the bastard."

THIRTY-NINE

By LUNCHTIME, Frank Dunn was still nowhere to be found. Even though it had only been a few hours since Ben issued the all-points bulletin, he'd hoped they'd get lucky and someone would spot the guy. It would certainly make his job a lot easier. Unfortunately, not everything always goes according to plan, he reminded himself.

Earlier, he and Tommy spent some time with Ron Kramer and Brian Woods in the Drug Task Force's makeshift workspace in the basement of the police station. After seeing where the team had been shoehorned, without even saying it, Ben and Tommy agreed never to complain about their cramped office again.

Chief Brent had ordered both Kramer and Woods to stay off the street for the next few days. He knew he wouldn't be able to keep them from reporting for duty, but if they were targets, he wanted to make it as difficult as possible for whoever was hunting his officers to find them. Reluctantly, Kramer and Woods agreed but offered to assist with the investigation in any way they could from the relative safety of the PCPD.

It was Ron Kramer who thought he might have the address of a woman Frank Dunn was reportedly involved with at the moment. How accurate the information was, he could not attest to, but it gave the detectives a place to start. While they went to track down the girl-friend, the two remaining members of the Drug Task Force said they'd work some of their own contacts and see if they could find Dunn. With their help, the rest of the department, and two other police agencies look-ing for the guy, it couldn't be too much longer before someone spotted him.

That was Ben's hope as he eased to a stop in front of an old four-story row house along one of the city's shabbier residential streets. Judging by the architecture, at one time these few blocks must have been a very desirable neighborhood. Though the houses were not nearly as magnificent and sprawling as the mansions along Grandview Avenue across from the park, they were stately in their own way. Or had been. Now, most had been converted into apartments whose landlords didn't feel the need to keep up with the maintenance of the buildings' exteriors. Chipped paint, shutters hang-ing by a single hinge, and cracked windows were the only features that made the row houses look as though they belonged together.

Double-checking the address he'd written in his note-book, Tommy confirmed they had the right house—413 Copperfield Avenue. Olive Bowan, Dunn's supposed girlfriend, lived in apartment #2. Taking a last drag of his cigarette, Tommy looked up to see the curtains drawn in all the windows on the second floor.

"It's a nice day, isn't it?" Tommy asked Ben, who was checking the apartment building's mailboxes to confirm Bowan's residence.

Ben had to admit, now that the scorching heat from the past several days was gone, the weather was much more pleasant. With a bright blue sky overhead, a light breeze, and colorful flowers springing from the ground in several places along the street, Ben thought how nice this street must have been when all of the houses were first constructed.

"Yeah," Ben answered, looking back at his partner who was still focused on the second-floor windows. "Why? What are you thinking?"

"It's nothing. Just, the curtains are closed. Middle of the day. Nice and sunny. Why are the curtains closed?"

"There could be a hundred reasons," Ben said, looking up. "She could work nights and sleep during the day. Kramer didn't know what Olive Bowan does for a living."

"I would have gone with her being a vampire," Tommy said, tossing the butt of his cigarette on the sidewalk and stamping it out.

"That could be another reason," Ben agreed.

"Somebody could also be hiding up there in the apartment and doesn't want anyone to see in."

"Yet another possibility."

"I guess we won't know the answer until we go find out." Tommy straightened his tie and started for the door.

"And just to be on the safe side," Ben said, putting a hand on his partner's arm, "I'm going to request backup. Just in case. If Dunn isn't in there, no harm, no foul. If he is, we're probably going to need some help."

"You take all the fun out of things," Tommy said, kicking a pebble down the sidewalk like a little boy whose mother just told him he needed to behave.

"Just give me one minute," Ben said walking back to

the car to radio Dispatch. "Then when we're finished here, I'll buy you an ice cream cone."

Tommy's eyes twinkled just like a child's. "Vanilla and chocolate swirl?"

FORTY

DISPATCH INFORMED BEN that a patrol car was just a couple of blocks away and would be there in a few minutes ready to assist if needed. Before Ben was able to sign off, he saw Tommy head for the apartment building's front door. Tossing the radio mic on the driver's seat, he went after his partner who was already stepping inside.

"Tommy! Wait for me."

"Well, hurry up," he said, holding the door open.

"Don't you think we should wait for the backup to get here?"

"Did you tell Dispatch where we were?"

"Yes."

"Will Dispatch tell the patrolman where we are?"

"Yes."

"Doesn't it make more sense for the backup to remain out front waiting in case Dunn gets by us and tries to do a runner?"

"Do we know if there's also a back way out of the building?" Ben asked with a raised eyebrow.

The wheels in Tommy's head screeched to an abrupt halt. "You win this round, Detective Winters."

Their playful banter took up just enough time. As Ben was feeling quite proud of his victory, the two watched as a PCPD squad car parked pulled up and parked across the street. From behind the wheel, Officer Buck LuCoco slowly emerged.

"Great," Tommy said under his breath. "If Dunn is up there, we're all dead."

Ben forced himself not to laugh. Though, he agreed with Tommy. LuCoco was not the best backup an officer could have. He'd end up winded just by pulling his gun out of its holster.

"Officer LuCoco," Ben said, meeting him on the sidewalk in front of the building. "Good timing. Tommy and I are heading up to speak with Olive Bowan on the second floor. Would you take a look out back and see if there's another way out of the building? If there is, radio in for another car so we can have both the front and back entrances covered."

Ben thought he heard LuCoco mumble a reply from behind the handkerchief he was using to wipe the sweat from his face. Whatever he said must have been affirmative, since he waddled off down the block to find the alleyway behind the set of row houses.

For a brief moment, Ben thought about radioing for additional backup himself. But the odds of Dunn actually being upstairs were pretty slim, he figured. And if there was a back entrance, he was confident LuCoco would call for another car…as long as he made it back before they'd been upstairs, questioned Bowan, and left. Ben couldn't understand how a man that out of shape could still be on active patrol duty.

Meeting Tommy back in the tiny vestibule just inside the front door, Ben could do nothing more than shake his head.

"I swear," Tommy began, "if I don't get my ice cream

because LuCoco has a heart attack while walking around to the back door of this place, I'm going to be pissed."

This time, Ben couldn't help but laugh.

"Alright, let's go," Tommy said, opening the inner door and stepping into a space about the same size as the vestibule.

Throughout some areas of the city, row houses like this, which were once occupied by a single family— sometimes for generations—had been split up to make separate apartment units. The way walls had been built to divide up the already existing floor plan were some- times very haphazard. Bowan's appeared to be one such building.

Immediately to the detectives' left was the door to the first-floor apartment. Directly in front of them were the stairs to the second floor. At some point in the past, this must have served as the home's entry hall, but now, Ben and Tommy could barely fit into the cramped foyer.

A faint smell of smoke drifted through the air as Ben and Tommy ascended the creaking stairs, peeling paint on the walls to either side of them. The inside of the building received just as much attention as the outside. It was always a shame to see a once dignified home fall into such a state.

Reaching the second floor, following their harrow- ing climb up a staircase that felt as though it could give way at any moment, Ben and Tommy found Olive's apartment. The brass number two affixed to the door dangled upside down from a single screw. Trying to return the number to its proper place, Tommy watched as it refused to stay and spun upside down once again the minute he let go.

One attempt was all he was willing to give it. Ignoring it any further, Tommy pounded on the door with the heel of his fist. The detectives listened for any sound coming from inside.

After a moment, Ben took his turn. This time, also announcing themselves. "Olive Bowan, this is the Parker City Police. Please open up."

This time, they could hear some shuffling coming from behind the door. A second later, the door was opened just enough to reveal a petite woman looking out from behind the security chain.

"Olive Bowan?" Ben asked, holding up his badge. "I'm Detective Sergeant Winters. This is my partner, Detective Mason. We'd like to have a word with you if we could."

Her eyes narrowed as she examined his badge through the opening. Ben was hoping she didn't just slam the door on them, making this more difficult than it needed to be.

"What do you want?" she asked, obviously satisfied that he was who he said.

"We'd like to ask you a couple of questions. It might be better if we did this in your apartment. May we come in?"

Olive stared at him for a long moment. Then closed the door and unhooked the chain.

FORTY-ONE

To PUT IT PLAINLY, the apartment was a complete disaster. Articles of clothing were thrown everywhere. A stack of pizza boxes lay tossed in one corner. Black plastic bags filled with who knew what dotted the floor of the combined living room and kitchen area. Glancing around the room, Ben felt his OCD starting to kick in and cause his heart to beat a little faster. He couldn't imagine how anyone could live in such a way.

Olive tossed a pile of clothes on the floor and slumped down onto a threadbare sofa that took up much of the open space. Picking up a pack of cigarettes from the cardboard box being used as a coffee table, she lit up and blew a ring of smoke toward the ceiling. Never once asking Ben or Tommy to have a seat. Not that there was anywhere they could.

Ben gave Olive Bowan a quick once over. She was definitely on the smaller side; maybe five-one at most. Long dark hair, to match her dark eyes, which both stood in stark contrast to her extremely pale complexion. The oversized T-shirt she wore revealed the tattoos that ran along both of her arms.

"Miss Bowan," Ben began, "is there anyone else in the apartment?"

"No."

Ben kept his eyes on her as Tommy glanced down the

small hallway toward what they could both only assume
was a bedroom and bathroom. Both doors were closed,
which didn't sit well with either detective. Tommy casually crossed his arms, allowing his hand to rest within
inches of his holster in case he would need to make a
quick draw.

"Alright," Ben continued. "We're here because we're
looking for Frank Dunn. We believe you two are...
friends. When was the last time you saw him?"

"Friends?" Olive snorted. "Really? Okay, fine. Frank
and I are *friends*. Whenever he's horny, he comes over.
When he's not horny anymore, he leaves. Other than
that, I don't see him all that much. What's he done now?"

Ignoring her question, Tommy asked one of his own.
"And when was the last time Frank was horny?"

Tommy couldn't see it, but he knew Ben must have
rolled his eyes.

Crossing her arms, Olive was going from indifferent
to defensive. They needed to be careful.

"I don't know," she finally said. "I guess sometime
last week. I don't write it down or anything."

"He's not here now?" Ben asked.

"What did I just say?" she snapped, sitting forward.

"And you haven't seen him in the last couple of days?"

"So...you're just going to ask questions and not actually listen to what I say? Is that how this is gonna go?
I said I haven't seen him since last week. That means
not in the last few days."

Olive's voice was rising, but Ben could see she was
telling the truth.

"I don't understand why you cops can't just leave
Frank alone."

"We need to speak with him," Tommy offered in explanation. "He might be able to help us with an investigation."

"Right. You want Frank's help? How dumb do you think I am. But if you actually think Frank would help *you*, then you're the dumb one."

Tommy thought it might have been worth a shot. He was wrong. It wasn't the first time and it wouldn't be the last.

Ben was just about to ask Olive if she had any ideas as to where Dunn could be when the bedroom door opened. In a split second, Tommy's gun was trained on the naked man stepping into the living room.

Certainly not fazed by the gun pointed at him, it wasn't clear if he was high or drunk. It could have been a little of both.

"Come on, baby," he slurred. "Come back t' bed. I tol' you not to answer the door."

"Rodney! Get back in there or cover yourself up," Olive ordered.

Before either Ben or Tommy could say anything, the door to the apartment swung open. Everyone turned to see Frank Dunn standing in the doorway. He looked much bigger than Ben had expected. But he matched his mug shot. Maybe even more intimidating looking in person.

From that moment, everything happened all at once. Dunn didn't notice the two men in suits, one of whom was holding a gun. The drug dealer was fixated on the naked man standing in—what he thought—was his girlfriend's apartment. As he charged at Rodney, Tommy spun in time to catch a shoulder check from the charging bull as he yelled, "Rodney, you fuckin' prick. I'm gonna kill you!"

Absorbing the hit as best he could, Tommy was knocked back a few steps, but managed to stay on his feet. Dunn however, lost his balance and stumbled forward, grabbing Rodney's naked waist. Both men hit the ground hard. Dunn was able to land a couple of blows before Tommy and Ben grabbed him from behind and pulled him off the bellowing Rodney.

Ben wasn't sure if Dunn fully understood what was happening. He was completely enraged by finding another man in Olive's apartment. As Ben and Tommy tried to subdue him, Dunn fought to get back to Rodney so he could finish the beating he began.

"Knock it off!" Tommy yelled. "You're under arrest."

Those words seemed to flip a switch in Dunn's head. No longer was he focused on the cowering naked man in the hallway, he became aware of his full surroundings. The trance-like state now broken, the drug dealer looked up at Ben then at Tommy, a fire burning in his eyes.

"The hell I am, you pigs!" Dunn growled as he jerked his arm free from Ben's grasp and landed a blow to Tommy's stomach.

An explosion of pain surged through his gut, all the air rushed out of Tommy's lungs as he fell backward against the wall. Releasing his own hold of Dunn allowed the giant to get to his feet and turn on Ben. Grabbing the detective by his shoulders, he was able to lift Ben off the ground a good two inches as he tossed him like a rag doll into Tommy who was just managing to regain his balance.

Scrambling to their feet, they followed Dunn out the door and onto the stairs. But instead of heading down to the first floor, he was racing up the steps.

"Where the hell's he going?" asked Tommy taking the stairs two at a time.

"Probably the same way he got in. The roof," Ben shouted, only a step behind his partner. "I never thought about there being a way in from the roof!"

"I guess you're not as smart as I thought you were."

"Very funny," Ben huffed, rounding the top of the stairs on the third floor.

Thirty seconds later, guns drawn, both detectives burst through the door leading out onto the roof. Dunn was already stepping over the low wall onto the roof-top of the house next door. For a big guy, he was moving pretty quickly.

Tommy was beginning to gain on him, when Dunn, unexpectedly, spun around and charged directly at him. Ben watched as the two men collided like two trains moving at full speed. Tommy was quick and athletic, but he was no match for the force of Dunn's size. The roof seemed to shake as the two hit the hot surface, sliding backward.

Dunn, now on top of Tommy, was an easy target for Ben.

Coming to a halt and leveling his gun, Ben shouted, "Get off him! You're under arrest!"

His eyes darting around, he realized Tommy was no longer holding his own weapon. It must have been knocked out of his hand when they hit the ground. Trying to search the roof while still keeping his eyes on Dunn, Ben saw his partner's gun only a couple steps from where the men had fallen. Unfortunately, Dunn saw it too.

Rolling off Tommy, he lurched for the gun. Tommy instinctively grabbed for Dunn's shirt to try and prevent him from reaching the weapon. For the second time, Dunn's size defeated Tommy.

In slow motion, Ben watched as Dunn grabbed Tommy's gun and twisted back to face him. The barrel of the gun glinting in the sunlight, already pointed in his direction, Ben did what he was trained to. He defended himself and his partner.

But Dunn wasn't going down without a fight. Both guns fired at the same moment. The sound of two shots exploded through the air, ringing out across the rooftops.

FORTY-TWO

1959...

CHRISTMAS AT THE ParkMar Hotel was a sight to behold. If there was one thing Billy Roscoe loved more than making money, it was Christmas. Which is why, like when he built the popular Downtown hotel, he spared no expense in decorating it for the holiday season.

Exactly one week after Thanksgiving, an enormous silver Christmas tree was put up in the lobby, surrounded by giant decorative presents and twinkling stars dangling from the ceiling above. Garland was wrapped around anything that didn't move and wreaths were attached to the outside of each guest window. From the roof of the hotel, Billy had a giant light-up Santa Claus in his sleigh hung so everyone walking by could see it. This went nicely with the candy cane ribbons wrapped around all the lamp posts by the city and the holiday wreaths strung up at each intersection.

Standing on the sidewalk, watching as the last piece of garland was hung over the main entrance to the hotel, Billy pulled the fur-lined collar of his overcoat tightly around his neck to ward off the chill. Even though he had far more important matters to attend to, he always oversaw the decorating personally. Christmas had never been a special occasion when he was a child, so now that he had the means, he liked to make a big deal of it. It was also the time of year he made hefty donations to a number of charitable organizations. Of course, there was no altruistic motive behind the donations. It was strictly for the publicity he would garner.

Blowing warm air into his glove-covered hands, Billy nodded a friendly greeting to two attractive women hurrying by carrying shopping bags full of gifts.

"It's beginning to look a lot like Christmas," Roscoe began singing under his breath as he turned to see Freddy Quinn and Marty Schulman turning the corner and walking his way.

Both men's breath circled their heads in puffs of white clouds as they spoke to one another. Billy was hoping the cold temperatures at the beginning of December meant a white Christmas was on the way. He could only hope.

"The decorations look great, boss," Freddy said, eyeing the wreaths now dotting the front of the building. "Is the Santa Claus going back up on the roof this year?"

"Tomorrow," Billy answered with a smile. "It's cold. Let's go inside and have a drink."

Not one to turn down a stiff drink, Freddy was right on Billy's heels as the three men walked into the warmth of the hotel's lobby. A few minutes later, they were comfortably ensconced in Billy's office, each with a tumbler of ridiculously expensive Scotch in his hand.

"Boys, I tell you, 1960 is going to be a fantastic year," Billy said from behind his desk. "The casino business in this town is booming. You just need to look at the deposits from upstairs to see that. And I'm thinking it may be the right time to expand the shipping business.

I've already talked to a couple of guys about selling the warehouse and building a bigger one on the other side of town."

"The warehouse over on Antietam?" Freddy asked, leaning forward.

"Well, considering that's the only one I have here in Parker, yes," Billy answered with a note of suspicion in his tone.

"Why sell it? You've got a great piece of land over there. You shouldn't give that up. Why not just buy another one nearby?"

"When did you become so interested in real estate?" Billy narrowed his eyes as he drained what was left in his glass. "Besides," he continued, "having one big brand new warehouse is better than two old ones. As head of my security, I would think *you'd* prefer to have all our cargo together in one place so you can concentrate our resources. Two locations could leave us and our shipments exposed."

Marty, always the father figure acting to defuse tensions, asked, "Who exactly have you talked to about selling? I'd think you'd want me in on that conversation."

"What is it with you two and the warehouse? Jesus! It's just an old building where we park the goods until they're ready to be moved on for sale. What inexplicable sentimental attachment do you guys have to the place?"

The lawyer let out a nervous laugh. "Billy, it's just my job to make sure your interest is looked after. And Freddy's right. That could be a very valuable piece of land one day."

"Fine. *If* I decide to sell the damn place, I'll make sure you're both the first to know. Speaking of which,

Freddy, I need to make a stop at the warehouse before going home tonight. Marty, do you want to come along? Since you're so enamored by the warehouse and all."

Marty shook his head and quietly finished his drink.

Billy didn't like being questioned by anyone. Let alone his top two guys over a stupid piece of land. What did it matter if he sold the warehouse and why did they care so much? Marty, sure, he dealt with the business and money side of things. Of course, he'd be brought in if a sale really was going to happen. But what was Freddy so concerned about?

For the first time, he wondered if Freddy was running his own thing on the side and using *his* warehouse as a front. Billy had never questioned his body man's loyalty or, to be perfectly honest, thought he would be smart enough to come up with a secret way to be making money. But if Marty was involved, for all he knew, they could be skimming off the take from the warehouse. If he wasn't able to trust them, there was no one he could put his faith in.

For months now, there had been moments when he'd noticed Marty and Freddy acting strangely. Like they were hiding something. Speaking to one another in hushed tones then quickly changing the subject.

Looking at the two now, Billy hoped he was just being paranoid. Freddy was an idiot and there was never a good explanation for what he was thinking. And Marty was right, he always had Billy's best interest in mind. But if Billy found out either of them was cheating him or working their own angle on his business, he wouldn't hesitate to kill them.

FORTY-THREE

"If BILLY SELLS the warehouse, it doesn't actually mean whoever buys it will find anything," Marty quietly pointed out as he and Freddy stepped into the lobby. "If they just keep using it as a warehouse, everything will be fine."

"Yeah, but if they do decide to do something else with the property and tear it down, they could find…" Freddy's voice trailed off as a hotel guest passed the pair heading for the elevator.

"I guess you should have thought about that before you killed," the frustrated attorney caught himself and, looking around to make sure no one heard him, lowered his voice. "Before you killed a cop."

"Hey! I didn't do nothin' to that cop. Remember that," Freddy snapped, his temper flaring. "I was trying to clean up your guy's mess. All you suits are the same. I was just protecting Billy."

"By burying the body of a dead cop under the floor of his building!"

Even using hushed tones, the two men were beginning to attract attention. Though no one could hear what they were saying, all one needed to do was look at them and their body language to know they were in the midst of a very heated discussion. Thinking it better to take the conversation outside, Marty grabbed Freddy's enormous bicep and pulled him in the direction of the door. Once outside and on the sidewalk, the street noise helped to drown them out. That, and the fact it was too cold out for anyone to stop long enough to pay them any attention. But the cold didn't bother Freddy Quinn or Marty Schulman. Both men's blood was boiling.

For months—since the incident—the two men had been skirting around the issue of what had happened at the warehouse that night. If they needed to discuss it in any way, they did it as quickly as possible and without saying anything that might arouse the suspicion of anyone around them. Though both men knew Billy had picked up on something. But he never asked.

Since it had been reported that the PCPD was ending its investigation into the disappearance of its officer, tensions between the two had eased slightly. The matter seemed to be closed and everyone came out of it unscathed. Except for Bert Ramsburg, of course. But everyone in Billy's orbit managed to survive. Now, with their boss thinking about unloading the property, there was no telling what a new owner might do with the building. If he tore the place down, they were bound to find the missing cop's remains, and then all hell would break loose.

After a few tense moments of silence, Freddy finally said, "Look. All you need to do is make it very clear to Billy that there is no financial benefit to selling the warehouse right now. If he sees he can make more money holding on to it and selling it later, then it buys us time before we need to worry about anyone finding anything."

"Or, you could always just get rid of the body," Marty

offered, allowing the condescending lawyer in him to come out.

If looks could kill, Freddy's would have obliterated him.

"Listen, you two-bit shyster," Freddy said, stepping as close to the attorney as possible without their noses actually touching. "We're gonna leave everything the way it is right now. Because if we go diggin' *things* up, that's a sure way to attract attention. As far as the world is concerned, Parker City Police Officer Bert Ramsburg ran away."

With that, Freddy turned and walked down the block leaving Marty standing in front of the hotel puffing clouds of hot air into the cold winter sky. The attorney simply could not understand how anyone could be as inept as Freddy Quinn. Sure, he had brawn, but no brains. Ramsburg's body *would* be discovered at some point. Leaving the remains buried was a bad idea. But Freddy was right in one regard. If everything just stayed as it was, everything was fine. Billy had been exonerated, even though he hadn't *actually* done anything... this time. Hank McMaster was still their guy on the inside of the PCPD. Freddy was still the muscle taking care of "security." And, thankfully, no one even knew Billy's silent partner existed.

For a split second, Marty thought that maybe it would all work out just fine. Then he realized the universal odds must be stacked against them. So all he could hope for was to have a massive heart attack and die before someone discovered the body so he wouldn't have to deal with it.

FORTY-FOUR

CHRISTMAS CAME AND went without any additional discussion of selling the warehouse on Antietam Avenue, which allowed both Marty and Freddy to relax and enjoy the festive season. It was difficult not to when their boss was in such a jovial mood. It always amazed Marty that a man as tough as Billy Roscoe, who could also be extremely dangerous if crossed, turned into such a happy, spirited fellow around Christmastime.

No holiday season would be complete without Billy's New Year's Eve gala. Since opening the hotel, the annual party was *the* event of the entire year in Parker City. Even members of some of the city's most uptight, blue-blooded families attended. When the food and drink were freely flowing—and it looked good for their image to make an appearance—then the stuck-up elites of Parker had no difficulty deigning to grace Billy's establishment with their presence.

As Billy worked his way around the ParkMar's elegantly decorated ballroom, he was happy to see that the trouble the disappearance of Officer Ramsburg had caused throughout the last half of the year had seemingly vanished. Both the mayor and chief of police were once again regular diners at the Derby Room and currently had full glasses of champagne in their hands as they smoked two of the most expensive cigars ever rolled. Gifts from their host, of course.

Billy couldn't help but wonder how long it had taken Chief Edgar Stanley to squeeze himself into the tuxedo he was wearing. Stanley was obviously not a man used to wearing fancy clothes. In fact, other than at the New Year's Eve party, Billy couldn't remember ever seeing him out of his uniform. An arrogant, foul-mouthed bully of a man, Roscoe knew he had to play nice because he never wanted to be on the chief's bad side. He could make it very difficult to conduct business in Parker. So, for tonight, the hotel staff would liquor him up, keep him well fed, and send him on his way sometime after midnight. As long as Stanley left happy, that's all that mattered.

The same applied to the mayor. Though Billy did enjoy talking with him. At least he understood the type of person he was—a politician with his own needs. Making his friendship fair weather at best.

Clustered in the corner, not far from the mayor, were the patriarchs of Parker City's five "ruling" families— state Senator Wilson Lee Baker; Henry Worthington, head of the Worthington Trust Company; Bernard Moss, Jr., owner and publisher of the *Blue Ridge Herald*; William G. Parker, president of the Appalachian Coal Corporation; and George Tildon, managing director of Tildon Industries, the region's largest manufacturing conglomerate. These were the men that ran Parker. Or so *they* thought, Billy sneered. Though he had to admit, their combined power and influence was substantial, he'd been able to do well for himself without their help. Or approval for that matter. They hated everything about him. And yet, they were still in *his* hotel on New Year's Eve, drinking *his* champagne, and eating *his* food. Billy knew it must be killing each one of the old men to see an "outsider" doing so well in their town.

"You sure know how to throw a party, boss," Freddy said walking up behind Billy, slapping him on the back.

"In less than an hour, it's going to be 1960! A new year, a new decade. I can feel it. It's going to be a good year," Billy said, his thousand-watt smile shining brighter than the crystal chandelier over his head.

"If you say so." Freddy shrugged, watching Billy cross to a group of ladies standing near the bar.

Turning, he stopped himself just in time to avoid running straight into the Kid. Dressed in an expensive tuxedo—one that probably cost more money than Freddy made in a year—he thought the Kid looked older in some way. More confident, somehow.

"Freddy!" he said, smiling. "I was hoping I'd run into you tonight."

"Well, you almost did. I guess tonight's the one night of the year when it's alright for you to been seen talking to the likes of me."

"Freddy... I just wanted to apologize. For the way I used to behave. And, thank you. Thank you for your help after what happened this summer. I... I just... I realized I needed to straighten up. My father isn't too far from retiring and I'm going to need to take over one day. I need to grow up. After...well, you know... I realized how stupid I'd been behaving."

Freddy found himself at a loss for words. He never would have expected this. Even though he hated to admit it, he appreciated what the Kid was saying.

Maybe he had misjudged him. He always knew he was smart. But now, he seemed to be self-assured and comfortable with himself. In that moment, he realized the Kid now reminded him of Billy.

"If it wasn't for you," he continued, "I don't know what would have happened. I owe you. I owe you a lot. If there is ever anything you need, if you ever need my help in some way, I want you to know, I repay my debts."

"But we should probably still keep our *friendship* quiet," Freddy said with a wry smile.

Returning the smile, the Kid answered, "It would probably be for the best."

FORTY-FIVE

1984...

THE AMBULANCE ARRIVED followed by two additional police cruisers. Their approach could be heard from several
blocks away as the familiar sound of sirens signaled their
approach. It took both paramedics along with the newly
arrived patrolmen to haul Frank Dunn down from the
roof. Ben followed behind, helping his bruised and bat-
tered partner down the stairs. Keeping an eye on things
on the street were Buck LuCoco and Officer Thompson, who had originally been securing the front and rear
entrances of the building before the shooting started.

Hearing the gunshots, Thompson had instinctively
raced toward the roof. There, he found Ben helping
Tommy to his feet and an unconscious Dunn with a
bloody hole in his shoulder. In complete control, Ben
ordered Thompson to call for additional officers and an
ambulance. As the uniform headed back down to do as
instructed, the detectives turned their attention to the
drug dealer.

The gunshot was superficial, but it struck with enough
force to knock the already unstable giant to the ground.
Hitting his head as he landed, it was lights out. He didn't
begin to come to until he was being loaded into the back
of the ambulance.

"Sure, now he wakes up," said one of the officers who helped carry him down the narrow staircase.

Handcuffs in place, keeping him secured to the gurney, the brute looked around through bleary eyes.

"Wha' the fuck happened? Where am I?" he mumbled, still trying to shake the cobwebs from his head.

"Franklin Dunn," Tommy said leaning against the back of the ambulance to steady himself, "you are under arrest for assaulting an officer, resisting arrest, and some other things we will charge you with later. You are also wanted for questioning in connection with the murders of PCPD Officers Joseph Noffsinger and Peter Vernon, and Lieutenant Hank McMaster."

Tommy continued to read Dunn his rights as the paramedics tended to his wound. Whether Dunn was paying any attention or not, no one could be certain. He just lay on the gurney staring at the ceiling of the ambulance. Ben made a mental note to read him his rights again when they got to the hospital just to be on the safe side. If he was suffering from a concussion, a lawyer could argue he didn't understand what was going on so the police shouldn't have been allowed to speak to him. Ben wasn't letting this guy get off on a technicality. Not when he could be the one responsible for the cold-blooded murder of three police officers.

Watching the ambulance pull away, Ben and Tommy headed for their car.

"When we get to the hospital," Ben said climbing in behind the wheel, "you should get checked out too."

"I'm fine," Tommy said, pulling out his cigarettes. "I'm just going to be a little sore in the morning. That's all."

The debate over whether Tommy should allow a doctor to give him a quick once-over continued the entire way to Tasker Memorial Hospital where Ben pulled in just behind the ambulance. The only time the two detectives weren't bickering about the need—or not—for Tommy to get checked out was when Ben radioed Dispatch to let the chief know Frank Dunn was in custody.

As the doctors in the ER worked to patch Dunn's shoulder, Ben and Tommy waited patiently a few feet away. Even though a nurse had offered them a room in which to wait, promising to let them know as soon as the doctors were finished, the detectives politely declined. They didn't want to take their eyes off Dunn. Even sedated, this guy could be dangerous.

That very same nurse couldn't help but notice Tommy appeared to be in some pain, so she offered to take a look at his bruises to make sure no serious damage had been done.

"I think that would be a very good idea," Tommy said as a smile that would put the Cheshire Cat's to shame appeared on his face. All Ben could do was shake his head in disbelief.

"I'll keep an eye on Dunn. Make sure you check his cognitive functions too. He doesn't always think straight," Ben suggested as he watched his partner and the nurse disappear into a side room off the ER.

Once Dunn was bandaged up and Tommy was given a clean bill of health and a couple of aspirin—and the nurse's phone number—Ben asked the attending physician if it would be alright to speak with the man now cuffed to a hospital bed. The doctor said he might be woozy from the sedatives he'd been given, but there was no reason they couldn't have a few words. And that's all Ben really needed. Just a few words.

Standing over the dealer's bed, Ben looked down at the man. Dunn was awake but staring at the wall.

"Frank? Frank, do you know why you're here?"

"Yeah. You shot me."

"Good. You're lucid enough for me," Ben said, then read him his rights a second time. Dunn grunted when asked if he understood everything he'd been told.

"I will take that as a yes. And it's not like the Miranda Warning has changed since you were last arrested. Or the time before that. You can probably recite it as well as anyone."

The remark elicited another grunt from Dunn.

"Frank, I need to ask you a few questions. Where were you two evenings ago?"

No response.

Ben raised an eyebrow.

"Okay. How about yesterday afternoon?"

Again, no response. However, this time, Dunn turned and glared at Ben. Refusing to break eye contact, Ben set his jaw and waited.

Finally, the dealer said, "You wanna stop dickin' around and just ask me what you wanna ask me? This is all such bullshit."

From the corner of the room where Tommy had been leaning against the wall, he asked, "Did you kill Joe Noffsinger, Hank McMaster, and Peter Vernon out of revenge?"

Ben noticed the slightest of reactions. If he'd blinked, he would have missed it. For a fraction of a second,

Dunn's eye darted toward Tommy as if he was surprised by the question.

After what seemed like an eternity, no doubt because Dunn was trying to figure out just how much trouble he was in, he asked, "What are you talkin' about? I dunno any of those people."

"Now that's not true," Ben said shaking his head. "Officers Noffsinger and Vernon were part of the PCPD's new Drug Task Force. They arrested you not too long ago. In fact, if I recall correctly from the report, Officer Noffsinger is the one who cuffed you. Joe was always very thorough with his details."

"And Lieutenant McMaster was the task force's supervising officer," Tommy added. "He was one of the people you threatened to get even with."

"I didn't kill no cops."

"Frank, I've seen your rap sheet," Ben said. "You're something of a big deal in Parker's drug world. But Noffsinger and his boys came along and started making things difficult for you. They arrest you but then you get off. Not before you threaten them though. Those are just the facts."

Ben pulled the plastic guest chair up next to the bed and sat down so he could be on the same level as Dunn.

"Are you telling us," he continued, "that it's a huge coincidence that three police officers you saw hurting your illegal business just so happened to end up being shot within two days of each other? And you had nothing to do with it? That someone other than you had a problem with all three of the same people?"

"I didn't shoot no cops. I'm not stupid."

Tommy couldn't help but laugh.

"Oh, no. You are, Frank. Believe me," he said walking toward the bed. "You killed three police officers and thought we wouldn't hunt you down. Then, you go and show up at your girl's apartment? Obviously, you're pretty stupid if you didn't think that was one of the first places we'd come looking for you."

Frank's anger boiled over as he tried to sit up and lunge at Tommy. The handcuffs locked around the bed rails kept him from moving more than a few inches.

"I think you hit a nerve, Tommy," Ben said to his partner. "But, to be fair, maybe Frank here isn't that dumb. He did have the idea to call Joe and get him to come down and meet him behind the Ramshackle."

"That's true," Tommy agreed. "But it also shows premeditation."

"I didn't call no one. I didn't meet anyone behind the Ramshackle. I ain't been to that place in weeks."

All of a sudden Dunn turned to face Ben. He'd thought of something. Ben could see it as if he was watching a cartoon where a light bulb literally went on over someone's head.

"When did this happen? You asked me where I was two nights ago. Right?" Dunn smiled, revealing a row of yellowing teeth. "There's no ways I coulda killed no one two nights ago. I was in the drunk tank over in Harrison County until yesterday morning."

Ben's heart stopped.

They'd have to call the Harrison County Sheriff's Department to check on Dunn's unexpected alibi. Even if he'd only been locked up when McMaster was shot, they knew the same gun had been used in all three murders. Dunn might not be the guy. And if Dunn wasn't the guy, they were back to square one.

FORTY-SIX

BEN REPLACED THE telephone receiver and stared blankly up at the ceiling. With one phone call, everything had just fallen apart. Their perfect suspect, according to the sheriff of Harrison County himself, had been picked up for drunken, disorderly behavior shortly after nine o'clock and spent the rest of the evening in the county lockup sleeping it off. Before he was brought in, he'd been drinking at a bar since around five o'clock.

There was no way Frank Dunn could have been in two places at once. He didn't kill Joe Noffsinger or Hank McMaster. Which meant the odds were incredibly slim he'd been the one behind the Harlequin who shot Peter Vernon.

The only suspect they had was completely in the clear.

Tommy didn't have to ask what was said on the phone, he could read it all over Ben's face.

"I don't suppose you want to break it to the chief?" Ben asked.

"Break what to the chief?" the unmistakable voice of Nick Brent asked from the doorway.

For the second time in a matter of an hour, Ben felt as if his heart had stopped. Standing up, Ben turned to the chief and explained everything that had happened that afternoon. Brent remained stoic, like always. He listened to how Dunn was apprehended, what was said at the hospital, and then what Ben just learned by speaking with Sheriff Mills. As Ben finished his recap of the day's events, the chief ran a finger over his bright red mustache. Both detectives appreciated the fact Brent was not a reactionary like his predecessor. If it had been Stanley standing in the office, Ben wouldn't have even been able to finish what he was saying before the former chief would have gone off on a tirade. Brent was taking it all in and thinking through their next steps.

The assumption was that the three officers had been gunned down because they were part of the department's war on drugs. When two of the men killed were on the PCPD's Drug Task Force, it was difficult not to jump to that conclusion. But what if the task force had nothing to do with it? What if they had been killed just because they wore a badge and their assignment in the department was coincidental? That meant every officer currently on the street could be in danger.

These were the thoughts the three men were discussing as they tried to figure out a plan to move forward.

"What still bothers me," Ben said, staring at his crime board and all of its notes, "is that the killer called and specifically asked Joe to meet him. He singled Joe out. If this guy was going to kill cops at random, why not just find one on patrol and do it. Why call a specific person?"

Tommy was following his partner's train of thought.

"Do you think this was all about Joe and the other two were just to throw us off the trail?"

"It worked," Ben pointed out. "For the last twenty-four hours, we've been on a wild goose chance."

"If you think about it though," Chief Brent started,

"he still tipped his hand by *only* setting Noffsinger up. He couldn't have known Hank was going to stop and buy milk or that Vernon would be on patrol and end up in front of the Harlequin."

"Those shootings do seem more opportunistic in nature," Ben agreed. "But neither location is a regular hangout for the police."

"Alright, so Frank Dunn was a dead end," Tommy said. "Since Joe's shooting was where this all began, we start with him. We need to see if someone was out to get Joe."

"Start digging into it tomorrow," Brent ordered. "You two have been running around for the last three days straight. Try to get a good night's sleep and start fresh in the morning. If anything happens tonight, believe me, you'll be the first two phone calls I make."

Tommy left shortly after Brent headed back to his office. He said he'd be in early the next day so they could hit the ground running. Ben, alone in the small Detective Squad's office, looked over the notes he'd written on the chalkboard one last time, hoping something might suddenly jump out at him. When no epiphanies came, he picked up the crime scene reports from the three shootings and stuffed them in his briefcase before turning off the lights. Maybe a clear head and a fresh start would be just the thing they needed. At least, that's what Ben was hoping as he closed the door and headed home to spend a couple of hours with Natalie.

FORTY-SEVEN

WHEN NATALIE HEARD the keys jingling in the lock and saw it was only a little after nine o'clock, she thought Ben must have made an arrest. Otherwise, she wouldn't have expected to see him home before she went to sleep. But when she saw his face as he dropped onto the couch next to her, she realized that wasn't the case.

With Nat curled up next to him, Ben explained how they'd been on the wrong path for the last twenty-four hours, leaving them back at the beginning. Frank Dunn had been the perfect suspect. Unfortunately, he had an air-tight alibi for two of the murders. For her part, Natalie listened quietly. She knew Ben just needed to talk through everything and get it all out of his system. Afterward, when he'd had some time to decompress, if she had any thoughts or questions, he was always more than willing to hear her out.

"So far, there hasn't been another shooting," Natalie pointed out. "It's been a whole day. Doesn't that help bolster your theory this all has something to do with those three particular officers? Otherwise, he could have just taken another cop out at any time today. It's not like he's been afraid to do it in broad daylight."

"That's true. Or," Ben thought for a moment, "he didn't want to push his luck three days in a row."

"My woman's intuition tells me this isn't just some random perp out there shooting police officers."

"A random *perp*?" Ben repeated her. "When did you start talking like that?"

"Isn't that what you call them? It's what they call them on TV."

"Oh, we call them that. And a lot more, depending on the situation and how frustrated we are," Ben said with a smile. "I can't even repeat some of the things Tommy has called suspects. He can be quite creative at times."

"I can imagine," Nat said, snuggling in closer. "Are you hungry? Do you want to go to bed?"

"Nah. Let's just sit here and watch television for a little while. I need something to take my mind off of everything."

"Alright. But I'm not going to let you stay up too late. You need to get some sleep."

"What are you watching?" Ben asked, stretching his legs.

"Well, I was watching *Cheers* before you got home. But it ended ten minutes ago while you were talking."

"I'm sorry. You should have told me to be quiet."

"It's okay. You're more important. Besides," she said with a grin, "it was a re-run."

Shaking his head, Ben leaned back and got comfortable. Within minutes, he was sound asleep.

FORTY-EIGHT

ARRIVING AT THE STATION, Ben couldn't help but admit the extra couple hours of sleep made a world of difference. Even though he still woke up with a knot in the pit of his stomach and an ache in his chest for the friends and colleagues he'd recently lost, his mind was focused. He was ready to take a look at the entire investigation from a fresh new perspective.

Beginning at breakfast, while Natalie bounced around the kitchen, he reread the crime scene reports cover-to-cover. There had to be something there that could help. A small detail that didn't make sense or appeared insignificant at the time. More often than not, it was the tiniest detail that could turn the tide of an investigation. Sure, every detective would like to find a telltale piece of evidence that would lead them directly to the offender within a matter of hours. But when there was no smoking gun or any other obvious clue...

"The devil is in the details," Ben mumbled under his breath.

"Sorry? What was that?" Nat asked as she pour herself another cup of coffee.

Ben looked up at her sweet face, not realizing he'd even said anything. "Oh. Sorry. I was just thinking. There has to be something we've missed. I don't care how good a killer someone is. They can't drop three bodies and walk away without having left a single clue."

Even after reviewing the files on a full stomach and a good eight hours of sleep behind him, Ben still couldn't find that *one* detail that made him say, "Aha!"

Frustrated, Ben wasn't going to let that deter him. He knew there was a clue somewhere that would lead to the unraveling of the case. He and Tommy just needed to find it. They were still waiting for the autopsies and official ballistics reports. Maybe there was something about the actual bullets used that would point them in the right direction. That's what Ben was hoping as he drove to the station.

Walking into his office, Ben decided he would request to have some uniform officers reinterview everyone from the Ramshackle. Maybe after a couple of days, one of the bargoers might have remembered someone or something out of place. Ben just hoped they could spare a few patrolmen for the task.

Before he even took off his jacket, Ben placed a call to Sergeant Kevin Bowers, commander of the PCPD's Patrol Division. Explaining how he hoped he could borrow a few officers to do some follow-up interviews, Bowers said he was happy to help find the cop killer that was on the loose and would send some guys up to get their marching orders.

Feeling as if he was actually in some sort of control of the investigation, even though they'd suffered a major setback with Dunn's alibi, Ben walked down the hall to the breakroom. At some point, he might have to deal with his very apparent addiction to caffeine. But that was a problem for another day.

Pouring himself a cup of coffee, he quickly scanned the top headlines of the newspapers sitting on the counter. The local papers were running stories about the three murdered police officers, as Ben expected. All wondered how long before the killer would be apprehended or if he would strike again. Skimming the articles, they reported as much as the department had given them. The reporters filled in the rest with their own information, though much of it was speculation.

Ben knew he wasn't going to find any answers in the newspapers, so after dumping more sugar than was good for him into his cup, he looked at *The Washington Post* to see what was happening outside of Parker. Much of the front page was taken up by articles about the current state of the presidential election, now that it looked like Walter Mondale would be the Democratic Party's candidate in the fall. The only thing worse than crime was politics, Ben thought, heading back down the hall.

"Sorry. I'd have brought you a cup of coffee if I knew you were here," Ben said, walking in and seeing Tommy standing in front of the crime board looking over the bullet points on each shooting.

"Don't worry about it," he said without taking his eyes off the photographs stuck to the chalkboard. "This alley is bugging me. We just assumed that the shooter ran into the Ramshackle. What if the other building is how he escaped?"

"It's a possibility," Ben admitted. "But the only door into that building was locked. Which would mean the shooter had a key. And that building is currently boarded up and abandoned."

The only sound in the office was the rattle of the

air conditioner as the two detectives found themselves lost in thoughts.

"You know," Ben said, breaking the silence, "there's one thing we haven't talked about. What if the shooter isn't a *he*? That's just something else we've been assuming. What if our suspect is a woman? That's not what my gut's telling me, but it's something we should at least consider."

"Okay, but the guys in the task force said a *dude* called asking for Joe," Tommy pointed out.

"She could have gotten someone else to make the call for her."

"Or we could be dealing with a Bonnie and Clyde-type pair."

Ben frowned. "I really don't want to think about that."

Tommy shrugged. Sitting down at his desk, he pushed some papers aside and asked Ben for the crime scene reports. Obliging, Ben took them from his briefcase and handed them to his partner, hoping he would have better luck with them. While Tommy was doing that, Ben thought he would take another dive into the files from the Drug Task Force. That was where he'd originally come across Frank Dunn. Maybe there was another suspect buried somewhere in the stack of folders.

As he was organizing the files into more manageable piles, the uniformed officers Sergeant Bowers assigned to help with the follow-up interviews arrived. After giving the men a quick briefing, Ben dispatched them to track down and speak with everyone who was at the Ramshackle three nights earlier. Once they were on their way, Ben was able to dig into the task force files again. He'd made a couple of notes the first time through, but nothing seemed as solid as Frank Dunn being the shooter.

Reading through page after page of dry, obnoxiously detailed reports, Ben wished real life was just a little more like the cop shows on television. If only the public realized how much of detective work was sitting and reading and doing research, they wouldn't believe it. To them, because of what they'd seen on TV and in the movies, it was all about chasing the bad guy through the streets until the pursuit ended with a big shootout.

Rubbing his eyes, Ben opened the next folder. Halfway through the report detailing a conversation Officer Ron Kramer had with an informant several months earlier, Sergeant Al Shepard knocked on the door.

"I'm becoming your personal delivery boy. I do accept tips for my service," he said smiling as he handed Ben a large envelope from the state police.

Surprisingly eager to read yet another report, Ben was hoping the medical examiner had had enough time to complete the autopsies and remove all the bullets from the three victims. If Ben was lucky, what Shepard was holding in his hands was the forensic analysis of those recovered bullets. They already knew the shell casings matched, but maybe the rounds themselves would lead them somewhere.

Tommy snatched the envelope out of the sergeant's hand before Ben could get to it.

"Thanks, Al," he said, tearing it open.

"Just skip to the summary," Ben said. "See if they found anything interesting."

"Forget interesting," Tommy replied. "I'm hoping they found something helpful."

"Why can't it be both?"

Tommy's eyes scanned the summary. Mumbling as he read, Ben couldn't tell what Tommy was thinking.

"Well?" Ben asked.

Tossing the report on his desk, Tommy confirmed that it was the official ballistics report. "And just as we expected, all five bullets match. They came from the same gun. 'Identical unique riffling' on each round."

Ben was about to say something then stopped.

"Wait. What did you just say?"

Tommy wrinkled his brow. "All the bullets match. It's just what we figured. They all had…"

"No," Ben cut him off. "How many bullets?"

Looking back at the report's summary, Tommy said, "Five. And they all came from the same gun."

Confused, Ben jumped up and walked to the crime board. Looking at the notes for each scene, he did the math in his head.

It wasn't complicated.

Something wasn't adding up.

"There are only supposed to be four bullets, Tommy." Pointing at the photos from each scene as he went, he said, "One shot for Noffsinger. *Two* for McMaster. And one for Vernon. One plus two plus one. That's only *four*. Where'd the fifth bullet come from?"

FORTY-NINE

January 1960...

Billy Roscoe watched the falling snow through the frost-covered office window. The arrival of the new year had brought with it a stretch of chilly seasonal weather. A wintery mix of snow and ice had been falling on and off for the last few days covering everything in the city with a layer of glistening white crystal. Though beautiful to look at, it made traversing the streets of Parker extremely difficult.

With the holidays behind everyone, there was very little motivating people to venture out in the sort of weather now blanketing the area. Shopkeepers and restaurateurs throughout the city were seeing a sharp decline in customers walking through their doors as more and more people chose to stay home, warm and cozy by the fire. On the fourth floor of the ParkMar Hotel, however, business was booming. Neither snow nor ice was able to keep the gamblers away.

The green felt tables called to the players like a siren's song, drawing them in every evening. The weather was no match for the excitement one felt watching the roulette wheel spin. Or the feeling one got drawing twenty-one at Blackjack.

Some people were beginning to call gambling a sickness. These were mostly the same people who believed America should still be living under Prohibition-era regulations. Billy Roscoe, on the other hand, thought a person's desire to gamble was nothing more than a small human vice. And he was happy to provide the service that so many Parker residents sought, albeit not one people spoke about publicly.

There was something magical about the game room Billy had built on the top floor of his hotel. Once through the doors, the sound of shuffling cards and ringing one-armed bandits was intoxicating. The glitz and glamour that surrounded players carried them away from their humdrum daily lives. It allowed a shoe salesman the chance to dream about hitting it rich playing Craps or a gas station attendant the chance to feel like a high-roller in Monte Carlo without leaving Parker City. Roscoe knew how to give the people what they wanted. Even if he had to break the law to do it.

"I think it might be time to start looking for a second location," Billy said, motioning toward the ledger sitting on his desk. "These numbers are making me very happy."

"The weather's not slowing things down?" the Kid asked from his seat on the sofa.

"Quite the opposite, in fact," Billy answered. "The colder it gets outside, the more we take in upstairs. But I'm afraid we might reach our capacity here at the hotel. Which is why a second gaming room makes sense."

"Any idea where you would want to put it?"

That was a good question. A second location in the city wouldn't be a bad idea. But it could also lead to additional exposure. Putting the new operation outside the city, or county for that matter, could spread things around.

But he needed to be careful. Billy didn't want to end up in a situation like with Bert Ramsburg. Their business couldn't afford *another* rogue cop conducting his own investigation. Even though Ramsburg disappeared, and nothing ever came of his off-the-books inquiry, questions still lingered.

"I'm not sure," Billy said turning from the window. "I think somewhere…"

Before he was able to finish his thought, Freddy burst through the door and charged into the room.

"We gotta go, boss!" he huffed, out of breath.

"What are you talking about? Go where?" Billy asked.

"Anywheres. We just need to get outta here. We're about to be raided!"

All of the blood drained from Billy's face as the Kid jumped to his feet.

"Raided?" they repeated simultaneously.

"By who?" the Kid asked. "I thought the PCPD was taken care of. Chief Stanley is downstairs in the restaurant right now. I just saw him."

"It ain't the Parker police. McMaster just called and tipped me off. It's the state troopers. The attorney general himself ordered the raid."

"Ferd's behind this?" the Kid asked, sounding surprised.

Both Billy and Freddy stared at him.

"Ferd?" Freddy couldn't help but sound like he was mocking the younger man.

Ignoring the tone in the thug's voice, he explained,

"Ferdinand Sybert. The state's attorney general. We call him Ferd for short. My father's known him forever."

Again, there was silence in the room until Freddy shook off the ridiculousness of the conversation and pointed out the police were on the way and they needed to clear out fast.

"Are you sure about this?" Billy asked. "Why didn't McMaster give us more warning?"

"He says it was a surprise to the PCPD, too. The AG got a tip and didn't know if he could trust the local police."

"Dammit!" Billy exploded. Reaching for the ledger on his desk, the telephone rang. Snapping it up without thinking that there wasn't time for him to be taking a phone call, he barked, "What?"

"Billy! Good. You're there. It's Marty." The lawyer sounded as out of breath as Freddy. "My secretary just called me here at home. State troopers and some U.S. Treasury agents just showed up at my office. You've got to get out of the hotel. They're on their way there next."

Thinking fast, Billy said, "We're heading for the house in Gettysburg. We'll be over the state line in less than an hour. I'll call you from there."

Slamming the phone down, Billy grabbed the ledger and his coat off the hook by the door and followed Freddy out into the hall.

"I sent Jimmy to get the car, boss. He's gonna be out back waitin' for us," Freddy said lumbering down the hall as quickly as he could.

"What about me?" the Kid asked from behind Billy.

"No one knows about you, remember? Silent partner and all," Billy said, struggling to pull his coat on while juggling the oversized record book. "Just calmly walk out the back door and go back to your office."

"And keep your fuckin' mouth shut," Freddy added.

FIFTY

"HOW THE HELL did this happen?" Billy shouted from the backseat as Jimmy carefully maneuvered the Fleetwood over the slick pavement. Sirens could be heard in the distance as they pulled away from the hotel.

"Were you able to give them the signal upstairs?" Billy asked rubbing his temples.

"Barely," Freddy said over his shoulder, sitting in the passenger seat next to his brother. "They might have been able to clear out the people, but there's no way they was able to move the tables and the equipment in time."

"Dammit!" Billy slammed his fist against the door. "I want to know who tipped off the attorney general and why we didn't know about it."

"Keeping an eye on that kind of stuff is Marty's business," Freddy pointed out. "Hey, you don't think it was the Kid, do you? He said he knows the guy."

"What possible reason would he have to do that?" Bill snapped. "He gets a nice take from our operation and he's scared to death of anyone finding out what he's up to."

"I guess that makes sense," Freddy agreed.

"Just let me do the thinking, alright. Once we get out of the state, we'll regroup and see what we can salvage," Billy said as the wheels of the Cadillac momentarily lost their traction on a slippery patch of ice.

"Sorry 'bout that, Billy," Jimmy said taking a firmer hold on the wheel. "It's getting hard to tell what's ice and what's road."

"I'd like to get to the house alive if possible, Jimmy."

Normally, from Parker City to Gettysburg it would be a straight shot up the highway. Under the circumstances, no one thought taking the most direct route was a good idea. If the state troopers were watching for Billy to run, that's where they'd be waiting. Instead, the escape would be done using all back roads, which had become hazardous because of the snow and ice.

There was no reason anyone would think Billy Roscoe would be heading to Gettysburg though. The epitome of a city boy, Billy couldn't stand nature and the country. But that didn't stop him from buying a farm outside one of the most historically significant towns in Pennsylvania several years back using a false identity just in case he would ever need to disappear for a while.

Sitting in the back of the car, Billy felt helpless. There was nothing he could do. He'd been ambushed. Even though there were plans in place if something like this ever happened, he hadn't had enough time to put them into action. Hopefully, Marty did what he was supposed to and kept all the "clean" files at his office and the...other files...hidden away.

As the Fleetwood continued to speed up then slow down as it wound its way along country roads heading north, Billy's mind was racing. There was going to be a way out of this. This wasn't the end of Billy Roscoe. Not by a long shot.

"Shit!" he heard Jimmy yell as the car skidded left then quickly pulled to the right.

From the backseat, Billy could feel the wheels completely lose their grip on the road as the car began to spin. The force of the unexpected motion threw Billy against the door, cracking his head on the window. As Jimmy tried to regain control, Billy was tossed into the door a second time. His head throbbing, all he could see were stars and snow…and a pair of bright headlights coming straight at the side of the car.

FIFTY-ONE

1984...

BEN SNATCHED THE ballistics report from Tommy's desk and began leafing through the pages. He couldn't understand how or why the crime scene techs would say there were five bullets. Only four bullets had been recovered from the three crime scenes.

Starting at the beginning, he quickly read through all the perfunctory information the lab was required to provide. The second page was where the analysis began. The first bullet the forensic team looked at was the one that had killed Joe Noffsinger. Ben turned the page and read the findings with regard to the two bullets that were removed from Hank McMaster. So far, so good. The details about the single round that was used on Peter Vernon came next. Four bullets.

Ben flipped to the next page which should have been where he found the summary explaining in less scientific terms why CSU concluded all of the bullets recovered from the victims were fired from the same gun. Instead, he found another page on analysis. Where had this bullet come from?

Tommy watched as a look of confusion appeared on his partner's face.

"Well? What is it?" he asked, feeling like a child

waiting to open his Christmas presents. "The suspense is killing me."

Ben didn't immediately answer. He was still reading. Turning to the final page, he scanned the report's summary, then turned back and reread the previous page about the mystery round. Slowly putting the papers on his desk, his mind was doing somersaults. This was information he'd never expected. How did this fifth bullet fit into the recent police shootings? He finally looked up at Tommy.

"The fifth bullet they examined," Ben said, "it was from the warehouse."

Tommy leaned forward in his chair. "What the hell are you talking about?"

"The warehouse where we found the skeleton. I'd forgotten all about it," Ben said, still trying to make sense of it. "Sergeant Bradford told me when they went back to do a second sweep of the place to see if they'd missed anything, they found a bullet lodged in the ceiling. According to this, they examined it at the same time they were looking at the bullets from our shootings and it matched."

"So, do we have another victim?" Tommy asked, looking up at the ceiling.

"The skeleton…" Ben said—not sure if he meant it as a statement or a question.

Searching his desk for the medical examiner's initial report on the skeleton from a few days ago, Ben said, "Okay, we know the skull showed signs of a single GSW. It isn't hard to believe then that the bullet the crime scene guys found in the ceiling is the one that put the hole in the skull."

"I can buy that… I guess. But what does *that* mean?"
Ben fell silent. Thinking.

"It means we need to find out more about the skeleton," he finally said.

FIFTY-TWO

THE ENTIRE LANDSCAPE of the investigation had shifted. There were now four victims. All killed with the same gun. But they knew absolutely nothing about the first victim except that he was male and in his forties or fifties. Definitely not a lot to go on.

After learning that the warehouse skeleton was somehow connected to the murder of the three police officers, Ben called the medical examiner's office and explained the situation. Politely, but firmly, he requested a full examination of the skeleton be made a priority. More intrigued than anything else, the assistant M.E. with whom he spoke said he would see what he could do.

Ben's next stop was Chief Brent's office. He needed to update him on what they'd just learned. No doubt the mayor would want to be briefed at some point. Hopefully, the chief could take care of that, allowing Ben to keep working. Though, he wasn't entirely sure of his next step.

Brent was just as surprised as Ben to find out the skeleton they'd uncovered was somehow connected to the shootings. Was it simply because the same gun was used? Or were the victims somehow linked?

Once they were able to determine the identity of the skeleton, it might shed some light on the matter.

Fully aware of how important it was to learn as much as they could about the mysterious skeleton, Brent offered to place a call to the chief medical examiner himself and stress the urgency with which they needed the information. Thanking him for his assistance, Ben went back to his office.

While he'd been in with the chief, Tommy had pulled out the missing persons files they'd started looking at before the shootings began, and was sorting through them, looking for males of the appropriate age.

"I thought you said once we had one of these fancy computer terminals, it was going to be so much easier going through old files," Tommy said, looking up at his partner with a scowl.

"Well, it will be. Once everything is computerized and all the department's files and cases are put onto the computer system. Then, all we will have to do…so I've been told…will be push a few keys and the information we need will appear on the screen."

"And when will that be?" Tommy asked, tilting his head like a Golden Retriever intently listening to his master.

"Sometime in the future," Ben said with a weak smile. "Until then, we do it the old-fashioned way."

Tommy handed him a stack of case files.

An hour later, the detectives had made progress but still had a way to go. They'd been working backward, starting with the most recent missing persons. Only a few matched the vague details for which they were searching. By the time they'd gone back through fifteen years of reports, they'd only come up with five possible matches. But Ben had requested files going back twenty years, so they still had a good number of cases yet to review.

"Ben?" Tommy said, closing one folder and picking up another. "What if the skeleton belongs to someone who didn't live in Parker City so we don't have a missing persons file on him?"

Without looking at his partner, Ben answered, "I was hoping you wouldn't think about that." Leaning back in his chair, he stretched his arms in front of him. "Once we see what we come up with, I'll ask the sheriff's department to go through their files and see if they can come up with anyone. Until we get any more on the skeleton itself, this is the best we can do."

As if on cue, Ben's telephone rang.

"This is Ben Winters."

"Ben, it's Shirley. I have Spurrier radioing in for you."

"Thanks. Put him through. It's one of the guys we sent out for the follow-up interviews," Ben said to Tommy as he listened to the clicks on the other end of the line.

"Detective, this is Brian Spurrier. I have something for you."

Ben reached for a pen and his notebook. "Go ahead. I'm ready."

"The first two witnesses I spoke with were busts. They couldn't remember anything more than what they'd already told Officer Thompson and Detective Mason. And that wasn't much to begin with. But the third person I just finished with, a Keith Rush, said when he was entering the Ramshackle at about a quarter to six on the evening in question, he saw an older man standing around back near the alley."

"An older man?" Ben asked. "What exactly does that mean?"

"That's the same thing I asked. But all Rush said was

'older' with gray hair. He didn't get a look at his face and he said he was wearing dark clothing. I know it's not much help," Spurrier said apologetically.

"No, Brian, this is more than we had before. No one wanted to give us anything. How did you get him to talk? Do I want to know?"

The officer laughed. "I didn't do anything out of line. Rush just said he was completely soused when he was questioned the other night so barely knew his own name. He hasn't had a drink for the last two days because he's been working, so was completely sober when I talked to him."

"I'll take whatever breaks we can get," Ben said.

After hanging up, Ben walked over to the crime board and made a note next to the Noffsinger crime scene that an "older man" had been seen by the alley just before the shooting. There was no way to know if the guy was the shooter or just someone passing by. But it was a new piece of information.

Watching his partner, Tommy said, "Maybe those two guys Kramer saw out front of the pawnshop saw this guy? It wouldn't hurt to ask?"

"You just don't want to look through the missing person cases anymore."

"Once again, this is why you're the chief detective around here," Tommy said with a smile. "But seriously, I'm going to go cross-eyed if I have to look at another one of these damn reports. Let me go track those guys down and see if they saw anyone. And I'll pick up lunch on the way back. On me. Just don't make me read another file right now."

"Alright. We'll divide and concur. You go see what

you can find out from them and I'll keep going through these. And I want a meatball sub with extra cheese."

"Done," Tommy said as he grabbed his jacket and ran out of the office before Ben could change his mind.

"Oh…teamwork," Ben said shaking his head. "It's a wonderful thing."

FIFTY-THREE

THE DELUXE MEATBALL sub from Giuseppe's made life worth living, Ben thought as he wiped the crumbs from his chin. Ironically though, Giuseppe's, one of the most popular Italian restaurants in the city, was actually owned by a Polish immigrant. But he didn't care where the chef came from as long as the homemade Marinara recipe never changed.

Lunch was the most fruitful thing to come from Tommy's outing, however. Though he'd managed to speak with the two men who'd been seen outside the pawnshop just before Officer Noffsinger was shot—a pair of brothers that owned the store—neither man could remember seeing anyone near the alley. They'd been too wrapped up in their conversation to notice anyone else. But if Tommy was looking for a television set or boombox, he'd come to the right place.

Tommy got the feeling the shop was a cover for something. What? He couldn't be sure. All he did know was that both brothers were idiots. So unless they were the best actors he'd ever come across, neither had the brains to be running an illegal operation without getting caught.

Leaving the store, Tommy stopped and took a seat on the stoop. From that vantage point, one couldn't see into the alley behind the Ramshackle. If there had been a guy there, the only way the brothers would have been able to see him is if he was standing in the opening of the alleyway. So, if they weren't paying attention, as they claimed, once he took a few steps farther in, he'd have vanished from view.

Tommy wasn't happy as he climbed into his Bronco and gunned the engine.

Like his partner, he felt there had to be *something* from one of the crime scenes that would give them a clue as to who the shooter was or his motive. No one just wakes up one morning and decides to become a cop killer. There was a reason for everything that had happened over the last three days. They just hadn't figured it out yet.

For his part, Ben would have liked to have gotten through the remainder of the missing persons cases, but shortly after Tommy left, he was called into the chief's office to meet with the mayor.

"We've gone a day without another officer being shot," the mayor said as Ben walked in. "Do you think he's finished?"

Pleasantries didn't seem to be on the agenda, so Ben jumped right in.

"Sir, I can't say one way or another," he apologized.

There was no way for any of them to know if the killer had done what he set out to do or if he was going to try and take out more police officers in the future. All Ben could do was brief Oland on where the investigation was at that point.

"You're telling me that the skeleton that was unearthed at that old warehouse is somehow connected to the murder of three Parker City police officers?" the mayor asked, with a heavy dose of skepticism in his voice.

"According to the state police's forensics team, yes. All four victims were shot with the same gun," Ben answered.

"And you don't know who the skeleton is or how long he's been buried?"

"Correct. We're currently working to identify the remains and hopefully the medical examiner will be able to tell us how long the first victim has been dead."

"This is unbelievable," Charlie Oland said turning to the chief. "Three murdered cops and they have something to do with a skeleton buried under a building for God knows how long."

"All we know is they were shot with the same gun," Brent said with a shrug. "Just let Detectives Winters and Mason do their thing. They'll figure all this out."

"They better, Nick," the mayor said with a sigh. "Otherwise, all of our heads are on the block with this one. And I'll tell you this. If there are any more shootings, I'm going to have to ask the state police to take over. I know you're good, Ben. But we need to catch this guy."

FIFTY-FOUR

By the time Ben and Tommy had gone through twenty years of case files, they'd only found a handful of men in their forties and fifties who were reported missing and whose cases were still open. A completely manageable number of cases on which to follow up. That just left the warehouse itself. They needed to learn the building's history—who built it, when, and who owned it between now and then.

Dividing up the tasks, Tommy took the list of missing men and the contact information for who reported them missing. While he was looking into what happened with each of the cases and whether the men had ever turned up, Ben was heading to the county courthouse to dig into old land records. Not exciting work for either detective, but necessary.

Ben was thinking about that as he walked the few blocks to the Samuel J. Tildon Courthouse. Named after the county's sheriff during the Civil War, the building had been completed a year after he died in 1876. Since then, the Reconstruction era courthouse remained the seat of the county's judicial system. An imposing structure with its distinct red bricks and enormous white columns, it made sense that anyone entering the building would feel intimidated. Especially if they happened to be the unfortunate individual about to stand trial.

In stark contrast to the courthouse's formidable frame, a beautiful flower garden had been installed leading up to the building's main entrance. The colorful array of flowers and sweet aroma scenting the air made the garden park a popular location for those working in the area to have their lunch.

Taking a seat on an ornate wrought iron bench bearing a small golden plaque indicating the piece had been donated by South Mountain Bank & Trust, Ben took a deep breath. The warm summer air filled his lungs. It was a beautiful day. If it wasn't for the three…correction, *four*, unsolved murders hanging over him, he could spend the entire day there relaxing. But a moment to clear his head before heading into the dusty records room in the basement of the courthouse wasn't going to hurt anything.

From his spot on the bench, Ben looked across the street to the Parker Historical Society building. The elegant brownstone, once the grandest private residence in the city, had been converted into a museum dedicated to the history of Parker City and County. It was also the scene of the Spring Strangler's first attack. Beverly Baker, one of the most influential women in the city had been found murdered in the townhouse. As the department's newly minted detectives, it was a baptism by fire for Ben and Tommy. When the case was finally closed, not only did Parker City receive national attention, but so did the detectives. Attention neither Ben nor Tommy sought or welcomed.

Shaking off the unpleasant memories, Ben decided he'd put off his mission long enough. It was time to venture into the courthouse and find out everything he could about the old warehouse on Antietam Avenue.

After signing in with the sheriff's deputy at the security desk, Ben followed the signs to the basement where he found the room that housed all of the county's land records. Stepping through the door for room B-117, Ben came face-to-face with a little man sitting behind a counter. The clerk reminded him of the "Time to make the donuts" guy in the television commercials.

Staring up at Ben over the rim of his glasses, the man asked in a dull monotone, "Can I help you?"

Producing his badge, Ben introduced himself. There was no reaction on the clerk's face.

"Can I help you?" he asked again with the same lack of emotion.

Tearing a page out of his notebook, Ben wrote the address of the warehouse and slid it across the counter. "I need to see all the records for this property, please."

"Is this official business?" the clerk asked, looking at the piece of paper.

"Yes. It's for an ongoing investigation."

The little man sighed and turned to his computer terminal. Ben watched as he punched in the address, then scribbled a code on the bottom of the notepaper. Standing up, the clerk disappeared through a door behind the counter without another word.

Pacing back and forth as he waited, Ben was trying to come up with all the ways in which the skeleton could be connected to the policemen who'd been shot. Admittedly, none of his ideas seemed plausible or made any sense. Hopefully, there was something in the land records that would connect the dots.

Fifteen minutes after he'd left the room, the clerk reemerged carrying a flat, rectangular file box. A card on the front matched the code he'd taken from the computer.

Handing the box to Ben, the clerk indicated a small table and chairs set up in the corner of the room where he could examine the documents. Carrying the box to the viewing area, Ben wiped away a thick layer of dust. Clearly, no one had touched this set of files in a very, very long time.

Surprisingly, the collection of pages was very detailed and comprehensive. Ben's greatest fear was that documents would have been lost or misplaced and his attempt to learn about the warehouse would result in little being learned. However, with the files that lay before him, he was able to trace the ownership of the property from the present day all the way back to when the warehouse was first built back in 1940. If this one folio was an example of how the county kept its land records, the court clerks should be proud. Too often, Ben had heard horror stories about how records were stored and lost and misplaced by municipal bureaucracies.

Going page by page through the box, Ben jotted down all the important information as he went. Even then, when he was finished, he decided to press his luck and asked the clerk at the counter if there was a way to have mimeographed copies of the documents made. Begrudgingly, the clerk said he would see what he could do but it would take some time. With that, Ben found himself sitting at the small table tapping his fingers awaiting his copies of the land records to be produced.

FIFTY-FIVE

THE AFTERNOON WAS in its waning hours when Ben returned to the PCPD with fresh copies of the land records in hand. Tossing them on his desk, he took off his jacket and hung it on the hook by the door. His eyes were red and itchy after sitting for hours at the courthouse in that dusty records room. But he'd found everything he was looking for. It was now a matter of figuring out how it fit into the case.

Tommy's jacket was still on the back of his chair, which meant he hadn't left for the day. Ben just didn't know where he was. Having left no message, Ben assumed he'd probably just gone for some coffee.

Proving once again why Ben should always trust his gut, it wasn't long before Tommy could be heard coming down the hall from the direction of the breakroom. Ben looked up from his notebook as his partner appeared in the doorway carrying a plate of chocolate chip cookies.

"Look what Lieutenant Whitcomb's wife sent in for everyone," he said, offering Ben an afternoon snack.

"She does know the quickest way to a man's heart," Ben said, picking two cookies off the plate.

"Funny," Tommy said in a somber tone. "I always thought the quickest way to a man's heart was through his chest."

He couldn't stop himself from laughing as Ben rolled his eyes.

"What did you find out about the missing persons?" Ben asked between bites.

"Yeah, well, three of the five guys who disappeared ended up reappearing. The most recent of those had gone on a bender and *woke up* in Atlantic City. Needless to say, his now *ex*-wife confirmed he is very much alive." Tommy finished a cookie and picked up another. "The two earliest cases, the contact information wasn't good anymore so I couldn't talk to anyone directly. I asked some of the old-timers around here if they knew anything. LuCoco was actually helpful. He remembered Cyrus Burns. Disappeared in '69. His body was found in the woods up in Catoctin. It was ruled a hunting accident. The other one…a Jim Peterman, no one remembers how that turned out."

Sitting back in his chair, Ben started thinking out loud. "Wouldn't it have made sense for someone to update the files for the three who turned up? And Burns when his body was found. I mean, that's sort of the point of keeping these files, isn't it?"

"Oh, Ben," Tommy sighed. "You're thinking too responsibly. These cases were in the '70s. It's not like the PCPD back then was known for its record-keeping ability. Hell, we're lucky just to know who was on the force at the time. The 1970s is like a giant black hole for this department."

"And that doesn't frustrate you?" Ben asked.

"Of course it does. But what are we going to do about it now? It's only been a couple of years since Brent took over and we're just now starting to see some real changes around here. Plus, a little birdie told me the chief's working on a comprehensive reorganization plan for the entire department. It can only get better."

Shrugging, Ben had to agree. Since Nick Brent moved into the chief's office, the PCPD was tightening up and becoming a more modern police force. It was slow going, but the groundwork was being laid.

Getting back to the topic of their missing persons, Ben said, "So, it's possible this Peterson…"

"Peterman…"

"Peterman…could be our skeleton?"

"He fits with the very little bit we know about the skeleton. James Alexander Peterman was a male and was forty-three when he was reported missing. So, yes, it's possible he's our mystery victim."

Tommy closed the Peterman file and handed it to Ben. Then, wiping some cookie crumbs from his tie, he asked, "And what did you find on your little research trip this afternoon?"

"I'm happy to say the county's land records are being kept a hell of a lot better than the PCPD's files are. I was able to trace the entire history of the warehouse from when it was built up to the current owners.

"Before the city expanded out in that direction, the land was part of a farm owned by the Easterday family. In 1940, they sold off a large part of the farm for industrial development. That's the year the warehouse was built by what I learned was a subsidiary of Westinghouse Electric. In 1955, the property was sold to a William Roscoe for his B.R. Freight company. In 1960, a trust purchased the company, though I couldn't find any information about them using it for any sort of operations. It's like they bought it and just let it sit empty. Then in the mid-'70s, the city condemned the property and seized it using its power of eminent domain. Early last year, the city sold it to the New Jersey developer who's building Parker Commons."

"That's a very comprehensive and boring list," Tommy said, leaning back in his chair and closing his eyes. "I have a question. How do we know our skeleton hasn't been in the ground since the warehouse was built?"

"Because of the bullet hole in the skull and the round CSU found in the ceiling. If there was no warehouse when the skeleton was shot, there would be no ceiling in which to find the bullet."

"You're so clever. Next question. How do we know the skeleton wasn't buried there back in the '40s?"

"We don't. That's where the medical examiner comes in. We need him to tell us how long ago our mystery victim died."

"You've just got it all figured out, don't you?"

"Yes," Ben said in a patronizing tone. "I do have it all figured out. I even know who our killer is. I'm just not telling you. I want you to figure it out for yourself."

Tommy frowned and said, "You know, sometimes you can be a real pain in the ass. I need to have a talk with Nat and make sure she understands what she's getting herself into with you."

Before Ben was able to respond with a quip of his own, the telephone on his desk rang. Sharing the exact same thought, both men involuntarily tensed. Had there been another shooting?

On the third ring, Ben picked up the receiver and answered.

"Detective Winters, this is Doctor Herman Dale with the medical examiner's office in Baltimore. We spoke earlier today," the voice on the other end of the line said. "I have some information for you. I'm going to have a courier deliver the full findings in the morning, but I figured since my boss received calls from your chief, Mayor Oland, *and* the governor today, I should give you the highlights sooner rather than later."

Ben assumed Charlie Oland was friends with Governor Hughes and asked him to help expedite the M.E.'s examination of the skeleton. Or maybe it was Chief Brent. He didn't know. But whoever it was, Ben appreciated the assistance.

Flipping to a clean page in his notebook, Ben began scribbling notes as the assistant medical examiner rattled off a list of details they'd discovered and determined during the examination of the bones. The most notable of the details was that "with no other clear evidence of cause, death appeared to have been due to a single gunshot to the head." The doctor went on to explain the bullet's trajectory and angle of entry and exit, but Ben knew the report would contain all of that information.

When Dr. Dale finally took a breath, Ben asked, "Do you have any idea when he was killed?"

Ben could hear the shuffling of papers. Then the doctor's nasally voice returned to the line. "We're placing the time of death somewhere between twenty-five and thirty years ago."

"Really?" Ben asked without even thinking.

"With what we have, that's the timeframe into which we can narrow it down."

"I'm sorry, doctor. I didn't mean anything other than I am surprised it happened so long ago."

Ben wasn't sure what to think. A murder that occurred some thirty years ago was in some way connected to the shootings just a few days earlier.

After thanking the assistant medical examiner for the call, Ben hung up and quickly reread his notes. If the skeleton had been buried for at least twenty-five years, that meant it wasn't Jim Peterman. In fact, it wasn't any of the missing persons they'd looked at because Ben had only requested files going back twenty years. And with those records being so shoddy, what were the odds the files going back even further were going to be any better?

Ben felt a serious headache coming on.

FIFTY-SIX

Taking the stairs two at a time, Ben was hoping the department's records room would still be open. At six o'clock, the odds were pretty good that Betty—keeper of the PCPD files—had already locked up and headed home for the day. On the off chance she was still there however, Ben didn't want to waste any more time. If he could go through the missing persons cases from the period when the M.E. placed the skeleton's time of death, maybe they'd finally have something to go on. Or, he thought, it could be another dead end.

How could a murder thirty years earlier have anything to do with the shooting of three police officers today? All they knew for certain was that the same gun was used in all four shootings. It didn't mean the killer from all those years ago was the same one picking off Parker City's finest now. The chance of that was slim to none.

Ben's mind was racing as he came to a halt in front of the door to the file room. Grabbing the doorknob and giving it a quick turn, his fear was realized. The door was locked. Betty had left.

"Dammit," he said under his breath, leaning his head against the door.

"Something wrong, detective?" a voice said from down the narrow corridor.

Ben looked over to see Officer Buck LuCoco lumbering toward him from the direction of the holding cells.

"I was just hoping to pull some files but it looks like Betty's already left," Ben said, the resignation in his voice evident even to someone as dense as LuCoco.

"You know," the officer said, stopping and leaning his hefty frame against the wall, "I'm sure we could rustle you up a key if it's that important. It's not like Betty has the only one. As a detective, I would have thought you could have figured that out."

Ben had to admit, reluctantly, he *hadn't* thought about that. Evidently, he was not in the best frame of mind. Especially if it was Buck LuCoco who was pointing out the obvious to him.

"You're right, Buck. But no. It's been a long day. It can wait until tomorrow."

"Suit yourself," LuCoco said as he started for the stairs.

"Just out of curiosity," Ben said. "How long have you been with the PCPD?"

LuCoco turned back to Ben biting his lower lip as he did the math.

"Well, I joined the force in 1955. So that makes it, what, twenty-nine years now. I'll probably be handin' in my papers soon. Time to hang up the uniform and go fishing."

Ben couldn't help but think LuCoco's retirement would not be that great of a loss. He was part of the PCPD's old guard and didn't like the way things were changing. But after thirty years he did have one thing going for him. He had institutional knowledge of the city and its history. None of the younger officers now joining the force knew what he knew.

"I don't suppose," Ben began, "you happen to remember any big missing persons cases from your first few years do you?"

LuCoco let out something that was a strange combination of a grunt and a laugh. Then said, "We didn't have 'missing persons cases' back in the fifties. Not the same way we have today at least. Everybody knew everybody else back then and knew where everybody was. No body just up and disappeared."

"That's what I figured," Ben said.

He'd known finding a report on a missing person from thirty years ago that miraculously matched the particulars of the skeleton which they'd unearthed was a long shot. Honestly, Ben wasn't even sure how far back the records went. For all he knew, he might have already gone through all the missing persons case files the department still had on hand. Twenty years of files that were getting old and faded was actually pretty good when you thought about it. Especially when they were being kept in a dank room in the basement of an old building that was inexplicably still standing.

Ben and Tommy would have to find another way to figure out the identity of the skeleton. Then, for the first time since Ben had known the grumpy, overweight officer, LuCoco did something helpful.

"There was Bert Ramsburg," LuCoco said after thinking for a moment. "He up and disappeared. That one was strange."

Ben felt a sudden rush of adrenaline.

"Who was Bert Ramsburg?"

"He was a patrolman with the department. A pain in

the ass kind of guy, you know? A real stickler for the rules. Every regulation had to be followed to the letter."

"I could see why you hated that," Ben said, hoping he didn't sound too condescending.

The disguised insult flew right over LuCoco's head.

"So, what happened exactly?" Ben prodded.

"Ramsburg was one of those guys always looking for a criminal conspiracy."

"Did he have any particular enemies?"

"Sure. Just like any cop. Anyone he ever slapped cuffs on. But Bert could be a real hardass about things."

"Anyone in particular, I mean."

"We're talking almost thirty years ago. I was new to the department. He'd been around a while. It's not like we was buddies."

"This could actually be very important. Just think, Buck."

Ben wanted to add, *just don't hurt yourself.* But since this was the most civil conversation they'd ever had, Ben wasn't going to throw the first verbal punch.

"If I remember right," the officer said, pausing to think about what he was going to say, "Bert was hot on an investigation. At least that's the way he made it sound. He thought there was something going on at the big hotel Downtown. The old ParkMar. He was looking into the owner. Boy, now there was a guy. He was always so flashy. He had this town eating out of the palm of his hand.

"Nobody knew it at the time, but Bert was right," LuCoco went on. "The ParkMar had a gambling room on the top floor. The state troopers and Feds raided the place and found it."

"But what happened to Ramsberg?"

"Oh. Right. He disappeared."

"You're killing me, Buck," Ben said, clenching his fists in frustration.

"He disappeared while he was looking into the hotel. The year before the raid, I think. Which was in…'60, January or February. It was the beginning of the year sometime. All hell broke loose around here that day. Stanley was furious because he hadn't been informed about the raid in advance and—"

"Buck, right now, I'm just interested in what you remember about the missing officer," Ben said as politely as possible.

"Oh, right. Everybody thought Roscoe got rid of him. The department looked into it, but there was no evidence."

"Roscoe?" Ben asked.

"Billy Roscoe. He was the owner of the ParkMar. And a bunch of restaurants around town. We come to find out, after the Feds swooped in, he was involved in a lot of illegal shit. Everybody thought he was a real pillar of the community but all the while, he was into all sorts of shady stuff. Made a fortune off it too, sounded like."

Ben had stopped listening.

According to the court papers, Billy—short for *William*—Roscoe was the owner of the warehouse on Antietam Avenue during the time the medical examiner believed the skeleton must have been buried. Finally. There could be a real break in the case. And even if this wasn't all related to the recent police shootings, Ben may have solved a case from the past he didn't even know he was working on.

FIFTY-SEVEN

"WE MAY HAVE a fourth dead police officer," Ben said, rushing into the office.

Tommy was on his feet, reaching for his jacket before Ben could stop him. "Another shooting? Where?"

"No. Sorry. The skeleton," Ben clarified. "It could belong to a missing police officer from back in the '50s."

"Excuse me? And how exactly did you come to that conclusion?"

Taking a deep breath, Ben started from the beginning, sharing the conversation he'd just had with Buck LuCoco. When he'd finished, Tommy sat back in his chair and crossed his arms without saying a word. Ben couldn't tell what his partner was thinking. It wasn't like him to be so quiet. Being that LuCoco was involved, Ben would have expected a snide remark at the very least. Instead, Tommy sat staring at him with a thoughtful expression.

"Are you going to say anything?" Ben asked after the silence became too much to stand.

"I'm trying to decide if you're grasping at straws because we keep coming up empty or if we just got really lucky."

"I will admit, this bit of information comes at the perfect time. Maybe the universe decided to give us a push in the right direction," Ben suggested with a shrug.

After another moment of deafening silence, Tommy leaned forward and rested his elbows on the desk. "I'll bite…for the moment. But what's next?"

"We find out what we can about Officer Bert Ramsburg's disappearance. A missing officer would have had to trigger an investigation. We need to look at the case file."

"Assuming it survived since 1959. That's twenty-five years in the basement."

"Yes. Assuming it survived. But Betty has already gone home for the day so the file room is locked tight," Ben said, slumping into his chair.

"You do realize we can get a key, right? I'm sure Betty doesn't have the only one in existence."

"LuCoco was also kind enough to point that out to me. Thank you very much."

"Great!" Tommy said, throwing his hands in the air. "Now I'm thinking like Buck LuCoco. That's a real kick in the crotch."

Ben smiled, then said, "He was actually helpful… this time."

"Okay, so tomorrow, first thing, we take a look at the Ramsburg investigation. Assuming there's a case file to look at. If we're lucky, we'll find something in it that connects to our current victims."

"That's exactly what I'm thinking," Ben agreed.

"But you do understand," Tommy said, "there is a chance the skeleton doesn't belong to the long-lost cop, right? Don't get me wrong. I'd love to solve a twenty-five-year-old cold case. But, I mean, that skeleton can belong to anyone."

"Maybe you're right and I am grasping at straws,"

Ben admitted. "But right now, it's the only potential lead we've got. Is it a coincidence that the day after the skeleton was uncovered police officers started getting shot? Maybe. But my gut tells me we're on to something."

"Far be it from me to disagree with your gut. It's never led us astray. So, I'll trust it for now. What time does Betty come in?" Tommy asked, standing and stretching.

"Eight-thirty."

Which is exactly when the two detectives were standing outside the door to the department's record storage room. No sign of Betty, Ben couldn't stop pacing. For his part, Tommy leaned against the wall nursing a large cup of gas station coffee he picked up on his way in.

"Ben… Ben… *Ben*! Would you please stop pacing? The floor is already worn out. You going back and forth isn't doing it any favors. Plus, it's driving me crazy. How much coffee have you had this morning?"

Trying to control his nervous energy, Ben planted his feet and stuck his hands in his pockets.

"Betty's late," he said.

"Maybe we're early," Tommy offered.

Ben had to admit to himself, he was being a little over-eager this morning. It was usually Tommy who would get worked up, leaving him to be the level-headed voice of reason. Now the roles were reversed. The worst part was, Ben wasn't entirely sure why he was *so* anxious. Even if they could tie Ramsburg's disappearance to the three shootings, that didn't mean they were going to be able to instantly determine who the killer was. But it would be a step in the right direction.

Baby steps, Ben told himself as he heard the door

at the end of the corridor open. Turning, he saw Betty navigating her way toward them. An older woman, she was clad in a raincoat covered in brightly colored flowers, carrying an oversized umbrella in one hand and an equally oversized purse in the other.

"Morning, fellas," she said, her raspy voice coming from under the rain hat pulled down low on her head. "You waiting for me? Sorry I'm late. The rain is causing terrible traffic this morning. You know, if you ever need to get in to look at a file after hours, the duty sergeant always has a key."

Tommy didn't have to say a word. Without even looking, Ben could tell his partner was making a face at him behind his back.

"We're looking for an old case file, so we thought it best to wait for you," Ben explained. He thought it sounded plausible.

"Just give me a minute to get in there and turn the lights on. Then I'll be at your disposal, boys."

"Take your time," Tommy said with a smile, knowing full well how anxious his partner was to get his hands on the old files.

A few minutes later, the three were huddled in Betty's cramped work area in front of row upon row of mismatched file cabinets. The only thing they all had in common was the layer of dust resting upon them. Other than a label on the front of each drawer bearing a numerical code, Ben couldn't see any way to tell what was in each cabinet. There must be some sort of system, he thought waiting for Betty to settle in.

Before she had even taken off her raincoat, Betty lit a cigarette, sighing after the first puff. The color of the bluish-gray smoke matched almost identically to the color of her hair.

"My husband doesn't like me smoking in the car," she explained as she shrugged off the flowered jacket. "So I don't."

"Do you think you should be smoking down here with all these old papers?" Ben asked innocently enough.

"Probably not," she answered as she booted up the computer on her desk.

"You're a woman after my own heart, Betty," Tommy said, flashing her a thousand-watt smile.

"Oh, please, honey. You couldn't handle me."

As they waited for the machine to turn on, Betty placed a pair of glasses on her nose with the thickest lenses either detective had ever seen. Finally, once the computer finished beeping and buzzing, Betty used her two index fingers to strike a few keys. Turning to Ben, she asked, "Alright then. What is it you're looking for?"

"Are the files all catalogued on that computer?" he asked.

"Sure are. I type in the file name you're looking for, the IBM here tells me which file cabinet it's in."

Ben looked at Tommy and said, "See, I told you computers were going to change the way we do things. One day, the case files themselves will be able to be stored on the computer and we won't need all these file cabinets."

"Hey, don't go putting me out of work, young man," Betty chastised.

"Couldn't you just file the cases alphabetically?" Tommy asked.

"Hey now," Betty said sternly. "You don't see me

coming up to your office telling you how to do your detectiving, do you?"

"He doesn't mean anything, Betty. He's just jealous because you know how to use a computer and he doesn't," Ben said pointedly to his partner, the consummate technophobe.

"It's not that I don't know how to use the computer…"

"You don't," Ben interrupted. "You think…"

"Boys," Betty cut him off. "I've got a coffee break coming up in a few minutes. Do you want to tell me what file you're looking for or are we just going to stand around talking about these machines?"

"A coffee break? Didn't you just get here?" Tommy asked.

"What's your point?" Betty responded, the smoke from her cigarette forming an ominous cloud over her head.

"We're looking for anything you have on the disappearance of Officer Bert Ramsburg back in 1959," Ben said, refocusing everyone on the actual reason for their being there.

"That's an old one. A few years before I started working here. Let's see what we have. *If* we have anything," Betty said, punching a long series of keys then waiting.

Neither Ben nor Tommy knew what was supposed to happen next. The computer screen at which they'd all been staring went blank except for a single flashing cursor in the upper left corner.

Eager for something to happen, Tommy asked, "What's going on? The screen's blank. It's not doing anything. What's supposed to happen?"

"Let it think," Betty said firmly, stamping out her cigarette in the full ashtray on her desk.

After another moment of nothing seeming to happen, a numerical code like the ones on the front of the cabinet drawers blinked on the screen. Scribbling the numbers on a small notepad, Betty said, "*That's* what's supposed to happen."

Ben and Tommy watched as Betty disappeared behind a row of file cabinets without saying another word. Neither was sure if they were supposed to wait there or follow her into the depths of the archives.

As if reading their minds, they heard her call from behind a row of cabinets, "I'll be right back. I have to go into the backroom for this one. If I'm not out in ten minutes, call for backup."

The detectives listened as a door creaked open somewhere out of sight. Then a few minutes later they heard the door close and the shuffling sound of Betty's feet returning. In her hand was a worn, discolored brown folder. It wasn't nearly as thick as Ben would have expected. The case file for a missing police officer should have been full of interview notes, reports, anything and everything the investigating officers came across. Opening the folder, Ben only found a few pages.

"Is this everything?" he asked, feeling there must be more information somewhere else.

"That's all there is," Betty said, directing his attention to the computer monitor with the single case file number. "If there was anything else, it would give me a whole list."

"I just expected there to be more."

"Well, hun," her Baltimore accent coming through

much stronger now, "I just keep track of where the files are. Not what's in 'em."

"Yeah," he said apologetically. "I know. I just… Thanks for your help."

"Now I'm going to need you to sign that you're taking that file out," she said picking up a clipboard and handing it to Ben.

FIFTY-EIGHT

"THIS MIGHT JUST be the most shoddy investigation I have ever seen," Ben said after rereading the Ramsburg case file a second time. "There is virtually nothing here."

Ben had crossed the line from confusion over the lack of information in the file to downright anger and frustration over the way the investigation of a missing officer was handled.

Other than a photo of Bert Ramsburg, the only other items in the file were a few sheets of paper with handwritten notes that were barely legible. Ben couldn't even find the names of the officers who were a part of the investigation.

"I'm the first to admit they didn't keep the best records back in the day," Tommy added, "but this is ridiculous. You don't think that somehow that Billy Roscoe guy was able to get to the file and remove evidence of his involvement, do you?"

"LuCoco said they never *found* any evidence tying him to the disappearance."

"I can see why, if that's the case they put together for the state's attorney back then," Tommy said tossing a Rubik's Cube back and forth from one hand to the other.

Holding the folder up and waving it in the air, Ben practically shouted, "Do you even think a state's attorney would accept this as a legitimate investigation?"

"No, but if Ramsburg was such a pain in the ass, as LuCoco led you to believe, Chief Stanley would have accepted it. Remember, he was running things back then."

Ben raised an eyebrow trying to understand what his partner was saying. "You think Stanley was somehow involved?"

"No. I'm saying he ran a very lax department and," Tommy paused as he reached over and picked the case folder off Ben's desk, "this would have been more than enough for him if the person running the investigation told him they couldn't find anything. He could have then told the state's attorney there was no evidence Roscoe was involved. Stanley carried a lot of weight in this town. Most people don't actually know how bad of a chief he was. And the ones that did, didn't care or were too afraid to try and get rid of him."

Ben rested his head in his hands as he tried to think about what to do next. He'd been counting on the file to give them a clue or point them in a new direction. He hadn't expected to feel like he'd run headfirst into a brick wall after reading it.

Absentmindedly staring down at his desk, Ben's eye caught the headline across the top of that morning's *Herald-Dispatch*. He suddenly had an idea.

Holding up the paper so Tommy could see he said, "Look at this."

"Yeah? 'Police continue to investigate cop shootings,'" Tommy read the headline. "I'll admit, it's not the catchiest headline."

"No, but it's an article reporting on the current investigation," Ben paused, waiting to see if Tommy picked up on his train of thought.

"That's what the newspaper does," Tommy said slowly, trying to figure out what his partner was getting at.

"Exactly. And…"

"And…?" The light bulb finally went off in his head. "And a missing police officer would probably have been a big story."

"Something the newspaper would have covered," Ben finished the thought.

"We need to read some old newspapers," Tommy said.

FIFTY-NINE

THE *HERALD-DISPATCH* building was, itself, a former warehouse across town from the PCPD. Back in the '60s when the *Blue Ridge Herald* and the *Parker Chronicle Dispatch* merged, the joint paper made its new home in the converted industrial building. Combining the two rival newspapers had been the idea of Bernard Moss, Jr., publisher of the *Herald* and one of the most powerful men in the city. It was the first paper in what was now a growing newspaper and radio empire for the family. Though Bernard, Jr. died back in the '70s, his son, Bernard B.Moss III, was now running the company.

Ben and Tommy had met the rising newspaper mogul three years earlier under very unfortunate circumstances. Moss's daughter, Penny, had been the final victim of the Spring Strangler.

Sitting in front of the *Herald-Dispatch* building looking through the rain-splattered windshield, Ben thought back to that horrible day. He remembered how it was raining then too. That was also the day he'd had something of a physical confrontation with the reporter Roger Benedict.

Dashing across the street, doing his best to dodge the raindrops, Ben tried to put those thoughts out of his head. He wondered if those memories would ever stop haunting him.

Stepping into the small reception lobby, Ben and Tommy shook the rain from their jackets. A young woman sat behind a desk with the paper's banner logo stenciled on it.

"May I help you?" the secretary asked as they approached the desk.

"Good morning." Tommy spoke first, as he usually did when they were about to introduce themselves to a pretty woman. Flashing his badge, he continued, "I'm Detective Mason, with the Parker City Police Department. This is my partner, Detective Sergeant Winters."

"What can I do for you?" she asked, wide-eyed.

It was Ben's turn. "We were hoping to take a look at copies of your old newspaper editions. Can you tell us who we would need to speak to about that?"

"Ummm," the young woman said as she bit her lower lip. "I think you should probably speak to our editor, Mr. Babcock. If you take the stairs, he's on the third floor. First door on the right."

"Thank you," Tommy said with a smile. "And what was your name?"

"I'm Lisa. Lisa Davis."

"Thank you, Lisa Davis. We'll be sure to tell Mr. Babcock you were very helpful."

The detectives walked away as a huge smile appeared on the secretary's face.

"You're terrible," Ben said starting up the stairs. "Do you even know you're doing it? Or is flirting just a reflex with you?"

"I can't help it if I make the girls go all warm and squishy inside. I guess I just have a natural charm."

"I think it's more like a sickness," Ben said as they rounded the landing on the second floor.

"Whatever it is, it gets the job done. She told us who to talk to, didn't she?"

"She would have told us whether you were *charming* or not," Ben countered. "It's not like we were trying to get any state secrets out of her."

"Must you always ruin my fun? Just because you're spoken for and aren't allowed to look at women anymore, doesn't mean I can't make new friends."

Ben rolled his eyes.

"I heard that," Tommy said from behind him.

Reaching the top floor, they found the editor's office right where Lisa said it would be. The gold embossed name of *Milford Babcock, Editor* adorned the frosted glass panel in the door.

The door was halfway open, so the detectives let themselves in to find they were standing in the editor's outer office. Another secretary, this one significantly older than Lisa, looked up at the visitors, giving them a quick once over. Not recognizing either of the men, her eyes narrowed.

"Can I help you?" The words were friendly but the tone certainly was not. This was a woman who did not like unexpected interruptions.

Ben performed the usual introduction of himself and Tommy, showing his badge to make it official, then explained why they were there and that Lisa directed them to speak with Mr. Babcock.

"I'm afraid he's very busy. If you don't have an appointment, you'll need to make one."

"As I said," Ben started, his voice pleasant but authoritative, "my partner and I are here on official police business and we need to speak with Mr. Babcock. If he can't help us, then we hope he'll be able to tell us who can."

Not pleased, the secretary pushed a button on her intercom and said, "Mr. Babcock, there are two Parker City police detectives here to see you."

There was no response. But a few seconds later, the door to the editor's inner office swung open. A tall man with a neatly trimmed beard and mustache stood in the doorway. Wearing a tweed jacket with leather patches on the elbows and a pair of glasses dangling around his neck on a chain, Milford Babcock could easily have passed for a college professor.

"I'm Milford Babcock," he said extending his hand. "You are Detectives Winters and Mason, I presume."

Taking his hand, Ben paused. "I'm sorry. Have we met before?"

"No," the editor said. "But Parker City only has two police detectives."

"Deductive reasoning," Ben said, shaking the man's hand.

Ushering them into his office, Babcock perched himself on the corner of his desk. An impressive feat, Ben thought, considering the amount of clutter covering the surface. The desk matched the rest of the office. Ben couldn't see a single bit of the wall for all the framed front pages and photos of Babcock shaking hands with various individuals. Some he recognized as local officials, others he could only guess at their identity. The editor also had a number of what looked like antique maps hanging on the wall behind his desk. There didn't appear to be an order to any of it.

"What is it I can help you with, detectives?" Babcock asked, cleaning his glasses with a handkerchief from his pocket.

Ben explained the reason for their visit. He hoped he didn't sound as frustrated as he was, having to now repeat himself once again. When he was finished, the editor tilted his head, a questioning look on his face.

"Is this in some way related to the shootings the department is investigating? Naturally, I have to ask."

Ben knew they needed to be careful with what they said. Especially since they were talking to a newspaperman. He should have begun by saying their visit was off the record, but since they hadn't told Babcock any more than they needed to look at old editions of the paper, no damage had been done.

"We can't say at this time. We're just hoping to do some research. And the *Herald-Dispatch* is Parker's newspaper of record so we couldn't think of a better place to come," Ben said, hoping that would satisfy the editor for the time begin.

As Babcock crossed his arms over his chest, Ben realized the man had a great poker face. He had no idea what he was thinking.

"You say you want to look at the papers from 1959? Well, that was before the *Herald* bought the *Chronicle Dispatch*. So, we don't have any of their archives. It was a messy takeover, between you and me. But you're welcome to take a look at what ran as the *Blue Ridge Herald*. If you need to see something from the old *Dispatch*, I think the library has their old editions."

Ben was extremely happy that Babcock was turning out to be more helpful than he expected. Leading the detectives down to the second floor and along a hallway that ran the length of the building, the newspaper's editor showed them into a room full of file cabinets and two microfiche readers.

Before leaving Ben and Tommy to their work, Babcock pulled the film cards for the papers from the time period from which they were interested, summer of 1959.

"If you need any later papers, they're all filed chronologically in these cabinets, starting here and going around the room in order," Babcock said before heading back to his office.

Pleased at how easy it was to gain access to the paper's archives, the detectives got to work.

One of the few pieces of information the case file contained was the last date anyone had seen Officer Bert Ramsburg alive. Ben decided to start with the edition of the paper from a few days after that.

Sliding the card with all of the miniaturized film pages onto the reader panel, a projected image appeared on the screen. Ben quickly scanned the headlines with Tommy standing over his shoulder. Three days after Ramsburg was last seen, there was nothing in the paper.

Tommy handed Ben the card for the next day's paper. Four days after he was last seen, still nothing. It wasn't until over a week later that a piece appeared in the paper reporting a member of the Parker City Police Department was missing. It was the top story, above the fold. And in it, it said Billy Roscoe, the "popular restaurateur and hotel owner," was being considered a suspect in the disappearance.

A few days later, another article ran stating that a witness, who they did not identify, saw the officer leaving the ParkMar Hotel on the evening he was believed to have disappeared. His patrol car had been returned to the station and signed in. After that, there was no evidence as to what happened to him. All of this was according to Hank McMaster, the officer investigating the disappearance.

Ben's eye froze on the name.

Hank McMaster was the one heading the investigation into the missing officer? That was certainly interesting.

It couldn't have been a coincidence that the day after they believe the missing officer's skeleton was uncovered, McMaster was shot to death. It could be the link they'd been looking for to tie the murders together. At least two of them. But what did Officers Noffsinger and Vernon have to do with it?

SIXTY

THE REVELATION THAT Hank McMaster was the officer in charge of the investigation into the disappearance of Bert Ramsburg twenty-five years earlier opened up an entirely new line of thinking. Assuming the skeleton unearthed at the warehouse *was* in fact Ramsburg, that connected the missing officer case from decades ago to the recent police shootings. Could it simply be happenstance? No. Because Ben didn't believe in happenstance, coincidence, or anything like that when it came to an investigation.

Spending a couple of hours at the *Herald-Dispatch* going through old editions of the paper, Ben and Tommy looked for every piece of information that had been reported back in '59. Though there wasn't much on the public record, there was a hell of a lot more than what was currently in the case file back at the station.

Both of the detectives knew Lieutenant McMaster had not exactly been a hands-on commanding officer during his time leading the department's Field Services Division. But that was after years on the force and rising through the ranks under a chief who placed more importance on loyalty and doing what needed to be done with as little effort as possible, than on regulations and doing what needed to be done *in the right way*. Regardless of all that, thirty years ago, there was no way Mc-

Master could have led such a slapdash investigation and gotten away with it. Especially if the state's attorney was involved. With only a few pieces of paper in the Ramsburg case file, Ben knew something wasn't right.

The final article Ben could find about the disappearance did a decent job of recapping the case but in the end, declared that the investigation had "stalled" according to McMaster. Making sure he'd written down all the pertinent pieces of information, Ben replaced the microfiche card back in the appropriate cabinet.

Looking over at his partner, who had fired up the second microfiche reader a short time ago, Ben wondered what he'd discovered that was keeping him so quiet. From over Tommy's shoulder, Ben saw a picture of what looked like a grand opening celebration. A line of men stood behind a ribbon stretched across the front of a building. There were too many in the group to see the front and tell what it was, however. In the center, stood a ruggedly handsome man in a perfectly tailored suit with a pair of scissors. Not a pair of the oversized ones people used to open businesses now, but a normal-sized pair that he could have picked up off a desk.

"What are you looking at?" Ben asked.

Pointing to the caption under the photo, Tommy replied, "I was curious to see this Billy Roscoe character. From some of the items we read, it sounds like he could have been Parker City's answer to Al Capone. So, I started pulling up papers and found this one. It's the opening of his restaurant, the Derby Room."

Ben scanned the crowd in the photo for anyone he knew. He recognized the city's former mayor standing

next to Roscoe. But other than that, these were all people from the past. From when he was just a little kid.

"You know what else is interesting?" Tommy said,
reading the article accompanying the photograph. "The
Derby Room was on the first floor of the ParkMar
Hotel—Roscoe's hotel where he had his secret gambling
establishment for all those years. Look at the address."

Squinting to read the blurry print being projected on
the screen, without realizing it, Ben said, "You've got
to be kidding me?"

The address of the building instantly clicked in his
head.

"I never thought I would ever say it, but I wish Chief
Stanley were still alive. He would have known all of
this," Tommy said leaning back in his chair. "We're just
too young to remember any of it."

The old ParkMar Hotel, home of the Derby Restaurant, was the building that now sat vacant and boarded
up, sharing the back alley with the Ramshackle Bar.

Ben felt as though more puzzle pieces were beginning to fall into place. And all those pieces that were
coming together were starting to point in the direction of the infamous Billy Roscoe. With everything
the detectives had learned so far, whether directly or
indirectly, Roscoe could be linked to three of the four
murder victims.

"We need to find Billy Roscoe," Ben said, adjusting
the card in the reader so he could see the photo again.
"Who are these two guys?"

"One of them," Tommy read, "is 'Fredrick Quinn,
an *associate* and head of hotel security.' And the other
is 'Martin A. Schulman, Mr. Roscoe's attorney.'"

"Schulman?" Ben mumbled, the name ringing a bell in the back of his mind. "Schulman."

Flipping through the pages in his notebook, Ben stopped at the notes he'd written down about the warehouse. Tracing his finger down the page, he stopped when he came to the details about the trust which had owned the building until the city seized the property. The B.R. Trust, which he guessed stood for *Billy Roscoe*, had been set up and administered by Martin A. Schulman, Esquire.

SIXTY-ONE

BILLY ROSCOE WAS looking more and more like their prime suspect with each new piece of information they learned. They didn't have a case yet. There was certainly no hard evidence. But they had a theory. And that was enough to get them started.

Back in the '50s, Roscoe was one of the most popular figures in Parker City. He was a businessman with the Midas Touch by all accounts. What people didn't know was that his most successful enterprises were illegal. Somehow, Bert Ramsburg got on to him and was conducting his own investigation into the fashionable restaurateur. Whether he found evidence that could put Roscoe away or not, he clearly got too close. So what did Billy Roscoe do? Like so many crime bosses before him, he made Ramsburg disappear. To make sure the body was never discovered, it was buried under the warehouse that housed Billy's smuggling business, though it was supposedly just a shipping and freight company.

That was the first part of Ben's theory. It laid the foundation for what was to happen decades later.

With the redevelopment of the Warehouse District, it was only a matter of time before Ramsburg's skeleton was discovered. Someone would put the pieces together after all these years and Roscoe would be on the hook for the murder. A crime with no statute of limitations, meaning he could still go to prison.

Back in the day, Hank McMaster, then just a patrol officer, was the one looking into his colleague's disappearance. Ben could only guess, but he must have found something at the time that would have incriminated Billy. As hard as it was for Ben to accept an officer of the law could be bought off, he had to assume that's what happened in this case. Roscoe got to McMaster and got him to throw the investigation.

With the discovery of the skeleton, however, the pressure would be on once again and Roscoe needed to clean up his loose ends. He couldn't take the chance of McMaster talking. That would explain why he was killed. If he knew something about the murder, now that there were actual remains, he would be a liability. Billy couldn't afford that.

"But that doesn't explain why Noffsinger or Vernon were shot," Chief Brent pointed out after Ben had explained his theory. "And you're taking a giant leap saying McMaster helped cover up the disappearance of a fellow officer. You said it yourself, Ben. You don't have any proof."

"We might have circumstantial evidence to that effect," Tommy said, walking into the chief's office holding a stack of papers in the air.

"What do you have?" Brent asked, a stern look on his face.

"It occurred to me," Tommy began, "after the lieutenant was shot, no one ever went through his office. We asked Kramer and Woods to look through Noffsinger and Vernon's desks to see if anything jumped out at them. But we never went through McMaster's. We were too focused on looking at a connection to drugs."

With a slight flourish, Tommy laid the papers he was carrying on Brent's desk. "I found these tucked in the bottom drawer under a bunch of magazines. It's the rest of the Ramsburg case file. There was no way the few handwritten notes we found in the file were all that an investigation into a missing police officer would have produced. A missing officer is going to generate paperwork. Ben keeps telling me how important paperwork is."

"And here I was thinking you never paid attention," Ben said.

"The point is…the lieutenant cleaned out the file because there are things in here he didn't want us to see."

"And what would these things be that he didn't want us to see?" the chief asked, beginning to look through the papers.

Tommy looked to Ben, then back to Brent, a weak smile on his face. "I'm not sure yet. Maybe just the fact *he* was the one looking into Ramsburg's disappearance. His name's all over these documents. It wasn't on any of the notes in the file."

The chief exhaled then leaned forward putting his elbows on the desk and clasping his hands together. Looking from one detective to the other, he agreed that it was a decent theory, if slightly far-fetched. But it was thin at best. The *only* thing they had that could lend credence to the notion of McMaster somehow being involved or caught up in Roscoe's machinations was that he'd apparently emptied the case file. But they didn't even have confirmation that the skeleton they'd found was *actually* Bert Ramsburg.

"Let's assume," Brent finally said, "everything you're saying is true. Why do I know nothing about this Billy Roscoe character? *If* he's such a vicious, hardened criminal, why haven't I ever heard of him until today?"

Both Ben and Tommy had grown up in Parker County but neither of them remembered anything about Billy Roscoe. They were just little children back when he was making waves in the '50s. And Nick Brent had only lived in Parker for the last seven years, having been recruited to the PCPD from Buffalo to fill the open captain's position. It stood to reason why none of them would know anything about Roscoe's history in the city.

But if he was still around Parker and worried about Ramsburg's remains being discovered, where *exactly* was he? And if no one knew where he was, why would he be worried about getting caught at all?

Ben was willing to admit, there were still a lot of questions that needed answers. Even though a few things were starting to make sense, the whole picture was still very fuzzy. He just knew they were on the right track.

"How exactly did you get turned on to this whole thing about Bert Ramsburg and Billy Roscoe anyway?" Brent asked.

"It was because of a conversation I had with Buck LuCoco," Ben admitted, somewhat sheepishly. "For all his faults…"

"And he has many," Tommy interjected.

"…he knows his history."

"Does he have any idea where we can find Roscoe?" the chief asked, crossing his arms and leaning back in his chair.

"I don't know. He's off today and there's no answer at his house. But I have Betty down in Records pulling anything she has on Roscoe and his associates, and Al Shepard was going to make some inquiries for me over at the courthouse."

Trying not to sound like he was patronizing his lead detective, Brent asked, "I'm assuming you already checked the phone book?"

"Yes. There are no Billy, William, B. or W. Roscoes listed. If neither Betty nor Al can come up with anything, I'll check with the state police and see if they have any information on his whereabouts."

The intercom on Brent's desk buzzed, immediately followed by the raspy voice of Mildred Greene. "Chief Brent, Sergeant Shepard is on the phone. He's looking for Detective Winters. Should I put him through?"

"Go ahead," the chief instructed.

Brent answered, then handed the phone to Ben.

As Ben listened to what Shepard was telling him, both Tommy and the chief watched as the expression of eager anticipation on his face was replaced with disbelief, then defeat. Replacing the receiver, Ben stared at the phone for a moment.

"I'm guessing that wasn't good news," Tommy said.

"No, it wasn't," Ben replied. "Al just spoke with Betty. Billy Roscoe and his driver, Freddy Quinn, were killed in a car accident in January of 1960. The same day the federal agents from the Treasury Department raided his hotel. Billy Roscoe's dead."

SIXTY-TWO

"I DON'T UNDERSTAND. I thought we had it," Ben said, the exasperation he was feeling evident in the way he slammed his fist—knuckles first—down on his desk. Shaking off the sting running through his fingers, Ben turned to the crime board where all the information they'd gathered on the murders created nothing more than a web of confusion.

First, they thought the shootings had something to do with the department's Drug Task Force. But then, because they thought they could connect Hank McMaster to the mystery skeleton, the theory shifted to a conspiracy begun over two decades earlier. Then they find out their number one suspect behind said conspiracy has been dead for twenty-four years and couldn't have committed any of the recent murders.

To try and lighten the mood, knowing the attempt could backfire, Tommy asked, "I don't suppose you'd be interested in hearing a theory involving the supernatural and Billy Roscoe coming back as a ghost?"

Ben slowly turned and looked at his partner from under a furrowed brow.

In response, Tommy simply offered his trademark grin.

"Okay. What if—?" Ben began before he was interrupted by the telephone. It was probably for the best, he thought. He wasn't entirely sure what he was about to say. Snatching up the receiver, he answered, then listened for a moment before scribbling an address on a piece of paper.

"We've got a body," he said to Tommy as he hung up the phone.

"Another cop?" Tommy asked nervously.

"Not this time," Ben said grabbing his jacket. "A woman over on the other side of town."

"What is happening to this place?" Tommy asked following him out into the hall. "It used to be so quiet. You don't think it's us, do you?"

"What do you mean by that?"

"Since we've become detectives there's been a marked increase in murders," Tommy pointed out, only half-joking. "I'm not saying there's any correlation, but someone might put two and two together and get the wrong idea."

"Sometimes it scares me, the way you think."

"It could be like that Mrs. Marbles character. She's a little old lady and people are always getting killed around her. Or…is it *because* she's around that people get killed?"

"What the hell are you talking about? First of all, I can only assume you mean *Miss Marple*. And second, and this may be the most important part, she's a fictional character! You're doing this just to make me crazy, aren't you?"

"A little bit," Tommy admitted with a smirk. "I'll drive."

SIXTY-THREE

Two PATROL CARS sat in front of a small, white ranch-style house in one of the quieter sections of the city. It was a decent working-class neighborhood where the residents clearly took pride in their homes. A small crowd of whom were gathered across the street, curious as to what had brought a police presence to their sleepy cul-de-sac.

Thankfully the rain had stopped, Ben thought as he stepped out of the car and adjusted the badge clipped to his belt. He took a moment to put the remaining thoughts of the skeleton/police shooting investigation out of his mind. This was a new case that deserved just as much attention.

Taking in his surroundings, the street reminded Ben of the one on which he'd grown up and his parents still lived. It was a pleasant neighborhood. Small, neat houses, all with well-kept lawns and flower gardens. He was sure the last thing any of them expected when they woke up that morning was a parade of police officers marching into one of their neighbor's homes.

Walking up the short driveway, the detectives were met by Officer Neil Thompson. A younger officer, Ben was impressed with the professionalism and work ethic he'd demonstrated in his time with the PCPD. If ever there was a chance to increase the ranks of the department's Detective Squad, Thompson was a top candidate to fill the spot.

"What do you have for us?" Ben asked.

"A dead female inside," Thompson said, looking over his shoulder. "The next-door neighbor had been calling the deceased since yesterday but was getting no answer. Her car was in the driveway and she hadn't said she was going away. So, just about thirty minutes ago, the neighbor... Mrs. Freda Reed...came over. No answer when she knocked at the front door so she went around back. Looked in through the kitchen door and saw a body. Ran back home and called us. Dunkin arrived on the scene about two minutes before I did."

Looking toward the house, Ben saw Officer Stan Dunkin standing on the front porch with an older woman in a dated housecoat. The detective assumed that was the neighbor, Freda Reed.

"Before forcing our way in the front," Thompson continued, "I checked the back door. It was unlocked. We were able to walk right in."

Impressive, Ben thought. He could tell by the look on Tommy's face, his partner was thinking the same thing. Most young officers would have just broken down the door in all the excitement to get inside. Thompson used his head and helped to preserve even more of the scene.

"I went in to check on the deceased. Well, I didn't know she was deceased at the time. But when I saw the blood and felt for a pulse...once I determined she was D.O.A., I backed out without touching anything else and called in for you guys."

"Nicely done, Thompson," Tommy said slapping the officer on the back. Then turning to Ben, said, "I'll take a look at the body if you want to call the coroner and talk to the next-door neighbor?"

Escorting Tommy around to the back door, Thompson stood outside as the detective stepped into the kitchen. Sure enough, a woman lay face down on the linoleum floor in a pool of blood. Not able to see her face, he couldn't tell her age. However, judging by her round, football helmet-style hairdo, he would guess she was "older." The brightly colored jogging suit with random geometric patterns gave Tommy a headache.

After a cursory examination, Tommy noticed some of the blood was already dry. More telling though was the skin. It had already begun to change color. Doing the math in his head, taking into account the neighbor hadn't been able to reach the deceased for at least a day and a half now, Tommy figured she must have been dead for close to two days or more. He couldn't figure out why the kitchen didn't smell worse if she'd been dead that long.

His natural instinct was to turn the body over to see what had created the blood pool but knew he couldn't move her. They'd have to wait for the medical examiner. Tommy hated having to wait that long. At this time of day, he thought looking at his watch, coming from Baltimore, who knew how long it would take for them to arrive?

Looking around the kitchen, there was an open soda can sitting on the counter and a couple of plates in the sink. The place was very tidy. Nothing appeared out of place and there didn't seem to have been any sort of struggle. It was possible the woman tripped, fell, and hit her head. Head wounds bled terribly. But the blood pool was nowhere near her head. Maybe she fell on a knife?

Hearing a noise behind him, Tommy turned to see Ben standing in the doorway.

"M.E.'s on the way," he said. "They'll get here… when they get here. Thoughts on the cause of death?"

"Until we can turn her over, I can't say. I don't *see* anything but there's a lot of blood. I haven't had a chance to walk through the house either. But everything looks in order here in the kitchen."

"Maybe we'll find out this was an accident then," Ben said, kneeling down to take a look at the body for himself.

"Did you get her name?" Tommy asked as he looked out into the living room.

"Yeah. Iris McKecknie. Age sixty-four or sixty-five. Her friend couldn't remember exactly. She was a widow. Lived alone. She was going to…" Ben stop mid-sentence when he looked up and saw Tommy's face. "What's wrong? What did you find?"

"What was her name?" Tommy asked again.

"Iris McKecknie," Ben answered, standing up and pulling out his notebook to make sure he'd gotten the name correct. "Yeah. Iris McKecknie. Why?"

Tommy was pale and Ben saw his hands were clenched into fists.

"Tommy, what's wrong?"

"That's not a very common name, is it?"

Ben thought for a moment. "Not really. I don't know anyone with the name 'Iris' or 'McKecknie.'"

"I didn't know anyone with that name until today."

Ben cocked his head. "What are you talking about?"

"Ben, we need to step outside and get the troopers from CSU over here right now."

"Who is Iris McKecknie?" Ben asked.

Looking down at the body lying on the floor, Tommy said, "Iris McKecknie is the witness who saw Bert Ramsburg leave the ParkMar Hotel the night he supposedly disappeared. I read her statement in the papers I found in McMaster's desk."

SIXTY-FOUR

THE LAST THING the assistant medical examiner said to the detectives as his team loaded Iris McKecknie's body into the back of the van was, "If you keep this up, we're going to have to open an office out here in Parker. I'm getting tired of driving out here from Baltimore every day."

"The drive's not that far," Tommy shot back, his own frustration at the number of times in the last week they'd *needed* to call the coroner rising to the surface.

There was now no possible way either Ben or Tommy could think the disappearance of Bert Ramsburg back in 1959 wasn't in some way connected with the recent shootings. The odds of another person who'd been involved with the investigation twenty-five years earlier turning up dead within days of discovering what they believed were the remains of the missing policeman were staggering.

Iris McKecknie hadn't just died. She was murdered. That fact was made painfully clear when the medical examiner turned the body over and discovered a single GSW to the chest. One of the state trooper forensic technicians found the spent shell casing under the oven, suggesting after it was ejected from the gun, that's where it rolled. Examining the casing through the plastic evidence bag, Ben knew it was going to match the others that had been recovered from the recent crime scenes.

"If it's not Billy Roscoe behind all of this, who is it?" Tommy asked, exhaling a cloud of smoke then dropping the cigarette butt and crushing it with the toe of his shoe. He and Ben were leaning against their cruiser watching as the state's Crime Scene Unit packed up its equipment to head back to the barracks.

Ben let the question hang in the air as he ran through the possibilities in his head.

He finally said, "Someone who would have something to lose if Ramsburg was found."

"Billy Roscoe," Tommy said, lighting another cigarette. "You sure you don't want one? It might help clear your head."

It was a habit he had. Before lighting up, Tommy would always offer Ben a cigarette. He'd never take one, as he'd never smoked a day in his life. But he always appreciated the offer.

"You don't think there's a chance Roscoe's still alive, do you?" Tommy asked.

Ben thought about that for a moment. Then asked, "If he *was* still alive, but no one knew it, why would he care if we found Ramsburg? Everyone thinks he's dead. No one would be going after him."

"Good point," Tommy said, handing the car keys to his partner. "You get to drive back to the station."

The pair continued to toss around possible suspects as they wound their way back to the PCPD. Though they could agree on the killer's motives, they had no idea who it could be. Billy Roscoe would have been the one with the most to lose if Ramsburg's remains were found. But he was dead. Which was a pretty good reason for him not to care anymore if anyone unearthed the skeleton. There had to be someone else. Someone with just as much on the line, who had just as much to lose if the Ramsburg case was reopened. But neither Ben nor Tommy knew who that was. It didn't seem like anyone was left from the Billy Roscoe heydays of Parker City.

"Except one person," Ben said as the two detectives walked down the hall to their office. "Well, maybe. The lawyer. He was in the picture. And he's the one that set up the trust that bought the warehouse…after the accident that killed Roscoe."

Talking through it, Ben understood the timeline now. Or, at least, he thought he did. Even with Roscoe dead, if his lawyer knew that the missing officer was buried under the warehouse, he wouldn't want anyone else getting their hands on the building. There were still people who could have been arrested back then, including himself. He needed to continue the cover-up.

"Do we know the lawyer is still alive?" Tommy asked, dropping into the chair behind his desk.

"No," Ben said, then handed Tommy his notebook turned to the page where he'd written the attorney's name. "Look in the phone book. See if we get lucky."

As Tommy pulled the phone book from the bottom drawer, Ben picked up the file that had been left on his desk. It was the accident report filed the day Roscoe and his driver, Freddy Quinn, were killed. Scanning the document, he saw that there had been two fatalities in Roscoe's vehicle, as well as the driver of the other car. According to the report, the accident was probably caused by bad road conditions—a heavy wintery mix falling that day. Then Ben read the name of the officer who filed the report. Hank McMaster.

"Maybe Billy Roscoe is still alive," he said under his breath.

"What was that?" Tommy asked.

Ben summarized the accident report and pointed out McMaster was the officer on the scene. If he was on Roscoe's payroll, he could have falsified the report. If the Feds were out to get Roscoe, this would have been the perfect way for him to get away and start a new life.

"But like you said," Tommy pointed out, "with everyone thinking he was dead, why would he be worried about us finding the skeleton? If he wasn't killed in the accident, does it make any sense that he would have stuck around Parker? If it were me, I'd have been outta here and started a new life where no one could find me like L.A. or… Mexico City."

"I have no idea," Ben admitted. "If he stuck around, people would have recognized him. He'd have to have moved on. Maybe with the help of McMaster and his lawyer. Did you find Schulman in the phone book?"

"Believe it or not, I think I did. There's a 'Schulman' comma 'Martin A.' over on Briarwood."

"Briarwood? That's a nice area. Some big houses over there."

"Just the kind of place where a mob lawyer might live," Tommy said, copying the address onto a scrap of paper.

SIXTY-FIVE

JUST AFTER NINE o'clock the next morning, Ben met Tommy in front of 1616 Briarwood Way. A rich, red-brick Georgian Revival mansion with stark white carved trim and columned portico, Ben counted four separate chimneys rising out of the roof from each of the house's corners. Like its neighbors, Schulman's home was surrounded by a large, immaculately manicured lawn and well-tended flower bushes.

Only a few miles from the desolate, deteriorating buildings in Downtown, Ben was once again struck by the juxtaposition he often found throughout the city. A street like Briarwood, where affluence was evident and put on full display, sat in bold contrast to the parts of Parker which had never recovered after the Great Flood.

"I could live in a house like this," Tommy said, getting out of his Bronco and straightening his tie.

"You could? You going to clean all those windows?" Ben asked.

"No. That's what I'd have a…"

"Don't say wife," Ben interrupted.

"…*maid* for. Mr. Smarty-pants," Tommy finished, then stuck his tongue out in child-like defiance. "It's this lawn I'd be more concerned about."

"What? You wouldn't have a gardener too? I think we can both agree, neither of us will ever live in a house this big. Now, can we get to work and go talk to Schulman, please?"

"Of course. Besides, I want to see if the floors inside are hardwood or marble," Tommy said with a smile. "I bet they're marble."

At the front door, Tommy rang the bell, then took one last look across the front yard as they waited for someone to answer. He knew Ben was right when he said neither of them would ever have a house like this, but that didn't mean he couldn't admire its splendor.

After a few moments, the front door opened and a stout woman in a gray maid's uniform stood before them. Hands tightly clasped in front of her, the expression on her face told the detectives she wasn't expecting visitors this morning and their arrival had most likely interrupted her cleaning schedule.

"May I help you?" she asked in a crisp, almost militaristic tone.

"Good morning. I'm Detective Sergeant Ben Winters with the PCPD. This is my partner Detective Mason. We were wondering if we might have a word with Mr. Schulman?"

Ben saw no immediate response. More often than not, when the police show up at the front door, the person answering becomes flustered, even inquisitive. Especially when they aren't expecting a detective to be standing on their doorstep. But the maid registered no reaction whatsoever. Her dark eyes looked them over from top to bottom before she asked them in.

"If you will wait here, I will see if Mr. Schulman is available. In the future, if you need to speak with him,

I would suggest calling ahead...or at least not showing up so early in the morning."

Ben and Tommy watched as she turned, marched down the hall, and disappeared out of sight.

"She told you," Tommy said.

"Yeah, well. You lose the bet. The floors are hardwood, not marble."

"So they are." Tommy had now become distracted by the magnificent flooring with its intricate inlaid decorative trim. "That maid might not have the best personality, but boy can she get these floors to shine."

"Please focus on why we're here."

"I'm just admiring the..."

"Mr. Schulman will see you," the maid said, reappearing through a door behind Tommy. Not expecting her to rematerialize where she had, he flinched. Ben stifled a laugh.

"This way please," she said leading the detectives into the room from which she'd just entered. "If you'll have a seat here, Mr. Schulman will be in momentarily. He's just finishing his breakfast."

"That's alright, we wouldn't like any coffee or anything," Tommy said after the maid had closed the door behind her. "I don't think she likes you, Ben."

Taking a seat in a large club chair next to the fireplace, Ben noticed a copy of *The Thin Man* sitting on the side table next to him. A fan of classic mystery novels, Ben flipped open the book and turned a few pages, stopping when he realized it was an original first edition of the Dashiell Hammett work. Signed by the author himself!

"I have first editions of all four Nick and Nora novels. And *The Maltese Falcon*," Marty Schulman said, standing in the doorway. "Gifts from a former client who enjoyed collectibles."

"It's in excellent condition," Ben said, carefully replacing the book on the table. Standing, he then introduced himself and Tommy as the lawyer slowly made his way into the room. A cane helping to steady his shaky frame.

In his mid-eighties, though Schulman's body was frail, his eyes were still sharp and alert. He took in every detail of the two police detectives standing in his sitting-room before Ben was able to get his name out. He might have looked fragile, but Ben sensed he could still be a force to be reckoned with.

"Please, detectives. Have a seat," the aging attorney said as he carefully lowered himself onto the sofa opposite the club chair Ben had found so comfortable. "I was wondering how long it would be before you came to speak with me."

"You were expecting us?" Tommy asked, raising an eyebrow.

"Of course I was. It was only a matter of time."

"Then you know why we're here?" Ben asked.

Marty smiled and leaned back into the deep cushions of the sofa. He was shrewd. He wasn't going to be the one to lead the conversation.

"Mr. Schulman, are you the Martin Schulman who was the attorney for William Roscoe?" Ben asked, taking out his notebook.

"Yes. I was Billy's attorney. But that was many years ago."

"But that's why you knew we would be coming to see you," Tommy said.

"Detectives, I am an old man. I would rather not waste time beating about the bush, as they say."

"Mr. Schulman, why do you think…"

"Please, call me Marty."

Ben wasn't sure if *Marty* had specifically waited to interrupt him, or if it was just a force of habit. Not allowing the detective to find his footing and fall into a rhythm. How many times had he used that tactic before? In court? During an interrogation?

"Marty, why is it you think we're here?"

"I can only imagine it is because of the skeleton you discovered under the old warehouse on Antietam. By now, if you are even a half-decent detective, you would have heard some stories and found out that at one point, I was the administrator of a trust that owned the property."

"Exactly what stories are you referring to?" Ben asked, as innocently as possible.

Schulman smiled and shook his head. "Detective, do we really need to play these games?"

"Fine," Tommy said. "Is Billy Roscoe still alive?"

The smug look on Schulman's face disappeared, replaced by one of sheer amusement.

"You think Billy staged his own death?" the attorney managed to say before breaking out into a hearty laugh. "Oh, my dear boy. Maybe you've read too many of those old mysteries."

"I'm not a big reader, Mr. Schulman," Tommy answered. "But I do know some mobsters have used the trick before."

Schulman laughed even harder this time.

Catching his breath, he said, "You think Billy was a

mobster? I can only imagine his reaction if he heard you say that. Billy was a *businessman*. Plain and simple."

"Whose businesses were mostly illegal from what we gather," Tommy offered.

"His businesses might have been unlawful, but they were victimless crimes. Billy was no comic book *gangster*. I was no *mob* lawyer. Billy never hurt anyone."

"What about Bert Ramsburg?" Ben asked. "It is his skeleton we found buried under the warehouse, isn't it?"

"Detective Winters," Schulman began, his voice was calm and haunting, "at this point, I think you know very well those are Bert Ramsburg's remains."

It wasn't lost on either Ben or Tommy how he'd phrased his answer. He'd confirmed the skeleton belonged to the missing police officer but did it in a way he could technically still deny admitting to knowing anything about the crime. Martin A. Schulman, Esquire might be a frail old man but he still had the mind of a wickedly sharp attorney.

Matching Schulman's tone, Ben said, "I'm not going to insult your intelligence or waste your time. I'm going to lay out everything we know for you.

"Those bones being discovered upset someone. They were never meant to be found. That's why you bought the warehouse all those years ago, to keep anyone from doing something like tear the place down. Everyone needed to think Bert Ramsburg just up and left Parker City. No body, no crime. Right?

"Which is why Hank McMaster did everything in his power back in 1959 to make it look like that's exactly what Ramsburg did. He even managed to get the state's attorney to believe Roscoe had nothing to do with it.

"As long as those bones stayed buried, everything was fine. But then the city condemns the property, taking it away from you. They turn around and sell it and work on the new Parker Plaza begins. Jump to earlier this week when a worker on the construction site falls through a weak spot in the floor and finds the skeleton.

"Something like that was bound to be reported in the newspaper. And people were going to start asking questions. Specifically, who did the skeleton belong to? Which meant anyone who knew about the mysterious remains and where they'd been all this time could cause a great deal of trouble if they talked.

"Which is exactly why we believe Hank McMaster was killed. He was the police officer who helped to cover up Bert Ramsburg's murder twenty-five years ago. He was the one person in the PCPD who knew exactly whose bones those were. And who put them there.

"It could have been a coincidence, admittedly. But let's be honest, what are the odds of that?" Ben paused, allowing everything he'd said to linger for a moment.

"I won't lie, detective," Marty said, tapping his index finger against his lips. "That is a story worthy of a Hammett novel. But, if I've been keeping up with local events, I believe *three* police officers have been killed. I'm sorry, I don't remember all of their names, but how were they involved?"

"That's a very good question," Ben answered honestly. "We now believe the murders of Officers Noffsinger and Vernon did have a purpose. To throw us off. To distract us from figuring out who the real target was. Hank McMaster."

"A little convoluted, don't you think?" the attorney

asked, stretching his arms out over the back of the sofa. "I don't think any of this will hold up in court. Unless you have some sort of evidence."

Ben smiled. "*Marty*, if crime made sense, you and I would both be out of business."

Schulman reacted with a genuine laugh.

"You're right though," Ben continued. "Right now, what we have could be considered circumstantial. But that's what's going to lead us to the hard evidence."

"See, there's been another murder that wipes away all doubt in our minds that this is all about covering up Bert Ramsburg's murder all those years ago."

With a furrowed brow, Schulman asked, sincerely curious, "Another murder?"

"Yes. It hasn't made it into the newspapers yet. Iris McKecknie was murdered. We found her body yesterday."

"Am I supposed to know who Iris McKecknie is?"

"She was the witness who worked at the ParkMar Hotel that *allegedly* told then-Officer Hank McMaster she saw Bert Ramsburg *leave* the hotel the night he *allegedly* disappeared."

Marty Schulman's jaw tensed ever so slightly.

Tommy, who'd been sitting quietly listening to his partner lay out their case, took over. "Someone is trying to tie up all the possible loose ends. Convoluted, as you say. But it all makes sense. And it occurs to me, counselor, you never answered my question. Is Billy Roscoe still alive? Because, if Hank McMaster helped him cover up the murder of a fellow officer, falsifying an accident report wouldn't be that difficult."

"Detectives, Billy Roscoe was killed in a car accident along with that Neanderthal knee-breaker of his, Freddy Quinn, the same day the hotel was raided. I will swear to that on the lives of my grandchildren. Billy Roscoe is dead.

"I'll tell you something else," Schulman continued, leaning forward. "Billy didn't kill Ramsburg. In fact, he never knew what happened to him. He knew nothing about it."

"We're supposed to believe that?" Tommy asked with a scoff.

"Believe what you want, Detective Mason. It's the truth. But your theory about someone trying to tie up loose ends is probably correct."

"If it wasn't Billy that killed Ramsburg and is now trying to cover his tracks, then who is it?" Ben asked.

The lawyer smiled. Then said, "The man who *actually* killed Bert Ramsburg. Billy's *silent partner.*"

SIXTY-SIX

STANDING IN FRONT of the sprawling estate, Ben recalled the first time he'd seen the enormous—and according to many old-timers in Parker City, "garish"—Art Deco mansion. It was during the Spring Strangler investigation when he and Tommy, against Chief Stanley's wishes, found the need to interview a potential suspect, who happened to be one of the most prominent men in the city and the patriarch of one of Parker's founding families. Ben never in a million years would have believed he'd be standing at the same door, three years later.

Things were different this time. Chief Brent was not afraid, nor part, of the old guard. Therefore, he told Ben if they had reason to believe they found the identity of Bert Ramsburg's killer, and the man responsible for the recent murders of three more PCPD officers, as well as Iris McKecknie, it didn't matter what his last name was. Brent promised to be the one to break the news to the mayor, taking that pressure off Ben as well.

Ben's unmarked cruiser sat in the roundabout in front of the house next to a cherry red Mercedes roadster and a brand new Jaguar. Behind them, three patrol cars blocked the driveway. Ben hoped this arrest would go smoothly and the handful of uniforms he'd brought with him, along with Tommy, was all that would be needed. Though, there had been a number of others who'd volunteered to join the team once they'd learned the detectives knew who was behind the shooting of their fellow officers. Even the chief said he would be joining them once he'd spoken with Mayor Oland.

The detectives had been surprised at how willing Marty Schulman had been to offer up the name of Billy Roscoe's partner after the verbal duel he'd tried to put Ben through. Even more surprised when he said he would testify with regard to his knowledge of what really happened to Bert Ramsburg. Long retired, and having no direct involvement with the '59 murder itself, the attorney knew there wasn't much the judicial system could, or would, do to an eighty-seven-year-old man.

Obtaining both a search warrant and an arrest warrant proved to be rather simple. Having to file the necessary paperwork and make sure all of their ducks were in a row, Ben and Tommy were concerned with getting a judge to issue the warrants. But Judge August Lewis—a recent appointment to the bench by Governor Hughes—who had no connection whatsoever to the former power structure of Parker, had no reservation signing the orders.

With an arrest warrant in hand, Ben rang the doorbell.

Next to him, Tommy stood, shifting his weight from foot to foot, anxiously awaiting the door to be answered.

"Can you imagine if Chief Stanley were still alive?" Tommy asked. "The last time, we just wanted to *talk* to the guy and he almost had a stroke. Now we're actually here to arrest him."

Before Ben could respond, the front door was answered by a gentleman wearing a suit that cost close to his full year's salary. His salt and pepper hair was combed to the side in a classic conservative style, just as Ben remembered. However, even though it had only been three years since the last time they'd spoken, the man looked much older. Even with all the trappings of luxury, he was beginning to show signs of his age.

"Detectives? What are you doing here?" Howard Worthington asked, the genial smile on his face slowly fading.

SIXTY-SEVEN

BEN AND TOMMY were surprised at how quickly Howard
Worthington crumbled. They'd hardly begun questioning him before he broke down and confessed to shooting Bert Ramsburg, claiming the whole thing was an
accident. Ben found it interesting that even after having been read his rights, Worthington was so willing
to admit to what had happened. But he was adamant
that he had never intended on killing the officer. There
was something about the way he phrased his confession that didn't sit right with Ben, but this whole case
seemed so far-fetched, what was one more odd detail?

Since Worthington wasn't known as anything other
than a friendly, charming, and charitable guy, it was
very possible he was telling the truth. Lending more
credence to the validity of his statement was his confirmation of everything Marty Schulman had said. He
used his family's money—without his father's knowledge—to invest in Billy Roscoe's hotel and gambling
operation. With that money and his inheritance at the
passing of his father, he'd founded South Mountain
Bank & Trust, one of the most respected and influential financial institutions in Western Maryland.

He swore that shooting Ramsburg had been a wake-
up call for him. He said he knew the minute the gun
went off he was in way over his head. Unfortunately,

the deed had already been done. But thanks to Hank McMaster, Billy's guy inside the police department, they'd been able to dispose of the body and cover up the whole thing.

After that, Worthington lived his life above board, following the letter of the law. Helping to keep him on the up-and-up was the fact the federal government swooped in and shut down Roscoe's illegal operations. That, and the fact Marty had been such a good attorney that the Worthington name was buried under so many levels of corporate paperwork and shell companies, no one ever knew about his involvement. If anyone would have learned about his connection to Billy Roscoe, his family's name would have been ruined.

When the warehouse was put up for sale by the city, Worthington got worried and tried to buy the property. Unfortunately for him, the city council sold to a Jersey developer. Howard could only hope when they tore the old structure down, they wouldn't discover the skeleton. The one thing he had going for him was that there weren't that many people left that knew he was the one who'd actually shot Ramsburg. If anyone really started asking questions, he figured Billy would get the blame. It didn't hurt that McMaster was now a lieutenant in the PCPD either. Once again, he would have been able to help "guide" any investigation.

Tommy pointed out killing McMaster was pretty stupid then. That was when things took an unexpected turn. Worthington denied having anything to do with the recent shootings. It was a declaration that left both Ben and Tommy at a loss for words. Howard Worthington was so willing to admit to Ramsburg's shooting, only to turn around and deny any involvement in the killings that they assumed were to cover up the original crime.

"What do you think?" Ben asked Tommy as the two stood in the grand entryway of Worthington's mansion. The two had stepped out to talk privately, leaving Worthington cuffed in his library under the watchful eye of Officer Spurrier.

"If we find the gun, he goes down for all the murders," Tommy said, hoping the search of the house would uncover the weapon. Another warrant was being executed across town at his office, in case Worthington had hidden the gun at the bank.

"There's something about how specific he was about it being an accident. His words were very precise."

Tommy thought for a moment. "Do you think he's trying to lay the groundwork for a defense? There's no statute of limitations on murder. It's not like admitting to the murder twenty-five years ago but not the recent ones is going to make a difference."

"That all depends on the way his lawyer presents the case, I guess," Ben answered, still trying to figure out Worthington's angle. "One *accidental* shooting could carry a lot less time than five charges of first-degree murder."

"We'll have time to figure it out," Tommy said confidently. "We got him for Ramsburg. We start there and…"

A gunshot rang out from inside the library.

Instinctively reacting—their academy training kicking in as it was meant to do—both detectives dropped into a defensive stance, weapons drawn. From the second floor, two of the officers searching the upstairs came running.

"Spurrier! Are you alright in there?" Ben shouted, preparing to enter the library.

When there was no response, Ben signaled to Tommy to enter low as he went high. Silently counting down from three with his fingers, Ben followed his weapon into the room with Tommy just a split second behind. Crossing the threshold, they saw Officer Spurrier lying on the ground, clutching his side, hands covered in blood, as Howard Worthington was being pulled through a door on the far side of the room.

SIXTY-EIGHT

BEN WAS SHOUTING directions to the uniforms in the foyer as he and Tommy pursued Worthington through the door on the other side of the library. Another man was with the banker. Where had he come from and, more importantly, who was he?

Carefully making his way down the short hallway, Tommy covering his back, Ben's eyes never stopped scanning the space in front of him. Whoever was with Worthington was armed and clearly dangerous. He'd shot Spurrier.

In the back of Ben's mind, another idea was beginning to take shape. Could Worthington have been telling the truth about not being involved with the recent shootings? Did he have some sort of dark guardian angel trying to watch out for him and cover up his decades-old crime?

From the corridor, the detectives found themselves stepping into a sitting room with floor-to-ceiling windows looking out onto the estate's backyard. A set of French doors stood wide open, revealing Howard Worthington and the mystery man quickly crossing the patio toward the lawn.

"Freeze!" Ben shouted, raising his gun and taking aim.

"I don't think they're going to stop. And I don't want

to chase after them into those woods," Tommy said, raising his own gun and firing a round into the air. "My partner said, '*freeze.*'"

The two men came to a staggering halt. Worthington's momentum, coupled with the sudden stop, caused him to stumble forward and land on his knees. That left the other man towering over the banker, a .9mm clenched in his hand.

Ben kept his eyes focused on the weapon. If he tried to make any sudden moves, there would be no choice. He'd have to take the shot.

"Drop the gun and put your hands above your head!" Ben ordered.

A tense moment followed as the detectives waited to see if the man would do as instructed, or if this was about to turn into a showdown of some sort. Thankfully, Ben's commands were followed. With the gun now lying in the grass, Ben realized he'd been holding his breath. Exhaling, he watched as Officers Grassman and Thompson ran past him and Tommy. Thompson helped Worthington to his feet while Grassman slapped his cuffs on the mystery man.

"Turn him around," Tommy said, holstering his gun. "I want to see who this dipshit is."

Grabbing the man's arm, the officer spun him around to face the detectives.

Even though he'd aged, the man still had the build of a former prizefighter. And the cold, dead eyes of a killer. Both Ben and Tommy recognized him instantly. Not only had they seen him at Worthington's house three years ago when they came to question the banker about Beverly Baker's murder—he'd answered the door and they just assumed he was the butler—but a couple of days ago when they were looking through old newspapers.

"Fredrick Quinn," Ben began.

"You're under arrest," Tommy finished.

SIXTY-NINE

EVENTS IMMEDIATELY BEGAN to snowball after the arrests. In addition to an ambulance arriving to transport Officer Spurrier to Tasker Memorial Hospital, a small fleet of backup units arrived, having been called in because of the shooting and unknown nature of the situation. PCPD officers and sheriff's deputies flooded onto the property, Chief Brent leading the charge. To everyone's relief, the situation was completely under control. In the library, Howard Worthington was under guard, as was Freddy Quinn across the hall in one of the house's several sitting rooms.

"What in the hell is going on?" Brent asked of his lead detective.

Ben smiled. "You're never going to believe the twist ending to this case."

"You say that's Freddy Quinn in there?" the chief asked looking over Ben's shoulder. "Didn't you find out he was killed in a car accident?"

"Freddy's got a lot to say, Chief. He's in with Tommy right now. And boy does he have a story to tell."

Both men, having been Mirandized a second time— just to make sure—were then loaded into patrol cars and taken to the station where the real fireworks began.

Worthington continued to deny any knowledge of

the recent shootings, while in the interrogation room next door, Freddy Quinn told a much different story.

"After that skeleton was found, Howard went nuts. He was afraid someone was going to find out what he did. Funny thing was, he was more worried about people findin' out he worked with Billy than that he offed a cop.

"Then, Howard gets a call from our good old friend McMaster. He wanted money to keep his fat mouth shut. He figured Howard paid him to keep quiet once, he'd do it again. But after all these years, Howard finally grew a set and told me to take care of things. So I did. He wanted the whole thing cleaned up."

By the end of the night, it had turned into one big old battle of He Said vs. He Said. Worthington's army of attorneys showed up and immediately began trying to discredit Quinn's statements, even though the tough guy was able to lay out a version of events that made perfect sense and didn't fly in the face of common logic and reason as some of the banker's claims were beginning to.

Sitting in the breakroom with Ben and Chief Brent long after the sun disappeared and the trio should have gone home, Tommy said, "This has got to be one of the most complicated things I have ever heard."

"It's definitely not going to be a cut and dry case for the state's attorney to make, but the story makes sense to me," Ben responded, finishing off his umpteenth cup of coffee since returning to the station with the suspects.

"We basically got the theory right. We just had the wrong people," Ben went on. "Worthington was the one trying to cover up the murder. So, he gave his factotum the order to 'take care of' anyone who could connect him to the murder. In so doing, of course, becoming an accomplice to another whole string of murders."

"He didn't think that through, did he," Tommy quipped.

"He's a banker. Not a criminal mastermind," Brent said. "I still don't understand why Quinn went to work for him."

"After the accident, Freddy says he knew Billy was dead just by looking at him. He knew he was in trouble because Billy was his meal ticket and the Feds were out looking for them. Not to mention, he'd just been in an accident and needed medical attention. That big scar on his face alone probably required a bunch of stitches. It was dumb luck that McMaster was the officer who showed up at the accident. Freddy got McMaster to say it was him who died in the accident with Billy."

"All the time it was actually his brother, Jimmy," Tommy offered.

"The only person he knew with the money and power to help him…and basically give him a new life, was Howard Worthington," Ben continued. "He was Billy's partner—which only a couple of people even knew about—and Freddy helped cover up Ramsburg's death, so he figured Howard owed him. After that, he just became a general aide-de-camp, if you will, for Worthington, just like he was for Billy Roscoe."

"The hell is an 'aide-de-camp?'" Tommy asked, raising his eyebrows.

"A gofer," Ben and the chief answered in unison.

"Good job," Tommy said, with a mock smile. "I just

wanted to make sure the chief here knew your fancy term."

"And Joe Noffsinger and Peter Vernon had to die for nothing," Brent said, the tone in his voice becoming very somber.

"They were Freddy's way of muddying the waters of our investigation. He'd read about the Drug Task Force in the paper. That's how he knew about Joe and was able to call and pose as an informant and set up an ambush. He knew if an officer was killed, the brass would show up at the scene. That was the only way he could know exactly where McMaster was going to be. He followed him from the Ramshackle and shot him at the convenience store. Pete was just the first cop he saw the next day. *That* was pure coincidence that he was on the task force like Joe."

"And look what it did," Tommy said. "It got us looking at drug cases."

"But you figured it all out in the end, boys," Brent said, leaning back in his chair and putting his hands behind his head. "That's all that matters. Now it's up to the court to decide what happens to these two."

"Hopefully we won't have another case like this… well, ever," Tommy said, looking out the window. "I don't like to think these are the sorts of crimes we're going to be dealing with now."

"You can say that again," Brent agreed.

"I don't know," Ben said, pausing for a moment. "I get the feeling Parker isn't the quiet little city we all think it is."

* * * * *

ABOUT THE AUTHOR

WHEN NOT SITTING in his library devising new and clever ways to kill people (for his mysteries), Justin can usually be found at The Way Off Broadway Dinner Theatre, outside of Washington, DC, where he is one of the owners and producers. In addition to writing the Parker City Mysteries Series, he is also the mastermind behind Marquee Mysteries, a series of interactive mystery events he has been writing and producing for over fifteen years. Justin and his wife, Jessica, live along Lake Linganore outside of Frederick, Maryland.

SOCIAL MEDIA HANDLES:
    www.Facebook.com/JMKiska
    www.twitter.com/justinkiska

AUTHOR WEBSITE:
    www.JustinKiska.com